THE
KLOWNS
OF KENT

STEVE HIGGS

VINCI
BOOKS

For Hunter
Follow your dreams and your heart and may neither steer you wrong.

Vinci Books

vinci-books.com

Published by Vinci Books Ltd in 2025

1

A CIP catalogue record for this book is available from the British Library. Paperback ISBN: 9781036708542

The EU GPSR authorised representative is Logos Europe, 9 rue Nicolas Poussion, 17000 La Rochelle, France contact@logoseurope.eu

By Steve Higgs

Blue Moon Investigations

Paranormal Nonsense
The Phantom of Barker Mill
Amanda Harper Paranormal Detective
The Klowns of Kent
Dead Pirates of Cawsand
In the Doodoo with Voodoo
The Witches of East Malling
Crop Circles, Cows and Crazy Aliens
Whispers in the Rigging
Paws of the Yeti
Under a Blue Moon
Night Work
Lord Hale's Monster
Herne Bay Howlers
Undead Incorporated
The Ghoul of Christmas Past
The Sandman
Jailhouse Golem
Sparks in the Darkness
Shadow in the Mine
Ghost Writer
Monsters Everywhere

The Eagle Tavern, Rochester High Street

I took a long draught of my pint and set it back on the bar. I didn't bother to remove my hand from the cold glass. I was confident the contents weren't going to last long. To my right, my office assistant James was drinking his pint in a similar fashion and to my left sat Frank Decaux, the owner of a local occult bookshop called Mystery Men. He had downed most of his pint already. All three of us were staring into nothing, our brains still wired from the events of the last two hours.

I took another swig of beer, savouring the cool, crisp taste as it washed away the smoke, adrenalin, and dirt. A little less than two hours ago Rochester High Street had been subjected to a zombie attack. I need to clarify that because the zombies had, of course, not been zombies at all.

They were perfectly ordinary people who had been doped with a neurotoxin and hypnotised. The drug ensured they stayed in the hypnotic state for an almost indefinite period and the hypnosis came courtesy of Dave Gough, a local hypnotist who went by the stage name 'The Great Howsini'.

The zombies were a smokescreen to distract people from the crime he was perpetrating. As people fled from their businesses, he and his wife robbed the tills and set fires to cover their tracks – why look in the cash register of a burnt-out building?

Frank, James, and I had discovered and foiled the crime by the simple expedient of running towards the zombies instead of away from them. My name is Tempest Michaels, and I'm an accidental paranormal investigator. Not that I investigate paranormal accidents, I'm a paranormal investigator and I came to that role by accident.

I joined the British Army when I left school at seventeen and enjoyed a career as a professional soldier for many years. I learned a lot and had no great desire for the career to end but the need for a large army diminished, the Ministry of Defence offered pay-outs for volunteers to leave, so I handed my uniform back and entered the world of civilians just a few months ago.

Adrift in a sea of endless options, I created my own next career as a private investigator but luck, or fate, or perhaps even God messed with the plan. My advert was misprinted, and I was presented as a paranormal investigator instead. I was angry at the time. I remember quite distinctly calling the paper and shouting at them for the mess. But while I was shouting at them on the office landline, complaining that I was trying to make a living and now had no chance of attracting a customer until they could rerun the advert, my mobile began to ring in my pocket.

It was a client calling with a case to solve.

To my great surprise, there was an endless supply of people with problems for which they had determined a paranormal explanation and they each needed someone to investigate. Suddenly that was me. The business has gone from strength to strength and recently a serial killer pretending to be a vampire murdered some people in my town and the case made national news. I solved the case, sort of, and the resulting publicity boosted enquiries even further, forcing me to hire an assistant and another detective.

So, here I was in a bar in Rochester drinking away the confusion and horror of the last few hours flanked by two people I would probably call friends but could most certainly call comrades.

Frank had arrived at my office on the morning the advert ran. His bookshop is located less than a hundred yards from my office. In it, he sells both fiction and non-fiction, comic books, toys, games, models, and anything and everything that had a tangible link to the paranormal. Frank has been a sounding board for me on several occasions and often comes with me on cases when I need an extra pair of hands. He is an absolute font of knowledge and has the heart of a lion. Unfortunately, the lion's heart is sheathed in the body of a middle-aged scrawny man.

James is the chap I had hired as an office assistant just a couple of weeks ago. He used to pretend to be a vampire but had given that up. The day after I hired him, he turned up for work dressed as a girl and insisted he be called Jane. His gender fluidity isn't an issue, let's be clear about that, but I do find myself wondering which version I will find each day, and since he doesn't change his voice ever, I can never figure out how to address him or her when he or she answers the phone. It's not a they/them thing, apparently. As James he wants to be address with male pronouns. As Jane it's the opposite. I'm sure I'll figure it out soon enough.

I took another sip of beer, the glass now nearly empty.

Amanda arrived a few minutes later, entering the establishment with her eyes searching. She spotted us almost instantly, looking weary at the bar. The first pint was in my bloodstream now and the second one, once ordered, would have an equally limited life expectancy. I was relaxed now at least.

'Hi, Tempest. Hi, fellas,' Amanda said as she reached us.

'Hi, Amanda,' the three of us replied as one voice.

'Had a busy day?' she enquired rhetorically. 'The high street looks like a disaster area. What did you do?'

'You remember hearing about the zombies?'

'Yeah. The police are all over the case but have no idea what's going on.'

'Well, the case got solved. Frank, James and I just happened to be here when they turned up in Rochester. I'll tell you all about it later but suffice to say that it has been an eventful day and I have no one to bill for it.'

Amanda is the other detective I hired to share the caseload. Actually, she suggested I hire her before I had got around to advertising a position and I took her on immediately. We had met a few weeks earlier when I was investigating the vampire serial killer case. At the time she was a uniformed police officer and still was, I suppose, as she is working out her last few days' notice in between putting in a few hours at the firm in her new role.

She is proving to be a real asset. She knows how to interview or interrogate people, she knows what we can legally do in pursuit of a case, which means I get arrested a little less often than I used to, and like me, she is able to assume there will be a perfectly rational explanation for every case we are presented with.

Unfortunately, I'm also kind of just a little bit in love with her.

Amanda is unfairly attractive. Her blond hair falls to her shoulders in a flawless cascade of natural waves. She has blue eyes that might have been carved from the heart of a glacier and seem to go on forever when I look at them. Her skin is equally flawless, her teeth are perfectly even and white and her lips – my Lord, her lips – they are wonderfully full and pouting and it is only rigid discipline, and the fear I might consider my life complete and just die on the spot, that prevents me from grabbing her and kissing them.

She is also dating a multi-millionaire playboy, and I stand no chance whatsoever.

'Sounds interesting,' she said, bringing me back to reality. I had been staring at her face again.

'Would you like a drink?' I asked, indicating the array of options behind the bar.

'Sounds great, but I have a shift in a few hours, so I'd better not. Actually, I came in to check you were all alive and report on the restaurant ghost case.' Amanda had been in the nearby town of Faversham this morning looking into a restaurant that was in danger of closing because of ghostly goings-on.

'What did you find?' I asked. Frank swivelled around in his chair to listen.

'The owner believes he has a ghost. Utterly convinced might be a more accurate term. Several of his staff have quit and he'd had customers running out screaming midway through their meals when the ghost has put in an appearance.'

'How is it manifesting?' Frank interrupted.

'Hmm?' Amanda replied with a raised eyebrow.

'I mean, what form is it taking? Is it a formed visible

apparition? In which case, is the apparition taking the form of a person or an animal or something else? Or is it just manifesting as noises or as a mist? Or it's able to produce ethereal energy to move objects?' Frank was ready to believe a paranormal explanation over anything else.

Humouring him, Amanda replied, 'It's just making noises, Frank. They are reporting footsteps and music in the upstairs dining room. The owner said that ...' She opened her handbag and pulled out a notepad to read from, 'the footsteps appear to walk across the room. Most evenings the sound of someone walking across the upstairs dining room happens. He claimed to have witnessed the footsteps go from behind him then right through him as the ghost crossed the room. Sometimes it comes back or goes in a different direction. The music is faint but intermittent.' She snapped the notebook shut. 'I heard nothing, but he's convinced he has a ghost and wants us to do something about it.'

'Groovy,' said Frank.

'You know what?' Amanda stared at the drinks behind the bar. 'I think I will have a little something. It's an hour before my shift starts.'

'I'm buying,' I said, only too happy to buy the love of my life a drink.

I am such a loser.

I made eye contact with the bartender. He was at the far end of the bar doing his best to chat up one of the waitresses. He sauntered over.

'Another round?' he asked.

'Yes, please and something for the lady.' Amanda settled on a white wine spritzer and plonked herself down on the bar stool next to mine while the barman made it.

'How long until you finish in uniform now?' Frank asked, making conversation.

Her eyes went upwards, doing mental calculation. 'I have four shifts left, I think. It will be weird to hand all the gear back in and never put it on again. But … also liberating, I think.'

'How so?'

'Shift patterns mess with my head. I don't like the routine, the uniform is hardly comfortable, and I'm ready for something new. Besides, working with Tempest as an investigator is far more interesting.'

I shifted in my seat and groaned a little at the reminders of just how interesting my career could be as pain flared in different parts of my body.

'Are you hurt?' Amanda asked, concern on her face.

'Just a few bruises and scrapes. Fighting zombies is an extreme sport.' I was playing it down, as was my natural style, but my injuries were hardly life-threatening.

'Given that you're an investigator and don't have to actually catch any criminals, you seem to get into a lot of fights. Should I expect the same?'

'Goodness no, Amanda. I don't know how I do it, to be honest. The likelihood of your life being endangered or there being any confrontation at all is probably quite small.' As the words left my mouth I wondered if they would prove to be true.

'So, how is the Klown investigation going?' Amanda asked, taking a sip of her drink.

Beside me, Frank drained the last of his drink and set the glass back down on the bar with a satisfied thunk. 'I think that is enough for now,' he announced as he stood up and stretched his lean frame. 'Thanks for the drink,

Tempest. I need to get back to the shop. It ought to be open and Saturday afternoon is one of my busy times.'

I got out of my chair to shake his hand. Behind him, James was getting up too.

'I'm leaving as well. My boyfriend is very concerned about me, so I intend to make good use of that.'

There was a quick round of goodbyes, and then it was just me and Amanda in a bar. I was breathing in her wonderful aroma – expensive perfume and sexy woman, and I was very conscious that with alcohol in my blood-stream the usual filter system that prevented my penis taking over my brain and using my mouth wouldn't be fully oper-ational.

In fact, Mr. Wriggly chose exactly that moment to voice his opinion. He thought I should spend the rest of the after-noon making Amanda forget all about Brett Barker and his fortune. He thought that Amanda had a very nicely shaped bottom and that I should try wearing it as a hat. I didn't disagree but thankfully managed to avoid telling Amanda about his ideas.

Instead, I told Amanda about the Klown case I was trying to investigate. Basically, it wasn't going anywhere at all. I had been hired by a lady to find her brother. He left her a note explaining that he was running away to join a cult of Klowns. He told her not to worry about him as he was with friends and had a purpose and was going to get rich. The bit about him getting rich was confusing, or it felt erroneous. I couldn't decide, but over the last few weeks, there had been growing reports of men dressed as clowns but with disturbing face paint. Instead of the traditional jolly smile. Instead, their make-up made their eyes look hollow or perhaps gouged out and their mouths were made to look like they had been sewn shut or cleaved open. Small articles in local papers had escalated to local television news reports and finally to national news as the tactics the Klowns were using also escalated from physical intimidation to actual bodily harm, then theft with violence, and onto grievous bodily harm. Then the assaults involved weapons, and speculation was that they wouldn't stop until someone was murdered.

The Klowns had been leaving graffiti all over the County – huge, daubed signs:

THE KLOWNS ARE COMING

Their appearances were mostly after dark, but not always, and they were popping up all over the place. The attacks seemed so random, and the selection of victims so disconnected that thus far no one had been able to find a pattern.

My task to find the lady's brother had proved easy though – sort of. I called his mobile phone number. He answered, and when he spoke to me he was very clear that he had no intention of coming home. So, I was faced with an adult male who of his own free will was doing what he wanted to do. He hadn't been kidnapped, I had no evidence that he had personally perpetrated a crime, and I couldn't come up with what I was supposed to do next. I could hardly go and get him and deliver him back to his sister - I had no right to do so.

'So, what will you do with the case?' Amanda asked.

'I think I have to call Mrs. Plumber and give her back her money.'

'Really? You've spent hours genuinely pursuing this case on her behalf. Surely you deserve to be paid for that?'

'It could be argued. However, I'm not comfortable

taking her money and delivering her nothing. I will call her and explain the situation later.'

'What about his location? The police would be very keen to learn where the Klowns are hiding. If they're all together, what they are planning, whether they would like to all turn themselves in perhaps.' She was being flippant, but also serious about wanting a lead that would get the police closer to catching the strange figure behind the violent crime spree.

'Yes, I should try harder to do something about that. This chap is probably the only Klown whose identity is known.'

'What's his name again?' Amanda pulled out her notepad.

'Adrian Plumber.'

She noted it down along with his phone number and a few details I had been able to obtain. I suspected it was a dead end, but I also know that sometimes it's necessary to pursue every lead because you can't tell which one would pay out.

'What did he do for a living, before he became a Klown?'

'He was a lawyer. Can you believe that? He practised tax law at a firm in London making what I must assume to be a pretty good wage.'

'A lawyer?'

I nodded.

'And he ran away to join a gang of criminals that like to dress as evil Klowns?'

'Yup.'

'I have said it before, Tempest, but there is a lot of weird stuff that happens around you.'

Amanda yawned and stretched in place on her bar

stool, lifting her arms high above her chest as she did. The action pushed her ample chest out, something that happened all too often for my pathetic libido to handle. I snatched my gaze away from her, lest I be caught staring, only to find that I was now looking into the mirror behind the bar and staring at her anyway. I dropped my eyes and focused on my glass.

Done with the yawning and stretching routine, Amanda slid delicately from her bar stool, gathered her bits into her handbag and wished me a good evening. She was off to get ready for work.

I refused to allow myself to watch her leave. I had to stop torturing myself with fantasies that I would ever have a relationship with her. Yes, she was utterly lovely to look at, spend time with, be around, but she was also my employee and almost certainly out of my league. I swirled the last of the liquid around in the bottom of my glass and made a decision.

I needed a distraction. A different lady upon whom my interest could be diverted. There had been a number of recent options when I thought about it, chief among which was a woman I went to school with. I hadn't seen her in years, until last weekend when she turned up at a baby shower for my heavily pregnant twin sister. She was one of the girls I secretly lusted after in my teenage years and would have, back then, cut off bits of myself to have seen naked.

Her name is Sophie Sheard. I had her phone number, I knew she was single, and I also knew she wanted me to call her. She made that part clear in a subtle yet very transparent way.

The two pints of beer were now fully in my bloodstream which had dulled the edge of the afternoon's drama and probably imbued me with a false sense of confidence. Whatever the case, I felt like it was a good time to make a move, so I chose to call her.

She gave me her number and an invitation to call last week. If I left it any longer my call might be less welcome. She might not welcome it anyway, I mused, but I wanted to find out. I didn't remember much about Sophie, other than she had been one of the really cool and pretty girls at school and that she had been friends with my sister. The phone rang for a while, and I was about to hang up when she answered.

'Hello?' she said hesitantly, probably because she didn't recognise the number on her phone.

'Sophie, good afternoon. It's Tempest.'

'Oh. Hi, Tempest,' she replied brightly, clearly excited that it was I calling her. It boosted my ego immediately.

'I was wondering if you might be available for a coffee or a glass of wine, or maybe even dinner sometime soon? It would be nice to have a proper catch-up.' I was inviting her out for a date but playing the romantic element down. It felt normal and natural to do so. I could have suggested we meet up and get to know each other better, but that had all manner of further connotations.

'That sounds wonderful. When were you thinking?'

Suddenly on the spot, I had no idea what to suggest. I was free every night in theory until a case demanded I be elsewhere. Fumbling for words I was just about to speak when she did.

'I have no plans for tonight if you are free.'

Suddenly I wished that I had no plans, but unfortunately, I did. 'Ah. Sorry, Sophie. I'm out with some chaps tonight. How about something tomorrow?' Big Ben probably would have told me to cancel my plans with him and the other guys and focus my efforts on getting laid. However, I wasn't the type to change my arrangements if a better offer arose.

'Yes. That sounds great. I'll leave the details up to you. I'm free all day, so let me know what you want to do and count me in.' It was an adventurous approach. I could come up with anything from cave diving to bungee jumping. However, I would, of course, arrange to take her for a nice lunch somewhere so we could chat.

'Thank you for being so trusting. I will book us a table for lunch at a nice restaurant and will confirm the time later. Does 1400hrs sound okay?'

'Huh?'

'I mean two o'clock. Does two o'clock sound about right for lunch tomorrow?'

'Oh. Yes. Two o'clock sounds fine. I'm looking forward to it already.'

We said our goodbyes and disconnected. I stared at the mirror behind the bar, telling myself that this was a good thing, that I had made a good decision. Sophie is attractive, she is single, and she is clearly interested in me.

Unconvinced, I gave myself a mental slap. It did little to remove the residual echo reminding me that she wasn't Amanda.

I hopped off my bar stool, grabbed my phone, and headed for the door. With two beers in me, I wasn't going to drive for at least an hour. I also needed to eat something, and I had to call Mrs. Plumber, so I tottered along the street, telling myself that the alcohol wasn't affecting my stride and arrived at my office ten minutes later with a foot-long sandwich and a bottle of water in a bag.

My office sits above a run-down travel agent shop in Rochester High Street. The entrance to it is around the back where there is a convenient car park. I rented the office from the chap who owns the travel agent shop, an equally run-down man called Tony Jarvis. He looked to be close to retirement and to have largely lost interest in the business. I also worried that he made very little money from his endeavours, yet he charged me a paltry rent that I was very happy to pay.

I opened the door at street level and jogged up the stairs to my office. The office itself is quite small but has enough room for an office desk and chair plus a small table and two more chairs by the window that overlooks the High Street, and I kept another couple of stacking chairs in a corner in case I have more than two visitors. A door leads through to a short corridor and a toilet that I share with the travel agent shop.

On my walls are Post-it notes from various cases, a map of Kent, which is where all my cases thus far have been, and a couple of whiteboards that come in handy when I am trying to visualise my ideas.

I sat at the table by the window and watched people going about their lives while I ate the delicious sandwich. It was more food than I really needed but I hoped it would absorb some of the beer. Lunchtime drinking isn't something I do more than a couple of times a year, not because I don't want to, but because I have little tolerance for alcohol and the practice tends to put me into a torpor for the afternoon. Today felt like one of those days when it could be justified.

My sandwich eaten and lips delicately dabbed clean with a napkin, I downed the last of the water and pulled out my phone. A couple of quick swipes and Mrs. Plumber's name and number appeared.

She answered on the third ring just as I was stifling a belch. It caught me off guard.

'Mrs. Plumber, this is Tempest Michaels of the Blue Moon Investigation Agency,' I managed after she had said, "Hello." twice.

'Oh. Mr. Michaels. Have you news?'

'Not exactly, Mrs. Plumber. In my last report, I explained that Adrian had spoken with me on the phone and that he intends to stay where he is.'

'Yes,' she said, expectation in her voice.

'The essence of the matter, Mrs. Plumber, is that he's entitled to do so. He's an adult. He hasn't been kidnapped and is not being held against his will. Were that the case, it would be a job for the police instead of me.'

'But can you not find out where so that I can get him?'

'It may be possible for me to track him down, Mrs. Plumber, but I must point out that I'm racking up a lot of hours with your case. If you wish me to continue, I can do so, but I believe that Adrian does not wish to be found. He refused to divulge his location.'

'Can you not track his phone?'

'I can, but it's not quite as simple as they suggest on television. I have already tried to do that, in fact, but it only works if the person's phone is switched on when you perform the search. Thus far I have not been able to locate him. He switched his phone off immediately after my conversation with him.'

'So, what are you saying?'

'Mrs. Plumber, I'm not confident that I will be able to help you to track down your brother and were I able to do so I couldn't hold him until you arrived. He's free to come and go as he pleases. The Klowns appear to be committing minor crimes but there is nothing to indicate that your brother is involved. I feel I should halt my investigation at this time and refund your initial payment.' It would leave me a little out of pocket for the work I had done this week, but my conscience would be content.

Mrs. Plumber was silent for a moment before she spoke. 'Tempest,' she started, using my first name for the first time, 'I'm worried about my baby brother. I think he's going to come to harm, and I mean to rescue him. From himself if necessary. Please keep the deposit and please find my brother. When you do, I will work out how to bring him home.' Her voice was full of emotion that sounded quite genuine. I knew I couldn't refuse her; I'm such a sucker for a lady in need of help.

'Very good, Mrs. Plumber. I will take whatever steps are necessary.'

We disconnected and I stared at the whiteboard on the wall by the desk – it was as blank as my mind. This wasn't even a paranormal case, not that it mattered because I had no idea where to start.

Maidstone Bowling Alley

I arrived home at 1612hrs. My office and home were only three miles apart, a fact I found thoroughly pleasing as I had no desire to commute into London every day like so many others in the area did. Behind my door, waiting for me, were my two faithful canine companions, Bull and Dozer. Were it not for them I would live alone and most likely be lonely. I had notions of living with a woman in the blissful, warm blanket of mutual love but thus far was finding such a partner elusive. My housemates instead were two miniature black and tan Dachshunds, brothers that had come from different litters but looked identical to most people. Of course, I could tell them apart just from the feel of their fur or from the sound of their bark, but then I lived with them and had them sitting on my lap every day.

Bull had arrived first. He was a proud and noble dog that held his head high and kept his tail ramrod straight. He could be found watching for danger, or perhaps squirrels, and he was everything a man could want in his trusted side-kick. I had gone back to the same breeder to get another one just like him roughly a year later. Bull's younger brother, Dozer, displayed some alternate characteristics though. He was a bit dopey, his expression, rather than give you the impression he was sizing you up, was one that made me think a cartoon thought bubble drawn above his head would be empty. He walked into things, he would lift a back leg to scratch himself and fall over, but he was arguably my favourite of the two. Not that I would admit that to Bull as he would widdle in my shoes if he knew. They were the most ridiculous dogs a chap could choose to have, but I loved them, and they came with the added advantage that ladies tended to cross the street to pet them.

They performed their usual routine of fussing around my trouser legs before running to the back door. I let them out and watched as they sped across the lawn, chasing away the wood pigeons that had been pecking at grubs in the grass. They vanished under a bush I probably needed to prune, so I left them outside while I wandered through to the kitchen to make myself a cup of tea.

I was going out bowling tonight with a few mates. A couple of weeks ago, my good friend Jagjit had suggested we do something different from just hanging out at the pub in the village and the idea of a night out bowling at the local alley had developed. The alley was walking distance for Big Ben, as he lived in the centre of town in a penthouse apartment overlooking the river. The rest of us were travelling into town together, or at least that had been the plan. Fighting a zombie hoard hadn't been on my diary for today and the event was having a knock-on effect on other plans. In the original plan, I was supposed to have been getting picked up by Jagjit at 1700hrs, but I had texted the chaps and ducked out of the food part of proceedings as I was no longer hungry after my sandwich and needed to attend to my body after the zombie battle. The chaps would still enjoy their steaks at the restaurant we had booked, and I would catch them up later at the alley.

The dogs reappeared from the garden, so I fed them and took them out for a proper walk around the village. The small village of Finchampstead is surrounded by woodland, crop fields, and vineyards, with paths that crisscrossed and circumnavigated the village. The setting made it a great place to live and a super place to walk a dog. I got back to the house at 1810hrs. I was expected at the alley for 1930hrs, so I had about an hour before I needed to be in a cab heading to town. I took myself for a bath, shucking my clothes into the laundry basket and checking myself in the tall mirror while the steam billowed up from the tap. I had cuts, scrapes and a bite wound to check out though thankfully none of them were worth being concerned about. I took a photograph of the bite mark wondering if I would end up with an album of stupid wounds from my cases. The bath was glorious and made me sleepy, so I stayed longer than intended and when I finally forced myself out, I found the two dogs asleep on my bed. I was tempted to join them and gave the concept of staying home some serious thought. In the end though, despite being in two minds, I felt compelled to do as I had planned. I hated it when people cancelled at the last moment, so I wasn't going to be the one that did.

By the time I arrived at the bowling alley, the effect of the two beers I had put away at lunchtime had worn off and I was looking forward to having a couple more. Jagjit was designated driver for the night, so I had a lift home secured already.

As I went up the stairs and into the Bowling alley, my nostrils were assailed by the myriad familiar smells it contained. Beer, burgers and other fried foods, and the grease or oil they used to dress the lanes. I took in a deep breath and held it, savouring the remembered scents. I was a big fan of a night out bowling though I couldn't remember the last time I had. Was it the simplicity of smashing things that spoke to my inner boy? Looking around, there was no sign of the guys but rather than send them a text to question their tardiness, I ordered a beer from the bar and settled down to wait for them.

Around me, I could see people of all ages, races, and beliefs. Many of the groups I looked at had a blend of exactly those demographics. Of course, there were also people who weren't so easy to categorise into a race or even gender. One person, probably a woman, looked more or less like a baked potato had decided to get dressed and go out for the evening. In addition to the rather unique body shape, its attire was a blend of colours that, if I were challenged to achieve the same, I might do so by forcing a rainbow and a unicorn into a blender. I might then throw in a grenade for good measure. The hair matched. He/she appeared to be happy though so any judgement about him/her stayed in my head. I liked that despite the craziness of the zombie attack today no one seemed concerned for their safety. They were out having fun.

'Hey, spunk ferret,' called a voice across the room in a volume loud enough to be heard over the general din of conversation. The voice belonged to Big Ben, a friend and former army colleague who often helped out on cases when I needed a little extra muscle. 'I hear you had some fun with zombies today.'

I turned around on my bar stool to face the chaps as they approached. At Big Ben's comment, many of the other patrons had paused their conversations to watch us. Partly this was because of the gregarious way in which Big Ben had announced his presence, and partly because at six feet and seven inches tall plus annoyingly good-looking, people tended to stare at him anyway.

Basic and Jagjit were ahead of him, but they all arrived at the bar together and we did a round of shaking hands. The young lady behind the bar appeared, guessing correctly that more drinks would be required. While she poured them and lined up the cold glasses on the bar, I regaled them with my day's activities and pulled up the sleeve of my polo shirt to show them the bite mark on my right deltoid.

'A real zombie bite mark,' Jagjit observed. 'Not many people around that can claim one of those.'

'Hur, hur,' Basic laughed. Basic's real name was James Burnham but had been given his nickname at some distant point in the past. I would never employ such an insulting term, but it was how he introduced himself. The name was in reference to his rather limited intelligence. He had a job collecting the abandoned trollies at a supermarket and he looked after himself well enough, but he lived with his mum and in all fairness, he was really, really thick. His I.Q. was somewhere around that of a dog or a pig or a school gym teacher. He was a good guy though and he contrasted brilliantly with Big Ben as a study in genetics. Big Ben could most accurately be described as an Adonis, like he was a more perfect or more advanced version of man, whereas Basic was a Neanderthal.

The chaps thanked me for getting a round of drinks in and we headed over to get shoes and roll a few balls. I hadn't been bowling for a long time and had never been with Jagjit and Basic. When it had been suggested as an activity a couple of weeks ago, Jagjit had asked if anyone was actually any good in case one of us was going to embarrass the others by turning up with his own ball and shoes etcetera. Basic told us right then that he was quite good, but the three of us dismissed the claim assuming he was confused about the numbers.

We were wrong. He was brilliant.

In every game we played that night he beat the next best score by over one hundred pins.

'How are you doing that?' Big Ben asked in game two as Basic had launched yet another bomb down the lane and scored his sixth strike in a row.

Basic had shrugged his shoulders and furrowed his brow which usually meant he had something to say and was considering how to arrange his words. 'I throw the ball at the pins,' he said.

'Ok. That's what the rest of us are doing,' I replied, encouraging him to share a little more of his magic.

He thought some more. 'Well, I line myself up on the place I want the ball to go then imagine myself standing right in front of the point I want to hit them. Then I roll the ball at the back of my head.'

All three of us had stopped to listen, wondering if there was going to be some genius top tip we could use. Now though, I could see both Jagjit and Big Ben were pulling the same face I was while trying to work out how to do what Basic had just described. Jagjit had suggested some side bets to make the games more interesting. A fiver each in a pot for each game; highest score takes it, and a fiver in for highest scoring game of the night. Basic swept up.

Ninety minutes elapsed and we were done. It had been fun but out of the four of us it was Basic who was looking pleased with himself. I checked my watch to find it was 2148 hrs. Not exactly late on a Saturday night.

'What shall we do now?' asked Jagjit. 'Get another pint

here? Or head into town? Or head back home and get a couple in the local?' The last suggestion was delivered with additional volume to make it quite clear what his choice was. He had been drinking diet coke all night and wanted to ditch the car so he could have a drink or two before bed.

I opened my mouth to check with Big Ben but found that he wasn't with us. 'Anyone see where Big Ben went?' I asked. We scanned the room but spotted him easily enough a couple of lanes down chatting with three quite attractive ladies in their early twenties. This didn't come as a surprise to any of us. Big Ben shagged more girls a year than most men could boast in a lifetime. He probably shagged more girls a year than many adult film stars. Worse yet, he put almost no effort into getting them into his bed. He just sort of turns up and girls volunteer for the task. I could be envious; the truth is I have been in the past, but all I wanted now was a woman who wanted to be with me.

'Let's go back to the pub,' I suggested, meaning The Dirty Habit in Finchampstead where Jagjit, Basic and I lived. We ambled over to where Big Ben was engaging the three ladies in conversation, being tactile and generally charming the pants off them. The question wasn't so much which one of them he was going to shag, but in what order.

'Hey, buddy. Remember us?' I asked.

'Oh yeah. Hey, Tempest. I would like you to meet Rebeca, Madison, and Nikki,' he said, indicating each in turn. 'They were having trouble with the computer system, so I gave them a hand.'

No doubt. 'Well, we are going to head back home. Can I assume you will be staying here?'

'What say you, ladies?' he asked smiling his best smile. 'Would you like me to hang around in case you find another task for my fingers?' They smirked and giggled at each other. Big Ben was going nowhere except home with one or more of his new friends.

Jagjit leaned in to shake Big Ben's hand. 'Catch you later, brother,' Basic did likewise but before I could, Big Ben stood up to whisper something to me.

'Want me to save one for you?' he asked quietly by my ear. I couldn't see how that would work in practice, but I was no one's silver medal and a quick shag with a girl I didn't know wasn't really my thing. I declined his invitation with a brief shake of my head.

We waved Big Ben goodnight and headed back down the stairs to the car park on the ground floor. I had four beers in me, and I wasn't paying much attention to my surroundings. Had I been, I might have seen them before we were at Jagjit's car, but very suddenly there were three men dressed as clowns blocking our path. I felt as much as saw Jagjit freeze next to me.

Under most circumstances, the appearance of some clowns ought not to cause alarm. However, the three clowns, which I then recategorized in my head as Klowns, were clearly men. They each wore a derivative of the same outfit which consisted of baggy trousers held up by braces, long-sleeved stripey shirts adorned two of them while the third had a satin effect white top with multi-coloured pom-poms down the front. On their hands they bore leather gloves and on their feet were battered looking but very functional boots, which, while slightly oversize in appearance, still looked like they had steel toecaps in them. To disguise their hair colour, or perhaps complete their outfit, each wore a wig. The wigs were identical in all but colour, the curly locks covering their scalps. From left to right the colours went blue, green, white. I observed that traditional humorous face paint with a broad smile was out this season. They still wore face paint, but it was applied to make them each look like serial killers. The one in the middle had done a particularly good job; his makeup gave his face an eerie effect by enlarging his eyeballs and extending his mouth. He looked part way between a ghoul and an alien creature. They were not small men, but they weren't huge either, nor did they look like they were in particularly good shape. If I had to guess their age I would say they ranged between late thirties and mid-forties. It was hard to tell with their outfits and makeup, but they were broad shouldered with thick necks and doughy but probably quite functional muscle under their shirts.

They said nothing while I took all this in.

'Evening, fellas,' I offered with forced false bravado. The three men each then hefted a weapon from behind their backs. Two had baseball bats, the third a wicked looking crowbar.

'Tempest Michaels?' the one in the middle asked. The question drew an involuntarily raised eyebrow from me and my pulse skipped.

This was no chance encounter.

They were blocking the path to Jagjit's car, so they not only knew enough to find me but knew the car my friend drove. A fact which they must have known in advance because I hadn't arrived in it and thus couldn't have been observed leaving it earlier.

We could attempt to go around them, but they were here for a fight. If I was going to get to the car the only way was through them. I could feel my anger rising. Whatever beef they had with me was now going to affect and involve my friends.

'I have a message for you, Mr. Michaels,' the one in the

middle spoke again. 'He wants you to know that this is your fault.'

He who?

I really wanted to know but I could ask questions later. 'Just one chance, gentlemen. Step aside or we go through you.' I was confident of my ability. I don't like to fight but I had training and experience, so when it came down to it, I was capable enough. I didn't like that they had weapons, but they were blunt ones and not too difficult to deal with if one knew how. If they had been carrying knives, I would have already run away. To my left, Basic was flexing his giant meaty fists, probably waiting for my cue. He was part caveman and part granite. He probably weighed about the same as Big Ben but in a package eight inches shorter. It seemed possible that he would just pick up two of the Klowns and throw them at a wall. If one hit him with a bat, I expected he would grunt and then eat the bat. Jagjit was slight though, doughy around the middle from too many of his mum's samosas and he worked in an office. Not that he was without the ability to defend himself, but I really didn't want him to have to go to work on Monday with a bruised face or a black eye.

My offer of an easy way out was met with a sneer from one and a chuckle from the other two. It was as expected. So be it, I conceded. However, as I bunched my muscles to spring into action, the Klown on the left took a pace to his right and knocked on the side of a Ford Transit van.

My adrenalin spiked as I realised the trap they were about to spring. I felt a little sick.

The van rocked a little from movement inside it and the back door opened to reveal three more Klowns. Now badly outnumbered, unarmed and with very little chance of anyone coming to save us, I did the only thing I could do: I attacked.

'Get to the car,' I yelled at Jagjit, slapping him on the arm as I went by him to jolt him into motion. This wasn't a brave move on my part, the car was our way out and I needed him behind the wheel as soon as possible. It was a great big 4X4 utility vehicle, and it would make a great weapon once it was moving. I had no time to communicate all of that though, so just got on with it and hoped he could fill in the blanks in my plan.

Darting forward, I went straight for the Klown in front of me: When outnumbered, even the odds. Quickly. I wanted to take one of them out of the game immediately and punch a hole for Jagjit to go through. From the corner of my eye, I saw the Klowns still exiting the van realise I was moving. They began to scramble but were too late to save my first target. Half a second had elapsed and the man I had picked had just begun to react, moving backward away from me as I had known he would. It placed him firmly into the category of easy target. I leapt off the ground and landed on his chest to ride him to the concrete. With my right hand on his face and my elbow high, I followed him down as he went over backward, and I drove his head into the ground with everything I had. Confident he was down for good, I rolled immediately to the right and swung my legs to take the feet out from under the Klown with the white wig that had been standing to my right. Jagjit flashed by.

The Klown didn't fall as I had planned though, so as I pushed off the ground to get myself up, he was able to grab my hair and viciously yank my head. It was a mistake. Both my hands went high over my head with my elbows forward to protect my face. Interlocking my fingers, I pressed down on his clenched fist to crush his knuckle joints. His grip failed instantly, whereupon I gripped his wrist, folded it up into his armpit and twisted. A simple blow to the throat was all it would take to ensure he was also out of the fight.

My hand arced towards his soft flesh. Then my ribs exploded in pain, and I was shunted several feet to the left. Too much time had gone by and the other Klowns were upon me. I went down to the floor, my legs no longer obeying my instructions.

As I glanced up, I could see a Klown with a bat closing on me. The ribs on the right side of my body were a solid ball of pain from where he had already hit me and I was struggling to draw breath. I stood no chance at all. In the second or so I had before the bat arrived to smash my skull, I saw that Jagjit hadn't made it to the car. It was still silent and stationary. Laying on the cold concrete with feet racing toward me, I worried about him. I couldn't see him though, but in looking around, I caught sight of Basic. He had one Klown by the throat and was kicking another in the head while he lay on the ground. I hoped he would have the good sense to scarper before the Klowns overwhelmed him too.

The Klown with the bat arrived where I lay gasping for breath, but he didn't raise his bat for another swing. To my surprise, he tapped the Klown with the white wig on the arm and the pair went either side of me and began to pick me up.

What the hell?

Still fighting for breath and worried I might lose consciousness, I was unable to offer them anything other than feeble resistance. White wig locked eyes with me, 'He wants you alive see. Otherwise, I would just gut you here and leave you for the rats.'

He wants you alive?

The Ford Transit was looming. Clearly, they were planning to put me in it, and we would go for a little ride somewhere. I was trying to shake them off but the pain in my ribs when I moved was unbearable. The lack of oxygen was making my pulse hammer in my head. With two of them dragging me to the van, I spied three more keeping Basic at bay. They all looked worse for wear and two had lost their wigs. Where then was Jagjit? Had they killed him? Or was he just incapacitated? Through blurry vision, I spotted a machete in the hands of one Klown. Basic could do nothing for me without risking serious injury. I wished he would save himself or get help.

We arrived at the van where the back doors were still open. White wig adjusted his grip, trying to manoeuvre himself so that he could get me inside. Sensing my last opportunity, I swung my arm to break his grip. I didn't want to go in the van, so no matter what, I had to escape right now. Whatever it was they wanted me for, I doubted we were going for cocktails, but as I tried to break free, the other Klown simply punched me in the ribs where he had hit me with the bat and as the fresh wave of pain hit me, I vomited.

As I emptied my stomach, the furthest most rear door of the Transit slammed shut and from behind it, Big Ben hit the Klown holding me with a road sign. The road sign was still attached to the pole it had been mounted on and at the other end, I observed as he swung it over my face, was a chunk of concrete where the sign had been ripped from the ground.

Big Ben twirled the pole, the concrete connecting with white wig's face and he let go of me instantly. I flailed my arms but found nothing to grab hold of so crashed to the ground again. A spray of blood from white wig's face hit mine. I was glad of it. He had it coming.

Laying on the ground, my vision blurred, I knew I needed to get up; the fight was far from over. Then though, I heard sirens. Lots of them. The Klowns all froze momentarily, then came collectively to a decision. They decided to leg it. To do so though, they wanted to get into the van that Big Ben and I were currently blocking their path to. Not that I was going to do much to stop them, lying on the ground as I was. Next to me, Big Ben hefted the road sign again with one muscular arm and extended the other arm towards them; come and get it, he beckoned.

Come and get it they did. I rolled away to my left to get clear of the van and give myself a chance to get up. The action of rolling over once though hammered home the point that I was broken. I could hear Big Ben trading blows behind me, but I couldn't get up to help.

The van's engine roared to life, and I heard doors slam shut. Then hands were grabbing my shoulders and lifting me again. I swivelled my head weakly to find a hand sheathed in a white glove holding me; another Klown trying to claim his prize.

'Leave him,' Someone shouted, 'there is no time.'

I was dropped roughly to the ground where I elected to stay. Seconds later the van peeled out of the parking space just as blue strobe lights began to dance off the concrete walls. Across from me, now that the van was no longer there, I could see Big Ben. He was sitting on the floor, propped against a car's tyre. He had both hands pressed to his lower abdomen where blood was seeping through his fingers. He had been stabbed.

A police car, then another swept past us and out of the car park in the direction the Klowns had gone. Two more police cars, their strobe lights flashing screeched to a halt beside us and uniformed officers spilled from the doors. I turned my head to look for Jagjit. As I scanned around, I spotted a Klown laying on the floor. It was the one with the blue wig that I had slammed into the floor. They had left without him.

Feet clad in coppers boots arrived by my head and then a knee as he knelt. I had come to know many of the cops in Maidstone, but this chap wasn't one of them.

'Sir? Are you hurt, sir?' he asked.

'I'll be fine,' I replied. 'I took a hit to my ribs. I may have a few broken ones. The big guy over there needs attention, not me.'

I looked across at Big Ben. There was a female police officer tending to him. Of course there was. She laughed just then, he was probably making a joke or saying something cool and guaranteeing a future shag.

The cop kneeling next to me finished saying something into his lapel mike, then turned his attention back to me. 'The paramedics are on their way. It's over now,' he said.

But it wasn't over. It was just starting. I had decided.

The officer was just doing his job, so I let him get on with it, his words washing over me. He had probably been at dozens or hundreds of scenes where he had to deal with the victim of an attack of some kind and so was acting in the way that suited his experience. This though was different. The Klowns had singled me out. They knew who I was and what car I would be in so they must also know where I live and possibly also where my friends and family live.

I was already involved in this case through Mrs. Plumber, yet I had been very much on the fringes. Now though I was in deep. If the police got these guys first, I was fine with that, but I was going to clear my workload and take on nothing new until I had the Klowns behind bars. If Mrs. Plumber's brother turned out to be involved after all then he was going down too.

The next thirty minutes went by in a blur of medical attention and police questions. While we were administered to, Jagjit reappeared looking sheepish and sad. He was sporting a fat lip and a bruise to his right cheek that was glistening red where the skin was almost broken. He had made it to his car, but before he could get the door open a Klown with a baseball bat was upon him and taking a swing. He had avoided serious injury but took a few knocks while fighting the guy off and had then made a run for it. He was ashamed to have run away, but we unanimously reassured him that it had been the right thing to do.

He thanked us, but I could tell he was still not happy. A cute lady paramedic took a look at Jagjit's face and had been openly flirting with him while she made sure he was okay. It may have been a professional manoeuvre to calm and distract him, but it seemed genuine to me. I was examined and loaded onto a stretcher. I was walking wounded and could move about, but they weren't going to let me do so and I offered no resistance. In the back of the ambulance, I wondered if Amanda might show up. She was working a shift somewhere tonight. I thought about sending her a text, but my phone was in my back pocket, the movements required to retrieve it less than appealing. Enough time had passed that I had been able to get oxygen back into my bloodstream. The adrenalin rush had left me feeling spent for a while, but I was more lucid now and could follow the conversation the police were having when the two cars returned from chasing the Klown van. They had followed them out of Lockmeadow, but they had lost them when they ditched the van and went on foot. The

Klowns had escaped, all bar the one I had knocked out. He was being tended to by yet another paramedic. One limp arm was handcuffed to the stretcher he was laying on.

I turned to Big Ben. 'How is it that you came to the rescue? We left you engaging in your usual sport of seeing how many girls you can shag,' I asked him.

'I remembered that I had left my keys In Jagjit's car. You had only just left so I ran after you. Phone signal is always bad here and you lot were heading into a concrete car park so there was no point in calling you. Anyway, as I got down the stairs, I could see the three of you facing off to three Klowns. I called the police while I circled around to come up behind them. It would have been four against three, and fairly easy with their attention split, but in the minute it took me to circle around you were already fighting and more Klowns had appeared. Then Bongo the evil dickhead Klown from hell hacked at me with a machete.'

'How are you feeling?' I asked.

'Not great, actually.'

'Scar tissue looks good on a man,' Jagjit offered, lifting the icepack from his face to speak.

'It does,' Big Ben conceded. 'But I fear this is going to cost me a few shags while I recover.'

'We are done here,' one of the paramedics said. He was standing above us and speaking to the officer in charge. Then he said, 'Ok. Let's go,' when he got a nod in return.

Big Ben and I were strapped in and were going to the hospital whether we liked it or not. Jagjit and Basic were asked if they wanted to come with us. They needed no further treatment, had given their statements and were free to go. I told them to get home. Basic lived with his little old lady mum and she needed him around to help her out.

Thankfully they didn't argue. We all shook hands, Big

Ben and I from our stretchers and as the doors to the ambulance were shut our two friends were getting into Jagjit's car. The pub in the village would be shut by now, which was a shame because it looked like Jagjit really needed a drink.

In the other ambulance, accompanied by two police officers, was the Klown with the green wig. He was still unconscious. He was under arrest, but I suppose since he wasn't able to talk or listen or anything else, the question-and-answer section of the evening would have to wait. I was beginning to worry that I might have done some lasting damage. Not that I really cared about the person beneath the daft outfit and make-up but were he to be badly injured it would most likely cause complications and questions back to me that I didn't wish to have to answer. Much easier if he came around with nothing worse than a headache.

It would be the police that questioned him, not I, so I hoped they would provide some answers. I had questions like:

- Who are you?
- Who sent you?
- Why am I your target?
- Who is it that wants me taken alive?
- Why are you dressed like a complete penis?
- Would you like to bleed some more?

I suspected that I wouldn't like most of the answers but getting them was necessary and it would be simpler if the police got them. I probably wouldn't voice the final question.

The journey from Lockmeadow in Maidstone to Maidstone A&E is roughly three miles and took about as many minutes. Big Ben and I were both quiet, keeping our own thoughts. The driver had ignored the red lights as he sped out of town on the Tonbridge Road, but it was late, and traffic was light anyway.

As we came to a stop, the backdoors opened to reveal the double-wide entrance into A&E. Even at this time of the day, it was busy with people coming in and out; doctors and nurses, paramedics in their green uniforms and the family or friends of people inside popping out for a quick smoke.

The stretchers were rolled out, Big Ben's first and then mine. The mild bumping and jarring far more painful on my ribs than I had expected. They were broken, of course, four of them down my right side under where my arm would naturally rest. It took nothing more than a brief examination by the first doctor available to confirm a diagnosis I was already sure of. There was little they could do other than give me pain relief. The bones were all in place and not splintered or likely to cause further damage. Most of the doctor's time was spent advising me on all the activities I should not do over the next six to eight weeks. He prescribed pain relief which a nurse appeared with moments later: Oramorph. It was morphine in liquid form. It would help me breathe, but other than that I just had to put up with the pain.

Not too far away, I could hear Big Ben charming the pants off several nurses. It hadn't taken him long to attract an unfair share of the ladies working on the ward. Looking across at them know I had to observe that most of them were young and attractive as if he had some form of invisible filter that prevented less attractive ladies from getting close. I turned to look at the nurse still hovering by my bed. She looked like a raccoon might if it lost all of its fur, developed a bad allergy that affected its skin and gained two hundred pounds. Life seemed a tad unfair at times. Big Ben had a wound to his abdomen that was almost ten inches long – can you guess what he compared the length to? The blow from the machete had been a glancing one mostly but it had also cut into his flesh and muscle. He would likely heal sooner than I and he didn't seem all that bothered by it.

I was though.

Some evil dickhead Klowns had set about my friends and me. I was incandescent with rage. What had provoked the attack? That was a question I really wanted answering? Why come after me when I'm accompanied by my friends? Why not attack me when I'm alone? I believed that I wasn't a violent person, that I only fought when I had to or was forced to. Right now, though, thinking about Big Ben bleeding on a car park floor and Jagjit going to work on Monday to meet with high-stakes clients and having to explain to his boss why he looks like he has been in a bar brawl, well I was ready to hurt some people.

I was gritting my teeth for my internal monologue and my jaw was starting to ache. I relaxed and flopped my head back onto the pillow.

'Tempest?'

I looked up. The voice was Amanda's.

'My God. Are you okay?' she asked. She was in uniform; her glorious blond hair was tucked up into her hat and she was devoid of make-up. She was still beautiful. Utterly, utterly beautiful.

'What are you doing here?' I asked her, rather than answer her question and spend time talking about me.

'I brought in a perp that went a bit nuts and put his head through a window. He's cuffed to my colleague and being treated just a few beds down. I heard Big Ben's voice and came to investigate. What happened?'

'Klown attack.'

'Klowns? You and Big Ben got taken out by some Klowns?' she said incredulously.

'And Basic and Jagjit,' I corrected her. 'They were armed, and it was six against three. Big Ben only turned up at the end.'

'Okay. But without wanting to butter your ego, you and Ben and Basic are like a small army. Basic looks like he couldn't only smash through walls but eat them afterward.'

'Nevertheless, we took a beating.'

'Are you okay?' she asked again. She seemed genuinely concerned.

I opened my shirt and showed her my ribs.

'Damn,' she whistled. 'Broken?'

'Yeah. Really, really broken.'

Her radio crackled to life. Whoever she was here with tonight needed her.

'I'll call you tomorrow,' I offered. I was glad to see her. It saved me a call. She patted my calf in an act of camaraderie. It was heart-breaking for me, but had she leaned in to give me a hug I probably would have tried to kiss her, so it was better that she didn't.

She vanished from view behind a curtain further down the line of beds and I found the button thing to summon a nurse. I asked for more pain relief and another thing of Oramorph was given freely.

I don't remember much else.

Maidstone Hospital

I awoke to my phone ringing. I was on a different ward to the one I had fallen asleep in. I was still coming around when Big Ben appeared in my field of vision. He snagged my phone from the bedside table and answered it.

'Blue Moon Investigations, Ben Winters speaking. How may I help you?' He winked at me as he listened to the person at the other end. 'It's your mother,' he mouthed 'Yes, Mary. Yes indeed. I'll pass that on.' He hung up.

'How're you feeling?' I asked.

'Fine,' he replied jovially. 'A little sore at the site of the wound but I can work that to my advantage. I believe it will shortly be raining blowjobs.'

'No doubt,' I said, laying my head back onto my pillow. 'What did my mother want?'

'Just to let you know that she and your dad were just leaving your house. They had fed and walked the dogs and stayed the night rather than go home. She also said that your dad found your rum and it's somewhat depleted.'

'Sounds about right.' At least the dogs had been well

catered for. They wouldn't have been bothered that I had failed to come home. They were well used to my parents and had probably been given treats to boot.

'Anything else?'

'The temperature in your greenhouse was too low to keep the plants in there alive through the winter so she has turned it up and you need to get your overwintering vegetables planted now or you will miss out.'

My mother was a constant provider of helpful horticultural advice. I had grown up with a garden that provided all manner of fruit and vegetables that she would then convert into pies and tarts and stews etcetera. My parents lived only a couple of miles away from my house and it took nothing more than a quick call last night to get them to leave their house and go to mine.

Soon enough, the doctors came on their rounds. They came to me first, led by a tall, slightly plump lady consultant with a gaggle of mostly female junior doctors following her. She instructed one to check my chart and make a recommendation, she didn't address me at any point which felt rude but also completely in keeping with National Health Service patient care. I was swiftly dismissed. The young male doctor recommended that there was no need for further treatment, and I should contact my local general practitioner if I needed further pain medication. While dealing with me, I had watched the consultant as she watched the young male doctor. Behind her were two equally young female doctors, one of whom had just got a look at Big Ben. He had removed his top so that his wound could be inspected when they got to him and now she was urgently nudging her companion and motioning with her head.

The consultant was finished with me, so I began to

slowly gather my things. I would wait for Big Ben so we could travel in a taxi together, but that is not what happened. What happened was the consultant lady stared at Big Ben with goggly eyes for half a minute while she tried to convince her brain to reconnect itself with her mouth. Big Ben was used to the attention and had most likely taken his shirt off just so he could distract the ladies. Just in case it was needed, which it wasn't, he smiled one of his magical smiles and made his pecs dance a bit.

Stammering, the consultant lady finally instructed the nudgy girl to get on with the task of checking his chart and determining if he was fit enough to be discharged.

'Um,'

'Come on, Doctor Stephenson,' snapped the consultant, who looked flushed and annoyed. 'You know how I hate mumbling.'

'Mr. Winters has suffered a penetrating abdominal trauma,' she managed, flicking over a page on his notes as if hoping the information she needed would leap from it. She was having trouble diverting her gaze from Big Ben though. He had now relaxed back onto the bed and fixed her with a smouldering stare of encouragement. I wondered if she might dribble.

'What are the dangers of abdominal wounds?' The consultant asked the group while also staring at Big Ben.

There were two young male doctors in the group, one of whom was staring slack-jawed at the aftershave model relaxing on the bed in front of them. The other one was immune. By dint of being heterosexual, I assumed. He was looking around the group in wonder, probably trying to work out what spell had bewitched his colleagues.

When no one else spoke, he started, 'Abdominal wounds are particularly likely to cause internal bleeding, which can be life-threatening due to the number of major blood vessels that run through the area. Peritonitis is an especially common complication if the weapon punctures the intestines.' He delivered the answer as if reading from a textbook. When he finished, he fell silent again, waiting for the consultant. Nothing happened. They were all just staring at Big Ben. Seeing the lack of impetus from his colleagues he stepped forward, grabbed the chart from the unresisting hands of Doctor Stephenson and then moved between the crowd and Big Ben as he moved in to inspect the dressing.

'How are you feeling, Mr. Winters?' he asked.

'I'm just fine, brother,' Big Ben replied in his usual relaxed manner.

'No temperature, no nausea?'

'Nothing at all. The wound is sore when I move, but they said it was superficial and would heal quickly.'

'Yes. Yes, this all checks out. Thank you, Mr. Winters. Please do not participate in any strenuous activities for a week and keep the dressing dry during that time. You will receive a letter advising you of an appointment to have the staples taken out. You are free to go.'

The consultant seemed startled as if woken from sleep to find herself in an unexpected place. 'What? Dr. Coruthers are you blind?' she asked fixing him with a glare. 'This man is clearly not ready to be discharged. The wound might produce all manner of complications.' Which she then went on to list. I understood very little of what she said but she made it sound like he would most likely explode if he attempted to leave the hospital. She moved closer to Big Ben and took his hand. 'Mr. Winters, I'm afraid you will have to stay here for a while at least. But don't worry, I will be taking very special care of you myself.'

Big Ben looked at the consultant. She was mid-forties by my reckoning, wasn't wearing a wedding band and was attractive enough to have held my attention. The younger female doctors were a mix of different races, heights, and levels of attractiveness but I could see that each one was considering the possibility of keeping Mr. Winters around as a positive action. She placed a hand on his tight toned, abdominal wall, made some hmming noises then placed it on one of his bulging pectorals.

'Yes, yes. Mr. Winters, I think is imperative that we keep you here for a day…'

'Two days?' enquired Doctor Stephenson, taking hold of his arm tactilely from the other side of the bed.

'Two days,' confirmed Doctor Harman, 'for observation. It would be irresponsible to let you go now when there could be… complications.' Her voice was getting huskier by the moment.

'Ladies, I place my firmness in your hands. I mean I place myself firmly in your hands,' Big Ben replied in his best bedroom voice clearly making the word order error on purpose.

Doctor Harman shook herself physically and somewhat reluctantly took her hands from his body. 'Doctor Stephenson see to it that Mr. Winters is found a private room where I can give him the best treatment.'

'Doctor Harman is this really necessary?' asked Dr. Coruthers, the only one immune to Big Ben's charms. 'Mr. Winters is clearly fit and healthy. The surgical notes state that the wound didn't penetrate the abdominal cavity…'

Doctor Harman cut him off with a wave of her hand. 'That will be all Dr. Coruthers, thank you. Do not question me on my rounds unless you wish to be back on geriatrics.'

The man closed his mouth. I guess working geriatrics wasn't a task he relished.

I picked up my phone and put it in my pocket. It looked like I was leaving by myself. Big Ben was grinning at me. When we locked eyes, he waggled his eyebrows to show he was up to no good. He was going to stay here and enjoy the company of whichever doctors, nurses, orderlies and other persons elected to sneak into his room. This wasn't untypical behaviour.

I bid him good luck, though I doubted he would need it and headed for the exit.

I had an advice leaflet which could be summed up as: Don't do anything. Don't exercise, don't do anything strenuous. Don't drive if I have taken pain relief. The list of don'ts went on for a while. Big Ben had it better than me and would heal quicker too. Nonetheless, he was out of action for seven to ten days while the wound healed. Once the stitches were out, he should be okay, but that was all moot because he was going to stay in the hospital and be used as a rather tall sex toy for the next couple of days.

There were taxis available from the hospital reception, so I hopped in the one at the front of the queue and caught a ride home.

My House in Finchampstead

As the driver pulled up outside my house, I checked my watch: 0956hrs. Nearly ten o'clock on a Sunday morning. I couldn't remember what I had planned for the day. Amanda and I had a few open cases but nothing that demanded my immediate attention. The fare was more than twenty pounds, so I handed over twenty-five, instructing the man to keep the change before I clambered tenderly out of the cab. Given how I felt right now, I reckoned the day was going to involve lots of sitting on my bottom on the sofa watching TV. The dogs would be happy enough with that.

I got to my door, fished for my keys and opened it, pausing so the two savage hounds could tumble out to greet me. I slowly bent down to pat and fuss them both but didn't pick them up as I often would; my ribs were just too sore.

Inside the house, there was evidence that my parents had been there in my absence. On the drainer were two clean glasses that my mother had washed up by hand rather than put them in the *infernal dishwasher*. The dogs buzzed around my feet and stared at the cupboard that contained their food and bowls. Like most dogs, they were everlastingly hungry and would ask for a second breakfast if the first was more than a few seconds ago. I felt certain that my parents would have fed them but called my mother to check anyway.

She answered on the third ring, 'Hi, Tempest. Everything okay?'

'Good morning, mother. Thank you for looking after the dogs last night and yes everything is just fine. The dogs are asking for breakfast. Did you feed them already?'

'Of course, Tempest.'

'I thought it would be so.' I scowled down at the two hopeful creatures still circling my feet and pointing to the cupboard with their noses. 'Shoo, the pair of you,' I instructed. Disappointed, they gave up and wandered through to their bed in the lounge.

'How are you feeling?' mother asked.

'I'm fine, mum. Just sore. I can't take a deep breath so I will not be going to the gym for a while but otherwise, there is nothing wrong with me and I will recover fully in a few weeks.' I knew that mum just wanted to hear that I was okay. She didn't like to consider that her children might be hurt or upset or anything else with a negative connotation. I expect most parents are the same regardless of the age of their children.

We chatted for a couple of minutes while she once again reminded me that I needed to plant my overwintering vegetables if I wanted a crop next spring. She had already forgotten my broken ribs and that I wouldn't be digging in the garden anytime soon. I bid her a good day and disconnected.

I needed a cup of tea. Tea is a great healer for me. It has been for as long as I can remember. I start every day with a cup, I make one every day when I get in from work, and I wanted one right now. They had offered me one in the hospital, but it had been terrible, making me wonder what they could have done to make it taste so bad. Tea is hot water over tea leaves with an option of milk and some sugar/sweetener. How does a person get that wrong? Anyway, I made myself a cup of tea and took it through to the lounge where I slowly eased myself onto the sofa. I had to put my cup on the floor to do so, which instantly attracted the attention of both my dogs.

Bull's head came up first, but Dozer wasn't far behind him. I gave a warning growl, but it did little to deter them. Edging forward as they were, I was caught halfway between sitting down and turning around again to retrieve my cup. It became a race, which I only just won, snatching the steaming cup from the carpet as they got to it. The beverage was too hot for me to drink still, so either or both of the daft hounds would have scalded themselves as they shoved their faces in it to steal a slurp.

As a consolation, I encouraged them onto the sofa to sit with me. As they settled onto my lap and curled up, I found Gardener's World on BBC2 where Monty Don was teaching me that right now was the perfect time to put in bare-root stock fruit trees and reminding me that I needed to get my overwintering vegetables in now if I wanted a crop next Spring. I sunk back into the comfortable depths of the fabric, a dog keeping me warm on each hip and the tea balanced on my right thigh.

I awoke briefly some time later when the sound of my tea being drunk reached my ears. I had fallen asleep, which didn't surprise me. Forcing myself to alertness, I let the dogs finish my tea. That the dogs had saved me from spilling it was my final thought as I drifted off again.

The next time I came to, it was my phone that woke me, its ring cutting through my slumber uninvitedly. I had to roll Dozer off my hip to get to it. He was either still asleep, despite the vibration and noise coming from under his head, or perhaps dead. I would check once I had worked out who was calling me. It was a number I didn't recognise, so I assumed it was a client. 'Blue Moon Investigations, Tempest Michaels speaking. How may I help?'

'Hello? Is this the man that investigates ghosts and what not?'

'I'm a paranormal investigator, yes,' I answered. The voice at the other end belonged to a man. He had a deep rolling baritone that gave me the impression he could sing. He sounded hesitant but not unsure of himself, if that makes sense. I gave him time to gather his thoughts.

'My colleagues and I may have a case for you,' he replied.

'Jolly good. Are you able to come to my office tomorrow morning?

'What? Oh, yes. I suppose we can do that.' I heard him speaking to someone, but in a muffled manner as if he had put his hand over the phone to mute the conversation at his end. 'Yes, that will be fine,' he confirmed.

'Shall we say 0900hrs?'

'What?'

'Nine A.M.' I translated. Civilians were so weird with how they said the time I thought to myself for the millionth time.

There was more conferring at the other end before he said, 'Yes, Mr. Michaels. That will suit us.'

I made sure he had the address and bid the fellow a good day. Then I realised I hadn't enquired what the case involved or even taken his name. I was slipping. The painkillers were allowing me to breathe and were taking the edge off the pain in my ribs but now I might find myself being engaged to look into a case of alien, killer-robot chickens. There were some crazies out there and many of them wanted me to prove their theories correct.

I focused on the television, the gardening show had ended, replaced by a political debate show of some kind. It was of no interest to me. I chose a news channel instead, catching it mid-way through a bland report. This one was on political unrest in a European country that I would struggle to find on a map. It soon ended though and went to adverts. The clock on my mantlepiece assured me it was almost 1100hrs so I would get headlines soon.

The Klown story had been on the headlines of the national news broadcasts several times recently as the scare tactics had changed to assault and then to assault with a deadly weapon. Initially, I had believed it was just one person, dressing themselves up and scaring people because they thought it fun or because they were a little deranged. My early assumption was wrong though. This wasn't a lone player, there was an extensive team.

The news headlines started, the two anchors talking to the camera in serious tones. I figured the Klown story would be third or fourth on the agenda, but I was wrong again. It was the lead story. I listened as they reported the first murder associated with the Klowns. Last night while I was being attacked there were yet more Klowns perpetrating a worse crime in Ightham – a village a few miles to the west. The victim was a man, no name released yet though his relatives had been informed.

Murder.

They had escalated their level of violence again. The report also covered the attack in Maidstone that I had been party to but in much less detail. A few injuries can't trump a murder. The camera swung to the female anchor where a map of Kent was superimposed on the screen next to her. She was showing where all the attacks had taken place thus far. They were scattered from the Hoo peninsular down to the Thanet Sound and right across the Weald. It looked utterly random. Ironically her next words were outlining how random the locations seemed. The camera switched then to the chief constable for Kent. He was sitting at a desk flanked by two other senior police officers. There were several microphones in front of him and flashes going off continually as photographers captured the moment for their papers or online blogs.

The news anchor finished up speaking just as the footage of the chief constable started. He said, 'I can report that this evening three persons in Klown costumes were seen running away from a house in Ightham. Calls for help were responded to by neighbours, who upon entering the property, found a man to have been repeatedly stabbed. Emergency services were called but the man died at the scene before he could be transferred to hospital.' He paused before continuing. 'This and the attack in the Lockmeadow district of Maidstone bring the tally of Klown related incident to thirty-five in the last two weeks. In a co-ordinated raid conducted by officers in seventeen towns across Kent, a total of twenty-two individuals have been arrested. The case continues at this time, and we urge everyone to be vigilant. If you see a Klown do not approach them, call the police on this number.' On the screen, a number in bold red letters was displayed. The television then went to split screen with the chief constable on the right-hand side and footage of the arrests last night on the left. I strained my eyes at the screen. In the flashes of film, they showed men being led out of their houses or being stuffed into police cars. They were not what I expected. They weren't of the same ilk as the men I fought last night. In fact, they looked to be mostly late middle-aged and out of shape as if the police had misunderstood the instruction and rounded up all the postal workers instead.

At the end of the report, I levered myself off the sofa. I was wrestling with my options for the day. I couldn't do much, but I was already getting bored with sitting on my bum. I have nervous energy, or at least I think that is how some would classify it. It manifests as an inability to sit still for very long unless I'm distracted by something that can hold my attention. Typically, I will sit down for a short period but then remember a task that I intended to perform and will get on and do that instead. Generally, if I have something that needs doing, I will do it. Is this a positive trait? Probably, but not always. Anyway, I was restless and in need of activity, so I made a new cup of tea, this time in a thermos cup with a lid and took both it and the dogs for a slow walk around the village.

It was cold out. The last of the overnight frost was still visible where the sun was yet to penetrate the shade. I zipped my winter coat all the way to the top and forced the Dachshunds into coats that had been specially made to fit their sausage-shaped bodies. They wore them with great reluctance, but they needed the extra layer to keep the cold at bay.

The village was quiet at 1127hrs on a Sunday morning. It was a quiet village anyway, but at this time of the day any churchgoers were in the church enjoying being preached to, it was cold enough to put children off playing outside and too cold to wash the car on the driveway, so I had been walking for several minutes before I saw my first person. As

I passed the pub, I realised that this was one of those Sundays where I could legitimately excuse myself from abstinence and have a couple of drinks. More normally, I do my drinking on a Friday or Saturday and spend a good hour thrashing myself at the gym on a Sunday. Gym wasn't an option today but almost tearfully I accepted that beer wasn't an option either. My painkillers were unlikely to mix well with alcohol, and I wanted the painkillers more.

As I turned off the main road and down a side street, I could hear a susurration. It sounded like a lot of people talking though I couldn't see anyone. I walked a few more yards and drew parallel with another street whereupon I spied the source of the noise. Outside a small, terraced house about halfway along the short street was a small crowd of perhaps fifty people. They were spilling off the pavement and into the road. Mostly they were chatting between themselves, but I observed that they were all looking at one house in particular. As I watched, a young man in his twenties took two paces and kicked the front door of the house in a manner that suggested he was trying to kick it in.

'Come out and face us!' he shouted when the door refused to yield.

This formed unusual behaviour for the village of Finchampstead where normally I would claim that nothing ever happens. I knew from experience that the relative IQ of a crowd was somewhere near the square root of all the people's IQs averaged. Crowds were dangerously stupid. Having formed, a crowd then wants to do something. People egg other people on. People whisper thoughts into other people's ears and before you know it they are setting fire to cars.

I looped the dog leads around a lamppost and left them

a good few yards away from the crowd before I approached. As I came along the street, I saw a car with crude spray writing all along one side and I knew what the crowd were there for.

The sprayed word was *Klown*.

No one had noticed my arrival, or if they had they had assumed I was just coming to join in. The young man stepped forward to kick the door again. As he drew back his right leg I pushed him over. So now I was centre of attention, all eyes on me. The shove I had given him pulled at my ribs a bit but I was refusing to show that I already wanted to go for a lie-down.

'What're you playing at?' asked a man just in front of me. I recognised him so perhaps he recognised me also. I didn't know his name, but it was a small village, so we had probably stood together in the queue in the shop before.

'That would be exactly my question also,' I replied, moving my gaze around so that I locked eyes with everyone in the small crowd. 'It's Sunday morning in our peaceful little village and you lot are trying to scare a man from his house.'

'But he's one of those clowns from the TV,' complained a woman in the front row to a chorus of "Yeahs." From many others.

'Does anyone know the name of the man living here?' I asked.

'It's Cliff Maxwell,' the same woman said, now sounding not quite so sure of herself.

'And you know this because?'

'Well, I live next door but one.'

'So, you are his neighbour. Has Cliff lived here long?'

'What has that got to do with it?' asked the young man

who had now picked himself up off the ground. I ignored him.

'I'm waiting,' I reminded the lady. I needed to be the one in control. I had to dominate the crowd until they came to their senses.

'As long as I remember,' she said reluctantly.

'Can you tell us all what he does for a living?' I asked, looking at the crowd rather than her. I was smiling now, my expression engaging and beginning to win over the people in front of me.

'He's a clown!' she delivered with gusto as if it were a crime in itself and she was revealing him as guilty.

'Do you mean that he's a children's entertainer?'

'Um.'

I addressed the crowd, 'Has anyone had Cliff around to their child's birthday party?'

'Oh, yes. He came to my Tommy's fourth birthday just a few weeks ago,' said a young mum. I noticed that she'd brought Tommy with her this morning to witness the lynching.

'Did he display any behaviour at the time that made you in any way scared? Did he stab, maim or otherwise murder you or any of the guests at the party?'

'Well, err no.'

This thing was over. I could see the uncertainty in the faces of almost all the villagers in front of me now. A few were less happy about it though. I pressed on, 'My dear fellow villagers, the man that lives here is a children's entertainer. Nothing more. The Klowns you have seen reports of on the TV are something else entirely. What on earth were you thinking? What were you going to do if you got him out of his house this morning? If he had run from the back door, would you have given chase? What then? Beat him to death?' A few people were starting to drift away from the back row. Slithering back to their houses hoping they could later deny ever being here.

'Hold on…' started the young man again.

'Did you vandalise his car?' I demanded angrily.

'What? No, I…'

'Who did then?' I snapped, cutting him off. He looked genuinely innocent, but someone had painted the man's car and there might be damage to the man's house yet. 'Where do you think you're all going?' I asked. People were now actively trying to be somewhere else. 'This poor man has been besieged in his own home by you, and his property has been damaged.' I reached behind me to knock politely on his door without taking my eyes off the people left still standing in front of me. Just then, a police car entered the street from the end I had walked from. I turned my head and sure enough, another police car was coming from the other end. The dispersing crowd were now trapped and had frozen.

Behind me, the door opened. Just a crack. I heard the safety chain catch the door. I looked over my shoulder to see a slim section of a face peering around the door at me. 'Mr. Maxwell the police are here. You're safe to come out now.

The police cars had stopped about fifty yards apart and the occupants were getting out. I spotted immediately that the car to my right contained PC Amanda Harper, my new work colleague and another officer I recognised as PC Hardacre. This would go smoothly now. Amanda spotted me and left PC Hardacre to the task of corralling the crowd so she could join me at Mr. Maxwell's door.

'Good morning, Amanda,' I said.

'Having a busy day, Tempest? I thought you were supposed to be taking it easy.'

'That had been the plan,' I conceded.

I explained quickly what had transpired. Mr. Maxwell felt safe enough to leave his house once he saw Amanda's uniform, so was able to regale her with a more detailed account of events from his perspective. He had called the police before I arrived.

I left Amanda dealing with the villagers and collected my dogs from where I had left them. As I said goodbye to Amanda, she told me this was the third such incident this morning. Vigilante crowds were targeting children's entertainers all over Kent. Mr. Maxwell had been lucky compared to some it would seem. Others had sustained injuries at the hands of their idiot mobs. I wondered then if across Kent there were men who owned clown suits barricading their homes for fear of attack.

The dogs pulled me to the park in the centre of the village so I would unclip them from their leads. I found it was a long way down to them with my ribs hurting the way they currently did, but I let them off and watched as they scampered away.

Soon enough, I was back home and surprisingly relieved to be back in the warmth of my house. Normally the cold does not bother me. I learned to ignore it a long time ago and had always held the opinion that it simply does not get cold in England. Not really. The opinion, of course, was born from having spent time in countries where it genuinely does get cold. I wondered if perhaps I was just feeling it more today because I was feeling battered in general.

I made a cup of tea and joined the Dachshunds who had already claimed prize spot on the sofa. I turned the TV on and settled down to do nothing, just like the doctors had told me I should. Once again, I fell asleep without drinking my tea and woke up to the sound of the dogs barking.

There was someone at the door. At least the dogs believed there was, so as usual they were making lots of noise and dancing around in front of it. It took me twice as long as it usually would to make my way from the sofa to the porch and I couldn't find the effort to shoo the dogs back into the kitchen, so I just opened the door and let them go. I was fairly confident the person outside wouldn't get savaged by them.

It was my parents. The dogs climbed their legs.

I said, 'Hello.'

'Hello, Tempest,' replied my mother. 'Do you have a lunch plan?' They were both dressed for church. I checked my watch to find it was 1317hrs. I had slept for over an hour. My parents had been to church, probably stayed for tea, biscuits and a chat and then come directly to me.

'I do not. I hadn't given it any thought actually. I was probably just going to grab something from the fridge.'

'Your father and I thought that might be the case, so we are here to take you out for lunch.'

Excellent.

'Would you like to come in while I find my shoes and coat?' I asked.

They nodded and followed me back into the house. The dogs plopped back over the door sill so I could close the cold air outside. I considered leaving the dogs behind as they could be a little bothersome in a pub at lunchtime – all the interesting smells getting them going, but I wanted them around me as often as I could manage it and I estimated I could slip them a few small pieces of roasted meat without ruining their dinner or upsetting any of the other patrons. As if reading my thoughts, they happily stuck their heads in their collars as I offered them.

Sunday Lunch at The Hen and Pheasant, West Farleigh

SUNDAY, OCTOBER 23RD 1351HRS

A thirty-minute drive later, the car tyres crunched across the gravel car park of the Hen and Pheasant in West Farleigh. As we exited their car, mother handed the keys to my father and instructed him that he was driving home. He didn't bother to put up an argument, it was a well-rehearsed charade because dad always drove home if it was daylight. His eyes aren't too good at night and mother did ninety percent of the driving, so he got to be the designated driver whenever they went out for lunch.

At the bar, I ordered a bucket of wine for my mother and non-alcoholic beers for my dad and I. Non-alcoholic beer isn't something I would typically imbibe. I got used to drinking it in Iraq many years ago when someone decided it would be an acceptable substitute for the real thing which, of course, wasn't allowed: Young, excitable and potentially irresponsible men, plus weapons, explosives and alcohol are not a recommended mix. The beverage failed to taste like the real thing in my opinion but wasn't awful provided one accepted it was going to taste different. My dad had over-heard me though.

'I think you would rather a coke,' he said in a mean-ingful and conspiratorial tone. 'I would definitely prefer one.'

I glanced at him. He checked to make sure my mother wasn't paying attention and showed me the hip flask in his jacket pocket. It would be full of rum and would indeed make the coke more interesting. I seriously considered it but, in the end, I declined although I got a coke for my dad so he could sneakily have a drink without my mum knowing. He grinned when I handed him his glass.

There was an open fire supplying welcome heat to the large dining room but a wide semi-circle in front of it where patrons had established it was too hot to go closer. We were escorted to a table way back in the depths of the pub which was next to a large window that looked out over the river. As I watched, a small pleasure cruiser went past, the skipper standing high up to see over the canopy as he steered.

On the drive over, mum and dad had both asked me about the attack and about the Klowns. I admitted I had no idea why they had targeted me or what they were trying to achieve in their attack or in general. Now, sitting at the table, the conversation continued.

'Surely they must have said something?' my mother insisted.

'They said lots of things, mother. Most of them are not repeatable. It wasn't exactly a conversation we were having.'

'I don't understand why they would just attack you. You must have done something to upset them.'

'Leave the boy alone, Mary,' instructed my father, knowing full well she would utterly ignore him.

'It's entirely possible that I have, mother. I simply do not know what that might be. The police are trying to find something that links the crimes they are already responsible for but are drawing a blank, so far as I know.'

'Ooh, is that lovely Amanda still helping you out?' Here we go.

'Yes, mother.'

'Have you asked her out yet?'

'No, mother.'

'Why ever not, Tempest. She's ever so pretty and is just the right age for breeding.'

My word!

'Mother,' I said with an edge of impatience, 'Amanda is already dating someone.'

'Is that because you didn't ask her out? I know how slow you are at making a move. You will never get a woman at your pace.'

My right eye twitched.

'Mary,' my father warned.

I tried to present an argument that would make sense to her, 'Mother, Amanda and I work together. It would be inappropriate for us to be in a relationship. It would certainly be inappropriate for me to make advances towards her. If there ever was an opportunity, it has passed and there is no point in discussing it.'

'Love always find a way, Tempest,' mother loved a cliché.

'But we are not in love, mother.'

'She might not be,' my mother said under her breath as she took a gulp of wine that nearly emptied the large glass in one hit. 'I need another glass,' she announced happily.

'Mum, if you continue to pester me about Amanda, I'm going to leave,' I threatened.

'Fine,' she drained the rest of her glass. 'Ooh,' she said,

excitedly tapping the table to get my attention. 'What about the girl from last weekend?'

'Hmm?'

'Oh, what was her name? You remember, Tempest. You went to school with her.'

'Sophie!' I exclaimed. I could feel the colour draining from my face.

Nuts! I was supposed to be taking her out for lunch today.

'That's right. Sophie. She's nice. Maybe you should ask her out.' At least for once, my mother was trying to fix me up with a woman I found attractive.

I slid slowly out of my chair, excused myself and went outside to make a phone call.

Sophie answered almost immediately.

'Tempest.' There was a definite snippiness to her voice. That she was monosyllabic was a clear indication of displeasure.

I elected to go with the "beg for forgiveness" strategy. It worked, but only after I explained I had spent the night in the hospital and still had morphine in my body. I detected a mothering instinct in her reaction to my news that I was injured. It wasn't necessarily a bad thing.

'Would it be acceptable to rearrange for tomorrow evening? I would very much still like to take you out for dinner.'

'That sounds lovely, Tempest. Shall we say seven o'clock?'

'I will pick you up at seven.'

We said goodbye and I wandered back into the pub. My steak was waiting for me. My parents were already tucking into theirs.

'Everything alright, kid?' my dad asked once he had cleared his mouth of half-chewed cow.

'Yes. I had a lunch date with Sophie arranged for today but forgot all about it. I'm seeing her tomorrow night instead.'

My mother beamed at me and raised her glass in salute. There was food in front of her though, so I was safe from interrogation for a few minutes at least.

I sat down and tucked into the succulent piece of meat on my plate. It was excellent and cooked just the way I like it. I abstained from dessert while my parents indulged themselves with a sticky toffee pudding and ice cream. It was too heavy for me, so I chatted amiably about nothing much and took the dogs to the bar to fetch mother another pail of wine.

By the time we left the restaurant, mum had put away about a bottle and a half of Pinot Grigio, the obvious result of which was that she fell asleep before we made it out of the car park. She would snooze in her armchair and wake in time to sing along with Songs of Praise on television later this evening.

On the way to their house, they dropped me at mine, but in the back of their car, my eyes had been getting heavy – the residual effect of the painkillers combined with limited sleep. Both dogs were asleep on my lap, one either side, making me warm which had added to the relaxed contentedness. Mum didn't wake up when we stopped. She was snoring loudly in the passenger's seat, her mouth open and hanging to one side. Dad asked if I needed him to come in and help me with anything which I thanked him for but had no tasks I couldn't perform for myself.

I waved him off and took the dogs inside.

The Klown case beckoned. However, it felt like too much effort to even spend time reading into it. There were numerous other tasks around the house and garden I was definitely not about to tackle, so resignedly I selected a book from my bookshelf and settled down to read. The dogs climbed onto my lap and presently we all fell asleep.

The Blue Moon Office

It was Monday morning, and I had risen at 0730hrs which was far later than usual. Getting a shower hadn't been a comfortable experience; raising my right arm to wash my hair a particularly painful chore. The two painkillers I took when I awoke, didn't begin to work their magic until I was making breakfast, and it wasn't until I was ready to leave home that I could move and breathe without wincing.

By 0850hrs I was trudging up the stairs to my office. I had silently bet myself a skinny blueberry brownie from the coffee shop that it would be Jane this morning and not James I would find at the desk.

'Good morning, boss,' hallooed Jane as I went in. I would have fist pumped my successful guess but might then have had to explain why. She was sitting at the desk wearing a blue satin top and a cashmere cardigan in a contrasting hue. I had asked her once where she managed to buy women's clothes to fit her frame and how they were always such great quality. The answer, she revealed was a website called, *Hers for Him*, where they sold second-hand ladies clothing tailored to the male shape.

'How are you feeling? Would you like coffee?' she asked. Until recently, it had been my habit to arrive at work with a coffee in my hand, but since my run in with Hayley, I was avoiding the place. Hayley and I had a brief game of hide the sausage two weeks ago and a few days later, after a receiving a text from me I had inadvertently addressed to Jane, she slapped me in the face in the street and called me several names.

'Indeed, I would. Thank you, Jane,' I answered as I passed her to take a seat by the window. 'Could you also get me a blueberry muffin? One of the skinny ones?'

'Goodness,' Jane said staring at me. 'I don't know whether to be alarmed or elated. You never eat cake, not even skinny ones. Is everything okay? Ignoring the broken ribs, that is.'

I smiled. Jane was right. As a practice, I don't eat cake, but I felt I could get away with it for once. She wasn't actually waiting for an answer, it had been a rhetorical question. She was getting up and putting her phone into her bag.

'Won't be long,' she announced. 'Macchiato or Americano?'

'The Macchiato please.'

I had clients due any moment. I had no idea what they wanted, what case they were going to present me with or even if they would turn up for that matter. I expected they would though, and sure enough, not a minute later, I heard the bottom door open and men's voices echoing up the stairs.

Making out what they were saying wasn't possible, but it appeared to be a discussion about whether they were indeed in the right place.

'Come up, gentlemen,' I called out. My request was rewarded with the sound of many feet trudging up the stairs toward my office. The chair I was sitting on was directly opposite the stairs, so I saw the top of a head followed by a face, then another head popped up behind the first and then another. The face of the first man was devoid of mirth, looking in fact as if nothing fun had ever happened to the man in his entire life. I estimated his age as late fifties. Most of his hair was gone and the ring of it above his ears was almost all turned to grey. He was clean-shaven, which must have been quite fresh as I spotted a small piece of toilet paper still stuck to his neck. He was almost all the way up the stairs now, so I could see he was quite short, perhaps less than five feet six inches. A small roll of body fat hung over the belt of his trousers to show the world that he was soft and pudgy. Very typical of the species.

I forced myself out of my chair without indulging myself with a grimace at my ribs and moved forward to greet them all.

'Good morning, gentlemen. Tempest Michaels, owner of Blue Moon Investigations Agency. Please come in.' I stepped back to allow them to file in. The three men who followed were all the same yet all also somehow different from the first man. Their ages were similar, their clothing as well but their heights and features couldn't have been more contrasting. The third man was well over six feet tall and as thin as a candy cane. He had long limbs like a spider and a long face as if someone had stretched it. The fourth man was less than four feet tall. I struggled with the right termi- nology. What was PC currently? Dwarf? Small person? I labelled him as *R2D2 stand-by* in my head and shook his hand anyway.

None of them had spoken yet. 'So, gentlemen. How may I assist you?' I prompted.

'We called you yesterday,' said the tall man. 'We need your help to stop the Klowns.'

'Okay,' I replied, coaxing him or any of the others to provide a little more information.

The dwarf/small person took up the explanation. 'There are fourteen of us so far and more joining every day. We are having to band together to stay safe, and we can't work. We don't dare put on our work clothes and no one wants to hire us anyway.'

'Hold on, sir. We need to back up a little. I feel like I have come in halfway through a conversation. Shall we start with some introductions.' I dislike when people fail to introduce themselves. 'My name is Tempest Michaels, but you know that anyway.' I looked at the man who was first to arrive and popped my eyebrows as a question.

'Oh. Err, David McLeash,' he blurted, as if startled by the need to say his name. 'Work name, Binky.'

Binky?

The second man told me his name was Mike Barfield then followed his friend and announced his work name as Mr. Cuddles. The tall man went next as he was next in line. His name was Kevin Brownfield, and I realised then why they were in my office and what they wanted when he told me his work name was Coconutty Honkster and honked a horn that was hidden in his pocket.

They were all clowns.

The final chap to speak was the munchkin. His name, he told me, was Richard Levaraugh and he went by the workname Big Dick. I had to fold my bottom lip over my top and pretend to get something off my desk so he couldn't see me trying to suppress my laughter.

'Can I assume that you are children's entertainers?' I asked.

'Indeed, we are,' answered Big Dick. I was trying to think of him as Richard, I really was, 'and we need your help,' he finished to a chorus of nods from his colleagues.

'Right then, chaps. Please grab a seat where you can and take me back to the beginning. I need to know everything.'

The chaps looked about themselves, then all moved to get to a chair. There were enough chairs, so each chap needed only to reverse a bit to find one, but instead, they pratted about, bumping into each other and occasionally pretending to trip as they manoeuvred to find a place to perch. Coconutty Honkster honked his horn several times as they shuffled and span. It seemed they couldn't operate without playing the fool.

Eventually, all taking a seat, they looked at each other once more, each seemingly waiting for another to take up the story. In the end, Richard (well done, Tempest) rolled his eyes in defeat and started speaking.

'We are here to seek protection for ourselves and our fellow clowns. We are being persecuted because the Klowns are hurting people. We formed a coalition of clowns so we could find safety in numbers or perhaps present ourselves as a body of clowns that are managed and thus separate from the mayhem being perpetrated currently.' The man handed me a card. It read: Clowns Living in Threat of Retribution in the South. I mumbled the words to myself a couple of times then laughed.

'You're aware the acronym for your little group spells CLITORIS?'

'Show me that!' said Coconutty Honkster. 'It does as well!' He honked his horn as he handed it to David

McLeash. A short debate ensued regarding who was to blame for the *damned silly name*. I felt forced to bring them back to the matter at hand.

'Gentlemen,' I prompted with some volume.

They bickered for another second or so before Big Dick took up the narrative again. 'We are being starved of business because no one wants to hire us in case we turn up and murder everyone. Clowns are very unpopular at the moment.' He went on to describe a few instances the four of them and some of their colleagues had suffered in the past week or so. Coconutty Honkster honked his horn in places during the dialogue when he thought it appropriate. The noise it made was beginning to annoy me. About halfway through the explanation, Jane returned. The chaps glanced at the stairs as the bottom door opened audibly and again as she clip-clopped her way up the stairs in her size eleven Mary Janes. Jane handed over my coffee without speaking and with no available seats she hovered near the door.

Mike Barfield did the gentlemanly thing and gave up his chair for the young lady, which Jane declined in her wonderful bass-baritone, much to the surprise of the four men. Thankfully, none of them saw reason to comment.

After a while, I decided I had heard enough. I had a simple question for them. 'Gentlemen, I empathise with your plight, but I'm struggling to understand why you have come to me. Surely this is a job for the police. They are already committing manpower and resources to track down the Klowns.'

The four men all stared at me and then glanced at each other with curious expressions. It was Richard who spoke first. 'But, Mr. Michaels, surely the police can't catch them.'

'Why ever not?' I asked, truly curious.

He looked confused when he replied with, 'Because they are from hell.'

'From hell?' I asked, my curiosity peaked.

'Well, we figured you would know all about this stuff. Surely, they must be demons or devils or something like that. The police can't catch them because they don't know how to. A demon circle will trap them and then you can banish them back to hell,' said David, glancing between me and his colleagues.

'Yeah. I've seen it on TV,' chipped in Mike.

I considered this for a moment. I had plenty of cases I could be pursuing. However, I was going to go after the Klowns anyway so it would be nice to be getting paid for it. Would I be taking advantage of them though? I considered it silently for a few seconds.

'Gentlemen, I'm willing to take your case, but I have to explain a few things first.' I locked eyes with each man, in turn, to make sure they were listening. 'There is nothing paranormal about the Klowns. They are just men. Ordinary men with a very unusual hobby. If I find them, I will ensure the police are brought to their location.'

'So, you will not be banishing them to hell then? asked Mike.

'No, sir. Wormwood Scrubs perhaps. But I need to make it clear that I'm an investigator. I investigate. I have no special powers of arrest, so when I find them, it will be the police who deal with them.'

The four men turned towards each other and began hastily discussing something in hushed tones. I couldn't hear what they were saying but when the horn honked once more, I wasn't surprised to hear Big Dick swear.

'Kevin, if you honk that ruddy horn one more time, I will shove it up your backside.'

'I have to honk it, Richard. It's my calling card,' he said with a honk, at which point Big Dick snatched the horn from him and tore the rubber bulb clean off the horn.

'Not anymore it isn't!' he claimed triumphantly.

With an impressively nonchalant delivery, Kevin reached into his jacket and produced another horn. He honked it with a smile.

'That does it!' shouted Big Dick, jumping to his feet. The effect of leaping off his chair actually made him shorter, but his face was thunderous, and he looked ready to kill.

'Perhaps we should wait outside,' said Mike, grabbing Big Dick's shoulder and spinning him around to face the stairs. 'You fellows conclude business here, please,' he said over his shoulder as he departed, pushing his short friend in front of him.

Jane walked across the room and sat in one of the now empty chairs.

'If you want me to pursue this case for you, I need to explain my rates.' I spent the next few minutes going over what I charge and explaining how the very nature of the case meant it wasn't possible to guarantee how long it would take to solve or even if I would. They were certain they wanted to engage my services though, so I shook their hands, took a deposit while they were still with me and bid them a good day. The horn honked twice more as Coconutty Honkster went down the stairs and several more times outside in the street before he was far enough away for the noise to no longer carry.

'How are you going to find the Klowns?' asked Jane after they had left.

'I honestly have not the faintest idea,' I replied. I wasn't lying. There just were no clues to follow at this stage. That hadn't deterred me before though, so I was going to put my best sleuthing boots on and see what I could find.

The first thing to do though was visit Frank. Frank knew all manner of weird stuff, so I wasn't going to be surprised if he already had some form of theory worked out for the Klowns. Of course, his theory would most likely be that they were demons from hell and that we needed to form a demon trap in order to pin them down and perform a banishing spell. Frank was a little out there, but his theories often gave rise to new ideas of my own. It was worth going to see him anyway, so I drained my coffee, dropped the cup in the bin and went out the door.

Mystery Men Bookshop, Rochester

The Mystery Men bookshop sits just off the High Street on a road called Northgate. The shop itself was on the first floor and almost invisible from the street unless one knew to look up. Frank did much of his trade via the internet as you might imagine but he also enjoyed a steady stream of patrons in the shop, all of whom found their way there quite deliberately and made regular purchases. Frank was doing alright.

He only had one member of staff, a nineteen-year-old, sexy, athletic little minx named Ivy. She went by the name Poison though and that was what was displayed on her badge. Her naturally black hair was usually accented with a colour which seemed to change more often than the weather. Today it was a deep-sea green hedging towards turquoise and matched her stretchy long-sleeved top. The top, and in fact her entire outfit had that distressed look about it as if the wearer had recently been in a terrible fight with a large dog. The effect was deliberate though so despite my reservations, I kept my mouth shut for fear of sounding like a dinosaur.

'Good morning, Poison. Good morning, Frank,' I called out as I went in.

Poison looked up. She had been leaning on the counter reading a graphic novel. 'Hi, Tempest,' she said, her voice laden with a definite sultry tone. There was a little heat between us that I was continuing to ignore for reasons that I myself didn't fully understand or would at least struggle to explain adequately to anyone else. She believed that she owed me her life and wanted to repay me using a fairly traditional method. I felt she was too young for me to be fooling around with.

Frank had his back to the door when I went in, caught in the task of pinning a poster to the wall behind the counter. The poster was for a Hallowe'en event in a week's time – some big jamboree in the grounds of Rochester Castle. 'Good morning, Tempest,' he said over one shoulder. 'Won't be a moment.'

He finished what he was doing and stepped down from the footstool thing he was on. My brain hadn't connected the bits of information to tell me he was standing on something. Frank is about five feet and four inches tall, so the extra step had only made him man height.

'What do you have there, Frank?' I asked, taking an interest.

'This?' he asked, turning back to look at the poster. 'It's a new event, actually. The Rochester Bloodbath promises to be a horror night that no other event can match. Lots of stalls set up, spooky sets to walk through where actors will be replaying favourite scenes from horror movies, that sort of thing. Poison and I have a stall there. I expect to turn quite a good profit and promote the business at the same time.'

'Sounds good,' I acknowledged. It would probably be great fun for those that were horror movie fans. Rochester attracted a lot of different events. The old, cobbled streets and narrow alleyways made it a unique place to bring people. Plus, the Castle and Cathedral grounds were open plan and thus perfect for setting up a stage or, in this case, a horror movie set.

Just as I was about to ask Frank about the Klowns and what he might know about them, his eyes bugged out and he started tapping his hand on the counter to get my attention. 'Ooh, ooh, ooh, I almost forgot,' he blurted with excitement.

'Forgot what, Frank?'

'Your competition.' He drew a blank from me. 'Your competition,' he repeated, nodding his head as if that would help me to understand him. 'Don't you know?'

I was still drawing a blank. I had no idea what he was on about.

'Tempest there is a new paranormal investigator in town. He set up shop just a few doors down from you.' This was news to me. Not welcome news either. I wasn't surprised that Frank knew before I did, he had some form of internal radar for anything with a paranormal slant. That the new guy was just a few doors down from my office was troubling though as if the person had deliberately put his business under my nose.

'Is there really?' Was all I could think of to say. 'Well, I wish him luck.'

'He won't need luck, Tempest. The clients are already overwhelming him.'

I didn't like the sound of this one bit. Thinking about it

though, I probably had myself to blame. My success with the vampire serial killer case and more recently the phantom case and others besides had made me into something of a minor local celebrity. That someone else had decided to cash in on the sudden popularity of investigating the paranormal should be no surprise. I made a mental note that I should go to see him, welcome him to the industry etcetera, while of course checking him out. I could tackle that later, for now, I had questions to ask Frank.

'Frank, what do you know about the Klowns?' I asked him, changing the subject completely.

'Funny you should ask, because I have just been doing research on exactly that subject for Lyndon.'

'Lyndon?' I felt like I was asking a lot of questions this morning or had more gaps than usual in my knowledge.

'Your competition,' Frank explained while beginning to look exasperated. 'Lyndon Parrish is a traditional paranormal investigator. He has all the gear. He knows about runic incantations, witch codes and how to close a circle. He carries holy water and a crucifix with him…'

'What you mean, Frank is that he believes in all the same hokum as you, whereas I do not,' I replied with a smile. Frank and I were on very different sides of the same belief system. Frank remained convinced that everything from crop circles to weeping Madonna's had something supernatural about them. I didn't.

'Yes, Tempest. That about sums it up. Shall we go and meet him?' he asked.

'Now?'

'I have this research for him,' Frank said, dumping some paperwork on the counter between us. 'I was about to go around there anyway. I can introduce you.'

I couldn't come up with a reason why I should not go.

Frank had already picked up the pile of papers and was hugging it to his chest to keep control of it. 'Lead the way.' I followed him back out of the shop with a quick wave goodbye to Poison who was already opening her graphic novel again.

That Frank was already doing research for the new guy bothered me. I had no right to claim Frank as my researcher, of course, he was nothing of the sort and I didn't pay him. He was someone that I had learned to respect though and possibly even rely on at times.

'Klowns then, Frank. What have you learned, please?' I asked as we walked along Rochester High Street.

'Not much, if I'm honest, but I already made an extra copy of the research in case you came asking for it. Here we are,' Frank announced as he headed towards a shop door.

We had gone past my office but only by about twelve yards. It was in the wrong direction for me, in that I always came in from the other direction and very rarely would I have passed the new business. Had I done so, I might have noticed the very new looking glass-front right under my nose. Casting my mind back, I could remember that this place had been empty for a while and had been covered up while it was being worked on recently. Clearly, the new owner had been getting it ready for business.

Above the glass front, the name of the business was displayed in large letters: True Paranormal Solutions. Large, glass windows sat either side of a glass door leading into the business. The bottom five feet of the glass was frosted so that one could see indistinct shapes inside but little more. The façade was very modern and inviting.

Frank pushed open the door with his left shoulder and went inside, leaving me standing in the street still taking it all in. After a few moments, I followed him in to find that he was nowhere in sight. The inside of the business was as plush and modern as the outside. It was everything my office wasn't. To one side was a reception counter made from chrome and even more frosted glass. Behind it, on a high stool, was an attractive woman in a business suit. Probably in her late twenties, she looked like a lawyer from a US TV show – all professional and glamourous with a side order of massively intelligent. She offered me a brief smile and a salutation but otherwise left me to look around.

On the other side of the office space was an area in which customers could wait. There was a middle-aged couple there now, looking slightly out of place amid the sleek surroundings in their ordinary clothes. They were sitting on one of a pair of plush-looking leather sofas which were arranged around a coffee table.

I looked around the room. On the far wall, opposite the entrance, were two office doors. One was blank, but the other had a frosted glass nameplate on the outside. It claimed the office in the name of Dr. L Parrish. Next to the door was a framed certificate. I walked across the room to inspect it. It was a Ph.D. awarded to Lyndon Parrish. He had studied paranormal psychology; a subject I knew nothing about. I moved on. Around the office were large, framed pictures of crop circles, the Loch Ness Monster, a grainy photograph of what one would assume is a flying saucer. Frank had many of the same photographs in his bookshop but, in contrast, his were ratty old posters held up with blue tac. The overall impression of the office and business was money. Lots and lots of money.

On top of the reception counter, was a cardboard holder in which I spotted a leaflet with the word *Rates* in the top left corner. I smiled at the receptionist and picked one up.

'Is there anything I can help you with today, sir?' she asked politely.

'Not just yet, thank you.'

'You will find our rates very reasonable,' she assured me.

Very reasonable? Compared to what?

Looking at the leaflet I realised that they were reasonable compared to mine. I honestly believed I charged a sensible, acceptable rate but the prices in front of me were undercutting mine by a good margin. I wondered how his business could turn a profit. I was making okay money from my work, but I was hardly rolling in it and my overheads must be a fraction of theirs.

My time to consider this was cut short as Dr. Parrish emerged from his office with Frank. The pair were deep in discussion.

'Oh, my word!' exclaimed Dr. Parrish as he noticed me. 'Tempest Michaels. The very man himself. In my office no less.' He was bubbling over with excitement. I couldn't fathom why.

I extended my hand, which he took. His grip was weak. I made no comment.

'Dr. Parrish?' I asked.

'Goodness, please call me Lyndon. I must say this is a real honour.'

'Why is that?' I really wanted to know why I suddenly seemed to be getting treated like the lead singer in a boy band.

'Anastasia, why does Mr. Michaels not have a drink?' he asked the receptionist. Somewhat flustered, she hopped off her stool.

'There is no need, really,' I said.

'Nonsense, Tempest. You're something of a personal

hero of mine. You gave me the confidence to set out on my own quest against the forces of darkness.'

'What forces?'

Frank leaned in to whisper in Lyndon's ear. His face turning from confusion to surprise. 'A non-believer?' he uttered in a hushed tone. He locked eyes with me again. 'Mr. Michaels, you do not believe in the supernatural forces, and yet you battle them anyway? It takes a lot to impress me, but my goodness you are quite the man.'

'Lyndon,' I started then stopped. I scratched my head as I tried to work out how to frame my question. 'Lyndon, there is no paranormal. It's all a load of rubbish and every one of my cases has proven that. What solution do you offer your clients if you do not solve their cases by presenting them with a rational answer?' The question felt like I was directly insulting him. Perhaps I was, but I could only assume that he was ripping people off by performing fake exorcisms or painting sigils on people's houses to ward off ghosts while charging them for his nonsense.

'You will have to forgive, Tempest,' said Frank. 'He would deny the existence of a lycanthrope even while it was eating his arm.'

'This is disappointing, Mr. Michaels. I had expected to exchange stories of supernatural adventures, of ghost hunting and bringing down foul beasts. Alas, it seems that will not be possible. I have to wonder though what happens to the spirits, ghosts and other creatures that you fail to tackle while you are offering your clients what you believe are rational explanations. You charge them for the pleasure of your time but do not catch, trap or otherwise dispose of the entity that has troubled them.'

Lyndon was neither small nor large. At just under six feet tall he was almost the same height as me but a lighter build. He looked very academic, which is to say that he didn't look very dangerous, but his ire was up; he was angry, and the anger was aimed at me. I had no interest in exchanging any further words with him.

'Good day, Dr. Parrish,' I said, smiling pleasantly. I offered my hand once more and like a gentleman, he took it and bid me a good day also. I nodded to Frank and left them both where they were. On my way out the door, I checked my watch: 1211hrs. I intended to investigate the ghostly footsteps at the restaurant in Faversham tonight, so I went back to the office to check on Jane, let her know my plan and that I was going home to rest.

Jane was sifting emails when I got back to the office. 'Anything of interest?' I asked her. It had taken some time to train Jane to see the crazy from the genuine cases. When she first started as my assistant, she was… well, actually she was James and dressed as a man… because she was one. But at the start, she had a propensity to believe the claims the clients made and would have signed me up to investigate every case.

'Hi, Tempest,' she said without looking up. 'We have another report of strange goings on at Chatham Dockyard, the ghost tours in Tonbridge believe they have an actual ghost now and there is a gentleman in East Malling that says his wife is a witch. I printed off those that might have some merit, highlighted passages for you to read and made up your usual folder to take home.'

I had no idea if all transvestites were this efficient, but Jane was able to admin the heck out of my office. I had managed perfectly well without an assistant for over six months before I hired her but couldn't now imagine how. She had worked for me for only a couple of weeks and at some point, would take a holiday of some kind. I worried that I would crumble without her.

To reply, I said, 'Jolly good. Have you much left to do? I'm going to go home and rest. I'm still quite sore,' I said, sort of patting my ribs as if she needed a reminder that I had an injury.

She looked up then. 'Of course, boss. I can lock up.'

I considered sitting down for a bit, I felt like I had overexerted myself but the effort of sitting down and then having to get up again at some point in the future sounded like too much trouble. Instead, I decided I would just go. I collected the folder Jane had made up for me and started to head for the door.

'Oh, err, Tempest,' Jane called before I could leave. 'It's my birthday on Thursday. My boyfriend wants to take me for a drink in Rochester and told me to invite some friends.' She stopped as if unsure what she wanted to say next. I made sure I was giving her my full attention, hoping it would encourage her to continue. 'Well, I um… I don't have many friends since the whole vampire club thing went south and I came out, so I was hoping you and Big Ben and some of the others might be available to come for a drink. I don't want my boyfriend to think I'm a total loser with no friends, I guess,' she said with her head down, so she didn't have to make eye contact with me. She looked up embarrassed as she finished speaking.

It occurred to me that I knew very little about my assistant.

'Jane, it would be an honour to come out for a drink with you and your boyfriend. I can't speak for the others, but I will enquire about their availability and let you know. I feel certain that they will be only too happy to join us. Where are we going?'

'The Warren.'

'What time?'

'Oh. Eight o'cl... I mean 2000hrs.' I smiled; she was learning to tell the time correctly.

'Right. I will speak with the others and let you know. I'm sure it will be a good night. I'm off to see Big Ben now actually, check on how he's doing in the hospital.' I had made the decision to see him in the last half second.

'Okay,' Jane said, smiling now with a degree of relief, having managed to ask what she clearly felt was an awkward question.

I said I would see her in the morning and left her where she was.

Maidstone Hospital

I pulled into the car park and for once found a parking space straight away and near the point where the car park was nearest the hospital. Heading through the main reception, I stopped as I realised that I had no idea where I was going. Big Ben had been spirited away by Dr. Harman and was probably being kept quite willingly as her personal sex monkey. However, I was willing to bet he would show up on the central registry and the lovely, wobbly old ladies in reception would be able to direct me to his location.

I was correct, so two minutes later I was arriving in his private room. I was a little surprised that the NHS had private rooms, I was used to being crammed in twenty to a ward, yet here he was squirreled away nice and cosy. I didn't bother knocking, even though the door was shut. It simply didn't occur to me. So, the sight I received inside was entirely my own fault.

I shut the door again, quickly leaving myself outside. Big Ben had seen me though and thrown me a grin from his prone position on the bed; it was an entirely typical thing for him to do. The other person in the room didn't see me, but then she had her back to me and her head down and appeared to be quite invested in what she was doing.

Standing in the corridor, I was calculating whether it was better to knock or go and find somewhere to sit until the visitor in his room elected to leave. Then someone tapped me on the shoulder and my bowel almost loosened itself.

'Whatcha doing, Tempest?' a voice asked from right next to my ear.

As my heart restarted, I turned to confirm that the voice belonged to Patience Woods. Patience is a police officer, a friend of Amanda's, and a larger-than-life black woman with boobs that probably created their own gravitational field. She was in uniform complete with radio, cuffs and all the paraphernalia they had to carry.

'Good afternoon, Patience. What brings you here?'

'That big hunk of man in there,' she answered, indicating the closed door with her head. I had no idea that she knew Big Ben. Considering it now though, it seemed perfectly reasonable that she would know him. He had shagged more than half the single women in the Country after all. And quite a few on the married ones probably.

'You, err, know Big Ben?' I asked.

'Honey, it's more like Big Ben knows me,' she replied with a wicked smile. I could imagine a night with Patience would be an adventure. I had no intention of finding out though, which was a decision based mostly on the principle that I had no desire to sleep with a woman after Big Ben had. I suspected I wouldn't fare well by comparison. Patience was looking at me. I was looking at her. The silence was getting awkward. 'Honey, why are we standing in the corridor and not going in that room?'

'Oh. Ah. Well, Big Ben is busy.'

Patience raised an eyebrow at me.

'He has a doctor in with him,' I explained.

Patience didn't look convinced. 'What is the doctor doing?' I guess my face told her enough. 'Huh,' she said, looking at the door. 'Time to go to work.' She straightened her hat, shuffled her belt a little to pull it up, then grabbed the door handle and threw it open.

Inside, the lady in her white coat stopped bobbing her head and leapt away from Big Ben in abject shock.

'Police, honey. This is a raid,' Patience announced at high volume as she strode into the room. She stopped as she got to the doctor. The poor woman was one of the young doctors I had seen doing the round with the consultant two days ago when I was here. Her face was bright red. She looked like she wanted to say something but had no idea what that might be. 'Wipe your mouth before you go back to the ward, sister,' Patience advised.

At the last comment from Patience, the girl fled the room, wiping her mouth with her sleeve as she went.

'That was fun,' said Patience. Her voice dropped an octave as it took on a sultry edge when she addressed Big Ben, 'Hi, lover.'

Big Ben chuckled. 'Hi, Patience.' He was shuffling back into his jogging bottoms and once they were back around his waist, I felt it was okay for me to enter the room.

'Hey, Ben,' I said.

'Hey, buddy. Come to rescue me?' he asked.

'Do you need rescuing?'

'Kinda. There has been a steady stream of visitors. I could do with some sleep.'

Patience put herself in the conversation, 'Sweetie, why are you messing with these skinny white chicks when you could be with me? Patience is gonna take you home but can't promise you all that much sleep.'

'Patience, dear. You do remember me saying that I have a strict one night, no second date policy?'

'Yes, honey, but there is no way you're able to resist another portion of Patience.'

He inclined his head, indicating that he didn't necessarily disagree.

'I'll come back,' I announced, heading for the door. I was getting uncomfortable with the continuous flirting and sex talk, largely because it reminded me how unlikely I was to get any.

'No need to go, Tempest. I have to stay here actually. Doctor Harman turned out to be right, I did have a nick to my bowel. I think someone got in deep doo-doo over not examining me thoroughly enough when I came in. They did a bit of surgery and fixed me up but there was a high risk of infection, so I'm on strong antibiotics and have to stay here for a while.'

'How long?' Patience and I asked simultaneously.

'Another couple of days maybe.'

'I just came to check in on you. Clearly, you don't need me, so I will leave you in this lady's very capable hands.' I was already heading out the door. 'Take care, brother. Call me if you need anything.'

Quite why I had thought Big Ben might need me to visit, I could now not fathom. I was just the type of person that tried to put others first. Maybe it was an army thing. There had been people under my command, and I had always made sure they ate before me, got rest before I did and when they were sick or injured or whatever, I always visited them and made sure they had what they needed. It was a camaraderie thing, or a leadership thing, or some thing.

I shook my head wryly, acknowledging that I was rubbish at working out what I wanted to say, even to myself. My car was where I left it in the car park, and I was home in less than ten minutes.

My House in Finchampstead

MONDAY, 24TH OCTOBER 1443HRS

Rather than go to the office in Rochester, I worked out of my dining room/office at home. I was still kind of half-arsing the Klown investigation because I wasn't sure what to do about it. There were other cases I could be working on, which I felt could be treated as a higher priority simply because I had a better chance of solving them. One of these was the ghostly footsteps I had sent Amanda to check out last Saturday. The solution to it seemed likely to be simple.

I called the number for the restaurant.

'Fennucci's, good afternoon,' said a young woman's voice with a very slight Italian accent.

'Good afternoon. This is Tempest Michaels of the Blue Moon Investigation Agency. Is Georgio Fennucci available please?'

'Just one moment,' she replied. It sounded like she had placed the phone down and walked away. I waited patiently for almost a minute before I heard someone pick it up.

'Hello?'

I explained once again who I was, but I now had the proprietor on the phone, and he was very pleased to be talking to me. He said that he had planned to call me today as he hadn't heard from the firm but was yet to find the time to do so.

There was no need for further discussion, so after assuring him that despite my firm belief that there was no ghost haunting his premises, I would visit him this evening and do my best to determine what was actually going on.

He thanked me and promised me a meal on the house for my efforts. Checking my watch, the time was 1521hrs. I needed perhaps forty minutes to get to the restaurant and park, leaving me three hours to fill. I needed to get clean, so a bath rather than a shower as I had plenty of time. First though, since it was so nice out today, I called the dogs for a walk.

They ignored me as usual until I went to the fridge, whereupon the noise of the light inside it coming on had its magnetic effect to drag them from their slumber and off the sofa. They arrived, skidding to a halt by my feet in the kitchen. I gave them each a small chunk of carrot and slipped their collars on.

They were happy enough with a slow meander around the village which gave me some time to consider the restaurant haunting. What equipment would I need? I made a mental note of a few items that I thought were likely to prove useful. Most of them were in my bag already but I wanted to take a tuning fork with me and couldn't remember where mine was. It was an odd artefact that I had picked up at a church jumble sale where my mother had been running a stall. She was selling cakes, and I had gone along to show my support. Where had I put it? I narrowed the search down to a few hopeful locations which

I would check when I got home. As I wandered, I discerned a niggling concern that I was forgetting something. Like there was a task I had committed to but could now not remember. It refused to surface and there was no appointment on my phone calendar which there would have been if it were work related because Jane was very good at organising my diary.

At almost the furthest point of the walk, fifteen minutes from the house, a gentle drizzle started. An ominous dark cloud had been visible over Bluebell Hill as we set off, my guess that it would move towards Maidstone had ultimately proven erroneous as it had instead made a beeline for me and the two Dachshunds.

Had we been closer to home and still on the outward leg, I would have turned around and headed for home. As it was, all I could do was quicken my pace and call instructions to hurry the dogs along. The rain picked up, driven by a breeze, fat blobs of it hitting the top of my head and visibly getting the dogs wet. I quickened my pace a little more, then noticed that the dogs weren't with me. Calling them had no effect, so I turned around and went back to find them safe and dry under a thick bush. They refused to come out, forcing me to get on my knees to clip their leads on so I could drag them from their refuge.

Ten minutes later, we were all back in the house, the walls of my entrance lobby were sprayed with muddy marks where they had shaken themselves, and the kettle was burbling away to make a nice cup of warming tea. I was soaked. However, I had to put up with my own wetness as the dogs would dry themselves on the sofa if I didn't intercept them with a towel.

As my tea brewed, I slowly pulled off my wet garments to throw them into the washer. Then, taking the hot beverage upstairs, I ran the bath I had already felt I needed. My ribs were hurting, the soreness there accented by having to struggle out of clothes that were sticking to my skin. I popped two of the strong painkillers I had been given at the hospital and swallowed them with a slurp of tea.

The painkillers did their magic, easing the pain in my side and spreading a general feeling of relaxed contentedness throughout my body. I awoke in the bath sometime later, confused by the darkness. I had no watch or phone with me so had no idea what time it was. Sliding out of the bath to flick the light on, I popped my head around the bathroom door to see the clock in my bedroom.

It was 1807hrs!

I needed to leave in a few minutes and hadn't fed the dogs or sorted out anything to wear. I fumbled and fiddled as fast as I could to get myself dressed, then had to convince the dogs to go into the garden and pee quickly – not a concept a Dachshund understands.

I drove a little more swiftly than I otherwise might have and somehow arrived on time. My rigid discipline that I was never late anywhere remained intact.

Fenucci's Italian Family Restaurant, Faversham

Having called the proprietor earlier, he knew to expect me and had set out a table at a point that intersected where he claimed the footsteps usually tracked. The restaurant was completely empty; I was the only patron. Okay, it was 1900hrs on a Monday evening but even so, a successful place would have people in it. The owner's name was Georgio Fenucci which sounded very Italian, unlike the man himself who sounded like he hailed from Essex. I wondered if the name was fake but refrained from asking.

He had opened the restaurant five years ago and had enjoyed a steady stream of clients ever since. That was until three weeks ago when the footsteps started to occur. On the first night that they manifested, he was in the kitchen when he heard a rush of people coming down the stairs from the upper dining room. Worried there might be a fire or some other disaster unfolding, he had rushed out into the restaurant still clutching a spatula in one hand, then watched in horror as almost all his customers disappeared out of the door. His staff had gone also, all except his wife and the slightly deaf barman.

He found his wait staff outside in the street and slowly convinced most of them to come back inside. Maria, one of the girls that had been working upstairs, explained what she had heard. They went back upstairs and, of course, there were no ghostly noises to listen to. Maria and the others had been adamant that they hadn't imagined it and corroborated each other's stories.

Georgio described being angry at the time because he suddenly had an empty restaurant and he had to throw food away. He did nothing about it though and since so many of his staff were telling him the same thing, he felt that he couldn't hold them to account or call them liars. Then the same thing happened the next night, after which, some of his staff quit and then the night after that. It was on the third night that he witnessed the phenomenon himself. By then he had become convinced that this was an elaborate hoax and had seated himself in the upper dining room to see if they dared to perpetrate it with him there.

Instead, he got the fright of his life as, clear as anything, an invisible person walked across the room, their footsteps audibly striking the floorboards. A few seconds later, he was alone in the room still rooted to the spot when the *ghost* ambled back again.

I listened to all this with my notebook out, taking notes while we were still downstairs in the bar area. He regaled Amanda with the same story on Saturday morning, but her shift pattern hadn't permitted her to stay for the evening to witness the event. There was one detail missing though.

'My colleague made a note that you heard music,' I prompted.

'Yes,' he replied. 'The ghost walks across the room several times most nights. Some nights not at all, but more often than not now the haunting occurs. It's usually accompanied by the sound of someone playing the cello. It's much fainter than the footsteps and I dismissed it the first time I heard it. After three weeks though, I believe the two noises are linked and I have the ghost of a musician haunting my restaurant.'

Georgio went on to complain about how his business was suffering and how he couldn't sustain the current level of income for very long. The phenomenon only occurred in the evenings, so he was able to conduct lunch trade, but the word was getting out and several customers who he considered regulars because they came in most weeks, had already stopped visiting.

I thanked him for his detailed explanation and went upstairs to find a seat. There was a lot of choice as I was the only person in the restaurant. Presently, a waitress appeared and took my order, returning a few moments later with a glass of ice and a bottle of sparkling mineral water. I had ordered carpaccio to start and a seafood pizza as my main course. I was hungry and looked forward to the food. While I waited, I pulled out a few items I felt I might need: a piece of chalk, a tape measure, a stopwatch and a tuning fork. I placed each on the table at the seat adjacent and to the left of mine so that they were within easy reach when I needed them, and so that I could grab them with my uninjured side.

Idly wondering how long I would have to wait for my food; I remembered that there was something niggling at me. I had forgotten to do something or was supposed to do something. It was the same feeling I had been wondering about earlier, but the memory still refused to coalesce. It was hiding in the corner of my mind, showing me glimpses but not revealing itself. I told myself that if I concentrated the answer would come to me. Just then I heard the door open downstairs. That I could hear the entrance door moving was a clear demonstration of just how quiet the restaurant was. I had instructed Georgio to not play any music tonight – I wanted as little background noise as possible, but the silence in the building was striking. Then I realised that it was Frank's voice coming from downstairs. He was talking with Georgio and there was a third man's voice in the conversation.

Clomping footsteps on the wooden stairs preceded the appearance of Georgio, then Frank and then Dr. Lyndon Parrish.

'Good evening, gentlemen,' I said to attract their attention. Frank and Lyndon both looked surprised to see me, so they weren't deliberately gate crashing. 'What a pleasant surprise. Won't you please join me?'

'Tempest,' beamed Frank. 'Lyndon plans to catch the ghost.'

I nodded, unsure what I could say to that announcement. I had my own theory about what was causing the phenomenon, and it was a little less than paranormal.

Lyndon said, 'Mr. Michaels, I must apologise. I had no idea you would be here.'

'Did Mr. Fenucci hire you?' I asked

'Goodness no, this is pro bono work. I'm new to the game unlike you, Mr. Michaels. I need to build up my reputation. This will do me no harm at all. Of course, had I known you were here I might have come along anyway to watch the master at work.' Lyndon strode across the room to shake my hand. Both he and Frank were carrying bags.

'Do you mind if Frank and I remain and attempt to catch the spirit?' he asked.

'No, please.' I indicated that they should carry on. I wanted to see what he planned to do.

Lyndon spoke briefly with Georgio who then departed. Then he laid his bag on the floor. From it he extracted a piece of equipment I recognised – it was a PKE meter. Mr. Reginald Parker had tried to sell it to me recently. I had all but laughed at him, but it seemed that he had found himself a customer after all.

Next out was a piece of clunky steel with a lid and a long electrical lead. Frank was emptying his bag at the same time. Onto the floor, he spilled several items of recording equipment and what looked like motion sensors with accessories like tripods to mount them on.

I looked at the few items I had on the table and smiled to myself. 'How is it that you plan to catch the ghost, Lyndon?' I asked.

Lyndon stopped what he was doing on the floor and stood up. 'First, we have to establish that there is a ghost. Not every report of supernatural activity has a genuine entity at the end of it,' he lectured knowingly.

Or none at all. Ever. I thought.

'Then I shall trap it inside a circle, and using this,' he showed me a fancy leather pouch with a drawstring at the top, 'I will anchor it to a new object and remove it from the premises.'

Frank saw me looking at the little pouch and answered my question just as I was opening my mouth to ask it. 'It's ghost dust, Tempest.' When he saw my continued curiosity, he spoke again. 'It's created from ectoplasmic slime by a process of desiccation, but it can only be performed by a single shaman in South America. The secret is passed down to only one member of the tribe on his death bed. It's incredibly rare.'

'No doubt.' I was continuously amazed at the odd stuff that Frank came out with and the vast variety of weird things he knew.

The waitress reappeared with drinks for Frank and Lyndon and my carpaccio. Frank and Lyndon showed no interest in food, but I tucked into my starter hungrily. It was as delicious as the dish always is and a generous portion as well.

Just a few bites in though, I heard the noise that had brought me to the restaurant. A very distinctive set of footsteps walked across the room towards me. The waitress screamed and fled, running down the stairs and very possibly out of the restaurant and into the street. Frank and Lyndon both jumped up from the floor and I had to go around them with my piece of chalk. Lyndon was shouting hasty instructions to get the recording equipment ready and fiddling with the little bag of super expensive ghost dust. Wincing at my ribs because I was trying to move fast, I got to where I believed the noise has started and made a mark on the floor, then drew a line across the floor following the footsteps that were still travelling across the room.

They went right through the table I had been sitting at but terminated just a few feet beyond. I caught up with them and crouched down. Reaching up with one hand, and without looking, I found and grabbed the tuning fork. I marked another spot on the floor with the chalk, ignoring the ruckus behind me: Frank and Lyndon were doing something complicated.

The footsteps started up again but this time I was ready for them. My hands were on the floorboards feeling the vibrations the footsteps were making.

'It's a classic non-forming, type three entity!' yelled Frank to Lyndon, excitement in his voice. 'This is huge!'

I had a different theory.

'Can you trap its energy?' Frank asked Lyndon.

'Yes, I think so. I just need to...' Lyndon scrambled across the floor ahead of where the steps were going. He was scribbling odd symbols on the floor with a silver marker pen. I stood up and followed the direction the floorboards went rather than following the footsteps. The boards went to the wall but looking down it didn't look like they stopped there.

Using the tuning fork, I tapped on a board then held the butt end of it against the board as it vibrated. Then I did the same again on the board next to it and the one next to that. Then I walked across the room to beyond where the footsteps had started and tried again. I got a very different result.

'Dammit,' Lyndon swore. 'It didn't work.' Whatever hokum he had been trying to do had failed apparently. He looked quite despondent.

I went back to the table and picked up the tape measure. I measured to the wall. Then I went to the point where the footsteps had started again and measured to the front on the building. The sound of someone playing the cello started. It was faint and sounded like it was coming through the floorboards. I smiled to myself, pocketed my tools and went downstairs.

I looked around for Georgio, but he was outside in the street. I could see him through the window with his arm around a lady wearing chef's clothing. I exited the restaurant and joined them in the street.

'Mr. Fenucci. Shall we put an end to your ghost problem?' My question was met with quizzical expressions. I ignored him for the moment and turned around to look back at the building. The restaurant sits in a long row of very old looking buildings all joined together like terraced houses. I would guess that they were easily four hundred years old and possibly even older than that. The front façade was constructed using solid looking wooden beams – I believe Tudor design is the correct term. The plaster between the black beams was bright white but that wasn't what I was looking at. I was looking at the windows of the upper dining room and what was adjacent to them on either side.

To the left, as I looked at it, was a shop that sold antique clocks and watches. The shutters were down to cover the large windows and protect the goods inside. On the upper floor there were lights on. I also noted that the shop had a new look to it.

'How long has the clock business been there, Mr. Fenucci?' I asked, pointing at it to remove any ambiguity.

'Oh. Err. Just a few weeks. I think. It has been empty since before we bought the restaurant. Nice girl that owns it now.'

'Is there really? Would you be so kind as to introduce me?'

'Oh. Err. I suppose I could.' He seemed sceptical.

'Indulge me please, Mr. Fenucci. I believe your neighbour holds the key to ridding you of the spirit that is haunting your premises.' I had already made my way to her door, which was a separate and unassuming flat wooden object with a door number and a doorbell. It was set at the leftmost edge of the building but had to be the door that led up to the apartment above the business.

I rang the bell and stepped back to wait as Mr. Fenucci joined me. I was just about to ring the bell again when I heard someone approaching from the other side. The sound of someone putting on a security chain and unlocking the door preceded the door opening and the face of a lady appearing on the other side. She was tall and thin and wore glasses that made her eyes look oversized.

'Good evening,' I said in my most congenial tone. 'Your neighbour, Mr. Fenucci has a small problem with his restaurant, and I was hoping I could ask you a couple of questions. My name is Tempest Michaels.'

'Hello, Tanya,' said Mr. Fenucci from his position by my right shoulder.

'Just a second,' she replied. She closed the door, fiddled with the chain and opened it again. Now that the chain wasn't attached, she could open the door more fully. She was wearing a pair of saggy looking tracksuit bottoms and a t-shirt. Her arms were exposed, and the skin was already doing goose pimples from the cool October air. 'How can I help you?'

'Do you play the cello?' I asked.

'Yes. I was just upstairs practising.' Her answer pretty much confirmed my theory.

'I'm really sorry for the intrusion, Tanya. Would you be so kind as to let us come inside for a moment?' She looked very unsure. 'I'm sure this will not take long,' I added.

I thought for a moment that she was going to say no but perhaps realising that the cold would be once again shut outside, she nodded and led the way back up the narrow flight of stairs to her apartment.

'What did you say this was all about, Georgio?' she asked as we emerged from the stairwell into a living area.

'Um,' Georgio started to mumble since I hadn't explained why were in his neighbour's place now.

I was looking around the room. 'Can you show me where you keep your cello, please?' I asked

Confused, she looked between Georgio and me, then

shrugged and led us further back into the living space. 'It's in here,' Tanya said as we moved from one room into a short corridor and then into another room. 'I haven't got around to decorating yet,' she explained as if embarrassed by the raw nature of the room.

It was bare floorboards. I walked to the window at the front of the building to check where I was.

'You still haven't told me what this is about,' Tanya said, getting a little impatient.

'My apologies. It's a little difficult to explain. We can hear you playing your cello from next door.'

'Oh goodness. Can you? I'm so sorry, Georgio. I never realised,' she replied sounding genuinely horrified.

'You play beautifully, Tanya. Please feel no reason to apologise. The bigger issue is the footsteps?'

'Footsteps?' she asked, utterly mystified.

I was in the process of taking out my tape measure but stopped and gave her the long explanation of why I was at the restaurant, what I had heard and why I was now in her house. As I did so, I pointed out to both Tanya and Georgio that the floorboards were one continuous piece of wood running between the two premises. They went under the wall which had probably been put in decades ago when the large original building was subdivided into several smaller ones. This wasn't uncommon in old buildings and when one looked at the front façade from outside in the street, one could see that it had originally been one building.

To test out my theory, I sent Georgio back to his restaurant while talking to him on my phone. With it on speaker, I advised him that I was moving across the floor in Tanya's room. Between us, we were able to prove that the noise from her room was travelling along the floorboards and manifesting as sounds in his upper dining room where the floorboards finally terminated and became the next floorboard. The faint sound of cello music was travelling through on the airwaves underneath the floor and would probably be inaudible if Georgio had background music playing.

I thanked Tanya for her time and assistance and returned to the restaurant. Trudging back up the stairs to the upper dining room I had to pretend that my ribs didn't hurt from the effort of just moving around. Lyndon was nowhere to be seen, and his equipment was gone. Frank was still there though, so I chucked him a quick wave before heading over to Mr. Fenucci to conclude matters.

My advice to him was to get a builder in to fix the floor. He seemed very relieved that the ghost was nothing more than noise from next door and happy that he would be able to easily fix the problem. I could offer no worthwhile guidance on what a builder might do or even charge for such a remedy, yet it seemed likely it would be a simple task. We shook hands, I told him my final bill would be through in a couple of days, and he told me my dinner was on the house. I, of course, said that his gesture wasn't necessary but offered little resistance when he insisted.

I checked my watch: 2037hrs. My carpaccio was stone cold having been left for most of an hour, but then it was supposed to be, so I ate it. Tucking in, I acknowledged how hungry I was.

'Well done, Tempest,' said Frank who was sitting opposite me at the table for four.

'That is very generous of you, Frank.' I couldn't remember Frank ever admitting that I had proven him wrong before. I felt no need to score a point though, so I let it pass. 'What happened to Lyndon?'

'He got a call from another client and had to rush off. He wasn't being paid to attend this case anyway.' Frank mentioning phone calls reminded me that I hadn't looked at my phone since I arrived at the restaurant. It was tucked in my bag next to my chair and had been there while I was solving the case. I picked it up now and checked it.

I had Seven missed calls. All from Sophie. I hung my head in defeat.

This was the task I couldn't remember. I had known there was something, but for some reason, it hadn't occurred to me that it might be a social engagement that I had forgotten. I genuinely sucked at dating girls. The last call was more than an hour ago. I switched to the text messages as there was an icon there showing me that four texts had been received. The texts started with a polite message at 1745hrs saying that she hadn't heard from me but that she was expecting me in an hour so was assuming I was coming and would be ready. The next message was a few minutes after I should have picked her up, checking that everything was okay. The next a few minutes after that, advised that I had better be able to provide a worthwhile explanation for standing her up two days in a row. The final message instructed me to do something quite improbable with a parsnip.

I needed to call her, so I excused myself and went out into the street where no one I knew would be able to hear the lady at the other end of the line screaming obscenities at me.

Sophie answered on the third ring. She didn't take long to start berating me. 'You've got some nerve calling me now, Tempest Michaels. I have never been stood up in my life, but you think you can leave me sitting in my house like an idiot, two days in a row.' It went on like that for a bit, so for brevity, I shall just say that I attempted to speak several times but never got more than half a word out before she launched into the next tirade.

After what felt like several minutes she finally ran out of steam and demanded I explain myself.

I took a breath, paused to see if she was going to start yelling again and simply said, 'Sorry.'

'Sorry? Sorry! Is that all you have got? Were you out with another woman? Is that it? Are you a player, Tempest?'

'As if I could ever be that lucky,' shouted Mr Wriggly

I ignored the voice from my pants. 'Sophie, I owe you an apology. I do not deny it and I have no wish to further bore you with my excuses. I'm in Faversham on a case. I can't explain why or how I managed to forget our date but would like to claim that I go on dates so rarely that when I was called to this case it didn't occur to me that I might have other plans.' So far, she had allowed me to speak. I pressed on. 'My intentions are unchanged. I would still very much like to meet you for dinner this week.' She hung up on me.

I looked at my phone accusingly. How was it that I managed to screw up my social life every time it threatened to get interesting? The phone went away in a pocket as I trudged back into the restaurant. Frank was still sitting where I left him.

'How are you getting home?' I asked him.

'I came in my own car. Lyndon asked if I wanted to go with him on the next case, but I said I would wait here for you. How did you know it wasn't a ghost?' he asked.

I poured more of the sparkling water into my tumbler and drank it. The ice was long gone but it was refreshing, nevertheless. 'Frank, my dear fellow,' I started. I wanted to explain once again that there are no ghosts, but I liked Frank the way he was – completely bonkers. In some way, his unshakable belief complemented my clinically sane examination of the facts. I started again, 'Frank not every bump in the night is a ghost. Not every bite is a werewolf, not every disease inflicted is a curse placed by a witch. This was just some loose floorboards in an old building. To me it was obvious.'

He nodded his head thoughtfully. Behind him Mr. Fenucci himself appeared carrying two pizzas; Frank had ordered himself one as well. 'Here you are, gentlemen. One Sicilian and one Fruits de Mer. On the house. You're very welcome.' He placed them in front of us with a flourish, looking like a man who had recently received wonderful news.

Steam was rising from them, bringing the scent of warm bread, melting cheese, garlic, herbs and other wonderful food smells with it. The pizzas didn't last long.

Frank and I enjoyed a pleasant evening meal together. Even though we occupy very different camps when it comes to the paranormal world, and it was a constant topic of conversation for us as both our professions centred on it, we were able to discuss business and other subjects with mutual respect.

Neither one of us wanted to hang around after we had eaten, so I bade him and Georgio good evening and headed for home. The roads were empty, which allowed me to enjoy the throaty roar of my German sports car's straight six, tuned, three-litre engine. I arrived home, to find the two dogs happy to see me but just as happy to follow me upstairs to bed once they had taken a quick trip around the garden.

My bed beckoned.

The Blue Moon Office

I slept badly. The injury to my ribs woke me every time I moved. At 0312hrs I forced myself reluctantly from my warm bed to find the painkillers in my bag downstairs. Once their numbing effect took hold, I drifted away, but adding all the sleep together I had probably achieved less than five hours, and I was tired when I got to work.

I arrived late. It was perhaps the first time I could remember being late anywhere since I was a teenager: the army beat the concept of lateness out of a person very quickly. Jane was oblivious though and when I arrived, she was typing up the invoice to Mr. Fenucci because I had sent her an email about the case before I got into bed last night.

My plan for the day was to start looking at the Klown case for my new clients, the clowns. Frank had furnished me with a pack of information but when he had outlined it last night it was all about demons that were recorded as having manifested as clowns at some point in the past and one or two demi-gods that had done much the same. It seemed unlikely to be helpful to me since I was certain this was a gang of cretins with criminal intentions.

Instead of looking into demons and demi-gods, I was going to research the victims thus far, examine the locations of Klown attacks and see what I could patch together from the available information. Amanda had been on a shift last night that had ended at 0300hrs and had promised to be in by lunchtime to offer her assistance. She was bringing information with her as the name of the murder victim from two nights ago hadn't yet been officially released.

For the next ninety minutes, Jane and I sat at the computer desk trawling through data on the attacks. There were numerous news articles, each of which allowed us to look at the information from a slightly different angle. We printed off a map of Kent and plotted the attacks as dots on it and looked into the people that had been targeted. Each of the people that had been chased or hurt appeared to have nothing in common until I found two women that had gone to the same school. They lived in very different areas now – one in Paddock Wood and one in Headcorn. Jane had been printing photographs of the victims and attaching each to an A4 sheet on which she had typed details such as age, location, occupation, time and nature of Klown attack. Thus far the two women were the only ones with a connection.

A couple of hours slipped past unnoticed when I heard the bottom office door open. Amanda called out as she came up the stairs. Coming into the office, she looked more radiant than ever; her smile welcoming but crushing my soul at the same time. Was it the influence of her boyfriend Brett making her glow? They had been dating for a couple of weeks now, so I had to categorise them as a couple. In many ways, it made life easier for me. I wasn't going to pursue a woman that was already involved with someone else.

'Good morning, Amanda,' Jane and I said almost simultaneously.

'Hey, guys. Whatcha doing?' she asked. She was carrying three cups of coffee in a handy four cup cardboard holder. Each one had a name on it. 'Ladies first,' she said as she handed one labelled Jane to Jane then took hers and handed the holder to me. I gratefully lifted mine and took a sip. It was strong and sweet with just the right amount of milky foam on top. The holder went into the bin by the desk as Amanda walked over to the wall where Jane was still pinning photographs.

'The murder victim,' Amanda started. 'His name was released an hour ago, did you get it already?'

'No, not yet,' I answered.

'Matthew Barrow, aged twenty-nine and resident of Igtham.' She put her coffee down to extract a notebook from her handbag. 'Unmarried. No children. Worked as a postman. No reason for the attack that the police can see.'

'Matthew Barrow,' repeated Jane as she typed the name into a search engine and started looking into the man.

'Did anyone see anything?' I asked her.

'No. No witnesses to the crime, but CCTV at a pub around the corner caught a shot of Klowns in a van driving away and they sprayed their usual message in his house.'

'What message?' Jane wanted to know.

'The Klowns are coming,' answered Amanda.

'Oh, that,' Jane said as she carried on working at the computer.

'Tempest, I only have a couple of hours. They are keeping us all busy and threatening extra shifts. The Klown attacks are attracting a lot of unwanted attention, so we are patrolling and investigating and being kept generally quite active. My shift last night was twelve hours, and I need a nap before I go back for my next shift. What shall we do?'

'What shall we do? Honestly? I have no idea. Jane and I are starting to pull together some details, but I don't really know where to start other than by learning all there is to know. I can't imagine that I'm doing anything the police are not. '

'This wouldn't be the first case you solve while the police scratched their collective heads.' Amanda's point was accurate but not necessarily part of a trend. I had got lucky a couple of times.

'Have the police interviewed all of the Klown attack victims?' I asked her.

'Of course.'

'Did they learn anything?'

'Nothing that was of any use so far.'

I thought on that for a moment. 'Maybe we should have a chat with them ourselves. Jane, do we have contact details for any of them?'

'Not yet,' she said without looking up from the screen. 'It will not take me long to find them though.'

'Let's do that.' My stomach growled at me. 'You want some lunch, ladies? I need to get a sandwich or something.'

'I brought food with me, thank you though,' replied Jane.

'Hey, I'm in. Where are we going for food?' asked Amanda. 'I'm hungry.'

The two us of settled on a tearoom a few doors along from us. Rochester has an abundance of places to eat and a booming tourist industry which is drawn there because of the old High Street, the castle and cathedral and the fact that Dickens lived there for much of his adult life. The tourist industry supported the vast array of tea rooms and restaurants so that even on a Tuesday there might be limited choice of where to sit.

At the bottom of the stairs, I held the door open for Amanda and closed it behind her. We turned left and emerged onto the High Street.

Before we went two paces, I touched Amanda's arm and said quietly, 'We are being watched.'

Amanda froze beside me at my announcement. 'Where?'

'Two hoodies across the road.' In the crowd of people, they stood out because they were the only ones not doing anything. There were other people standing stationary but those were engaged in conversation, or texting, or looking in shop windows. Between the people moving in all directions, these two were facing the office and staring right at it. We couldn't see their faces though as they both wore oversize hoodies that were pulled right up to hide them.

They realised they had been spotted as I directed Amanda's gaze towards them. I was setting off in their direction, assuming it was what they wouldn't expect – few run directly towards a threat which is why it's almost always the right thing to do. However, if my move confused them at all it didn't show. They threw back their hoods to reveal Klown make-up beneath.

A woman about to pass in front of the Klowns screamed and suddenly all eyes were on them. The crowd freezing as if caught in time.

Amanda and I were advancing across the street towards them, our estimated time of arrival at their location was about three seconds. Less if they came towards us.

'You're both under arrest,' shouted Amanda as she brandished her police ID. She followed up with instructions to get on their knees, but as expected, neither one paid her any attention.

'I'll get the girl,' the one on the left said, smiling an evil, awful smile. He started towards us, but his colleague, accomplice… however you wanted to think of him, stuck out an arm to bar his way. 'Hold on. How come you get to deal with Miss Sexy Tits, and I get the bloke that looks like he just left the gym?' he asked.

'Well…' his colleague started only to be cut off again.

'You actually have to walk in front of me to get to her. Why don't you fight the guy that we came here for since he's right in front of you and I will have a quick wrestle with Lady Funbags. It shouldn't take long, then I'll give you a hand,' he said, advancing on Amanda.

'I don't think so, dickface. Haven't you just spent all morning telling me all about how you were going to show him how tough you were.' The two were staring at each other now, almost chest to chest. 'I distinctly remember you saying that you were going to give him a beating he wouldn't forget. Now it's fighting time and suddenly you're all afraid.'

'Are you looking to get a beating first? How about I slap you silly then deal with the target and then maybe take little lady love bumps for a date somewhere,' he said, poking his colleague in the chest.

'Try it,' the other one instructed, grabbing hold of a handful of sweater.

'I think that's about enough with the boob comments,' Amanda announced sounding bored. 'Let's get this done.' She threw her bag to an empty bench a few feet away and cracked her knuckles.

It brought the Klowns attention back to us. Their argument dissolved instantly, and they both came for me, but they only took a pace before they stopped again. 'Hold on,' said the one on the right, bringing a halt to proceedings once more. 'We forgot the message.'

'Oh yeah. The message,' acknowledged his companion.

'He wanted you to know that all that has happened and all that will come to pass after we kill you could have been avoided if you had just kept your nose out.' He looked across to his mate. 'Did I miss anything?'

'Yeah. Time to die,' he sneered and once again they both came at me.

I looked for weapons. Neither was holding anything that I could see but then the distance between us was gone and it was too late to do anything other than fight. I was pre-injured, if that is even a word, so I let the Klown come to me, hoping he would commit to a punch or kick that I could convert into a hold and incapacitate him. As Amanda and I had closed the distance to them, I had sized them up. They were both taller and heavier than me and the one on the left as we faced them was the taller and heavier of the pair. With Amanda on my left, she had drawn the straw to deal with him and the bit of my brain that always wanted to protect women had been telling me to somehow swap with her. There was no time for such things and even if there had been she was likely to deal with this better than I anyway. They both went for me though as if Amanda was of no consequence and soon learned what a mistake that was. As I met with the Klown closest to me, I noted that his comrade suddenly vanished from sight when Amanda removed his legs.

I wanted to watch Amanda - to make sure she was alright, but if she needed my help, I couldn't offer it right now. A fist flashed out towards me, the sunlight glinted off what I thought was a collection of rings but realised almost too late was a knuckle duster armed with spikes. It was precisely the move I had hoped for though. It would be simple for me to step inside the punch while spinning to place my back to the attacker. I had practiced the move hundreds of times in various classes. Catch his right arm with my left, right elbow high going back into his face or throat. Pull down with the left arm and duck under it and suddenly the attacker is bleeding from his face and lying on the floor with me on top of him.

Yeah. Didn't happen like that.

I caught the punch and span but as I lifted my right arm everything went wrong. My pain killers had worn off and I had no power in my right arm with which to hit him. I ended up just backing into him so that we were basically spooning in the street.

'What the…?' he asked from right next to my left ear.

He shoved me hard in the back, forcing me to break my hold on his arm. To my left, Amanda had her man on the floor in a head lock, but he was fighting her. He too had a knuckle duster and was trying to punch over his head to get to hers.

Klown dickhead one, the Klown that I had thus far had little success with, came at me in a huge haymaking lunge. He was trying to get me with the knuckle duster, which told me that it was probably his only move. He wasn't a fighter then; he was a big guy with a weapon, full of false bravado because there were two of them and they were armed. I imagined that they had told themselves this would be easy.

If he knew about my ribs, he was failing to target them. However, if his intention was to kill me or cause serious injury, he looked to be more than capable, and Amanda couldn't hold off both if I was unable to deal with him.

From the crowd, someone shouted, 'Bravo!' A quick

glance revealed that Amanda had her man on his front now with both hands behind his back. She was sitting on him. That a crowd had formed to watch the spectacle but were doing nothing to help the little blonde lady said volumes about human mentality. Did they think this was a show put on for the tourists?

Another haymaker punch swung harmlessly by as I span away. He was slow, not uncommon in big men, but having missed me several times, he accepted that his tactic wasn't working. I saw the change in his stance and in the next second, he came at me with both hands trying to grab me. Keeping my feet apart and balanced, I parried his hands away. But I was using only my left arm; my right arm I kept tucked into my body. Any attempt to use it would result in incapacitating pain, so it was held in a boxer's defensive pose where I could pretend it was ready for the big punch if I got an opening. Keeping his focus on me, I had circled him around so that I was now between him and Amanda. I couldn't allow him to interfere with her restraining the other Klown.

Barely a minute had passed since we came out of the office, fights are always so quick, but I was feeling the effort, and my right arm was getting difficult to hold up. It seemed to me that he noticed my discomfort as he changed his stance again. He led with a kick which came low and on my right side. I couldn't block it with my left arm, so I moved into it to take the blow early on. In doing so, I had given away any distance advantage I had, which exposed me to his next move. He grabbed my right arm and the pain in my ribs made my head swim. I was going down.

I tried to focus on his face, looking for advance warning of the next blow, hoping I could go with it or twist away from it. He had hold of my right arm though and I couldn't pull it from him. Just then though, as I was looking at his face, it disappeared. It just exited stage-left from my field of vision. In its place was an enormous boot. The Klown's body followed its head, flying off to the left. I was rid of the Klown it seemed, but he failed to release my right arm as he went, causing a savage tug to my injured side. It finished me off and I tumbled to the floor in a pile.

'Are you alright, Tempest?' asked Basic, leaning over me.

I gave him a thumb's up with my left hand. It seemed easier than speaking.

'Hur, hur,' he laughed. Basic laughed a lot.

I was able to raise my head a bit so I could see that the Klown Basic had kicked showed no sign of movement and Amanda's Klown was incapacitated. Then raised voices drew my attention. Coming towards us through the crowd were two uniforms. They arrived slightly out of breath, but ready for action. They spotted Amanda and it was clear they recognised her. From her position still sitting on top of the still protesting Klown's back, she gave the cops a little wave. Sirens heralding the arrival of more police and an ambulance split the tranquillity of the ancient stone around us. I continued to lay on the floor. It wasn't exactly comfortable, but I really didn't want to move.

Presently, a green box appeared by my head and a paramedic appeared above me. 'I'm ok,' I told him. 'I'm just having a rest.' I explained about my ribs and was rewarded with the promise of some medication. They wanted to take me to the hospital, but I knew there was no need. I thanked them and forced myself into a seated position.

Amanda was a few feet away talking to Chief Inspector Quinn. He and I had met a few weeks ago, the day after I had met Amanda, actually. He didn't like me. The two

Klowns were in handcuffs and being led away and the crowd had been pushed back but had grown in numbers. Lots of them had their phones out and were recording the scene. No doubt I would be on YouTube tonight showing people my incredible fighting skills - something to look forward to.

Amanda saw me sitting up and came over to check on me. 'How are you feeling?' she asked.

'Same as before. My ribs hurt. Did you get anything from the Klowns?'

'Nah, they won't speak. CI Quinn will be interrogating them shortly back at the station, but there is no ID on them just the same as the last guy we caught. I wanted to check on you, but I will have to go soon. They have recalled all officers. With an attack in daylight, they have called for rein-forcements from other counties, so we have to show that we are using all our available resources here first.' I guess that made sense. 'Is there anything I can get you?'

'No. I'll be okay. Where is Basic though and what was he doing here?'

'Ah. Actually, Basic is here because I hired him.'

'Hired him?'

'As protection for you.' I opened my mouth, but she kept talking so I couldn't get a word in. 'Just for a few days. From your description of the attack the other night, it seems likely that they targeted you deliberately. Today's attack right outside your office confirms it. You're injured and can't defend yourself as you normally would, so you need someone around that can help. Big Ben is out of action and Basic said he could take a few days off from the super-market to help out.'

I nodded. I might not like it, but it made sense. My pride, my sense of manliness was wounded from the suggestion that I needed a bodyguard. I was big enough and tough enough to take care of myself. Except I wasn't at the moment. If Basic hadn't come to my rescue, I might not have survived the most recent attack. I really didn't like it, but I swallowed my pride and kept my mouth shut.

'What's going on?' asked a voice that I recognised as Jane's. 'I noticed flashing lights from the office window when I got up to make a tea and was starting to wonder why it was taking so long to fetch a sandwich.'

'We got distracted,' I said.

'Yes. I see that.' I would have to sit down for a proper chat about the Klowns with Jane later. It felt very possible they might target her also.

Amanda checked her watch. 'Do you need to go?' I asked her.

'No, no. I can hang on for a bit,' she replied, but it was clear that she was being polite.

I said, 'There is nothing more you can do here. You need to feed yourself and get to work. You should go.' I spotted Basic eating a kebab and sitting on a bench just behind the crowd of people watching us. 'Basic is here. Don't worry about me.'

'I think you will have to go to the station anyway, Tempest. They are going to want to question you about your involvement.' Of course, they would. I had been attacked twice in a few days.

I clambered to my feet, wobbling a little as I did so. Once I was up, I had to bend over a bit to lower my head until the sparkly lights stopped dancing in front of my eyes. 'I'm fine,' I lied to Amanda and Jane's concerned faces. 'I just stood up too quickly.'

Basic saw me and gave a wave. CI Quinn saw me also and detached himself from the officers he was talking to.

The show was over anyway; the police were packing up and moving out.

'Mr. Michaels, another busy week for you. Would you care to tell me why the Klowns are targeting you?'

'I wish I knew.' It did seem that I was part of their plan though. Maybe if I could work out why, it would be possible to solve this case.

'I will need you to come to the station, Mr. Michaels. You are free to do so at any point. However, right now would be as good a time as any.'

I nodded my head. 'I'll be along shortly. Within the hour.' CI Quinn appeared to be content with my answer, he turned away to deal with other business as I looked around for Jane.

I spotted her chatting with Basic and sharing his kebab. They were both sitting on the bench. 'Hey, Tempest,' Basic called as I approached. 'Why don't sharks eat clowns? Because they taste funny. Hur, hur, hur.' I smiled to be polite. Good old Basic.

'Basic, I believe Amanda asked you to hang out with me for a few days.'

'S'right,' he said around a mouthful of kebab.

'I need to go to the police station shortly. You don't need to come with me. I should be safe enough there.'

'Amanda said I was to keep you safe and to thump any of dem Klowns if dey came near you,' he replied.

'Okay. Well, I need some lunch so shall we meet in a few minutes?' Basic was already getting to his feet, clearly intending to accompany me wherever I was going. 'I'm just going in that shop over there for a sandwich, Basic. You can watch the shop from here. Please finish your kebab.' I added that I would be fine since he didn't look convinced and left him to finish shovelling bits of meat into his mouth.

I returned a few minutes later with a turkey and swiss sandwich wrapped in greaseproof paper that was tucked inside my shoulder bag. Basic had finished eating and had clearly wiped his greasy fingers on his jeans to dry them. The empty kebab container was in the bin next to the bench and a pair of pigeons were underneath his seat and edging close to a few scraps he had dropped.

As I approached, Jane got up. 'Tempest, I forgot to tell you that I got a call just after you left the office. You have a female client visiting tomorrow morning at ten o'clock.'

'What is it pertaining to?'

'Same case. The Klowns. She was crying a lot so I couldn't make out all that she was telling me. She wanted to see you in person though, said she had information and wanted your help.'

Information. I checked my watch. it was entirely possible the information was nothing, but I felt a pull to check it out anyway. I tapped a finger on the face of my watch idly while I debated what to do. CI Quinn was expecting me, and I actually wanted to get him on my side for once. He could be helpful to me if our relationship was less antagonistic.

Decision made, I hauled my keys from my bag. 'Ready when you are,' I told Basic, at which he leaped up and off we went. 'I'll see you in the morning, Jane,' I offered back over my shoulder while we were still within earshot.

Basic had another joke for me as we walked. 'Hey, Tempest. What material do you use to make a clown outfit? Poly-jester! Hur, hur.'

Maidstone Police Station

The journey to Maidstone police station wasn't a long one, but the Medway Towns road infrastructure could be testing at times and often got clogged up. Usually, it took nothing more than a broken-down car or a goods lorry unloading outside a business, to cause a large tailback. We were fortunate today and suffered no such delays.

I checked my watch as we got out of the car: 1413hrs. I wondered if I would get anything out of this afternoon or if I would just be stuck here for hours. Basic and I walked around to the front entrance of the station and went inside.

The officer on the front desk noted my name and why I was there and asked me to take a seat. A dozen uncomfortable looking polypropylene chairs were arranged in two rows and welded to a bar so they could only be moved as one unit. It probably just kept them tidy. I slumped, already bored, into one of them, and started waiting. I'm not a fan of waiting, for the simple reason that it's usually open-ended. The wait stops when someone else decides it should. Today, I was in the hands of CI Quinn.

120

He made me wait.

After thirty minutes, I got up to have another word with the desk officer, a polite request that he convey to CI Quinn that I was going to leave in fifteen minutes if he hadn't found time for me before then. I suspected, actually, that it wasn't CI Quinn I needed at all. I was only giving a statement and thus I could probably give it to anyone.

The fifteen minutes ticked by with no change to my situation, so I got up and left the station, taking Basic with me. I was disappointed I hadn't been taken seriously because I wanted to be involved in what was going on. Two attacks in the space of a few days was no coincidence and from the messages the Klowns had delivered, I was convinced targeting me was very much planned. However, as I went out the door, I heard my name being called and I turned to see CI Quinn standing next to the desk officer. Conceding that it would be simpler to just get on with it now he was finally ready, I went back inside and allowed him to escort me through to a back room. Basic remained in reception, content I would be safe from Klown attack while I was here.

'Mr. Michaels, I will have a PC take your statement shortly, but I wanted to speak with you myself as once again you appear to be causing trouble that I cannot charge you with.' If he was looking for a reaction from me, I denied him the pleasure. He continued regardless. 'How is it that I find you at the centre of the Klown attacks?'

Instead of answering a question I was sure he knew I had no answer to, I tilted my head slightly, examining him as if he were a curiosity. He was being foolish, so I was treating him as a fool. 'I need to speak with the men you have in custody.' I made it a statement, not a request.

'Certainly not,' he scoffed.

'They have targeted me twice, Quinn. Do you think it a

coincidence? I'm given to understand they are being tight-lipped. Do you not think it might be worth seeing if they open up to speak with one of their intended victims?'

He smiled at me and gave an amused chuckle. I thought it fake, but it sounded real. 'I'll send in that PC,' he said on his way out the door.

Giving my statement didn't take long; a few minutes only, after which I collected Basic from reception and thankfully escaped the police station. Then, I headed into town as there was an errand I needed to perform.

At the top end of Fremlin Walk in Maidstone town centre, was a florist. There were other florists around, or I could just order flowers online, but I liked to pick my own – it made the decision to do so more intimate. In the florist, I could see which flowers looked good, so that was what I did. I owed Sophie an apology, no matter whether she accepted it or not, or ever spoke to me again, it was right that I acknowledged my failing.

I selected and paid for a spray of freesias they would deliver to her address. I had no idea where she lived but I did know where she worked, so I sent them there with a note.

I got back to Finchampstead at 1717hrs. Basic was happy to be dropped at home. I watched him go inside before driving around the corner to my own abode. Happy dogs greeted me at the front door, then scampered off to the back door so they could scare the wood pigeons from the lawn.

With the world shut outside, I settled into a peaceful evening routine of feeding myself and getting an early night in the hope I could make up for some of the sleep I had been missing.

Outside the Blue Moon Office

Despite the early night and my fatigue, I slept fitfully again. The painkillers kept the ache in my ribs at bay but movement in my sleep woke me every time. My continual grumping and groaning had caused the dogs to get off the bed during the night. They had retreated beneath me, where a folded single duvet provided a refuge in which they were supposed to sleep anyway. I gave up on sleep at 0702hrs, carried the Dachshunds downstairs and went through to the kitchen to find the kettle. Tea would help. It always does.

Presently, the dogs barked to come back in, waking me from my sleep-deprived daze where I had been staring at the mug of tea in front of me. I opened the patio door and followed them back through to the kitchen as they shot through the office in search of kibble.

A minute later, I was back in my home office and firing up the computer while the dogs wolfed down their breakfast. A text from Amanda telling me there had been yet another murder had arrived while I slept. She also told me that all police were now on duty rotation until further notice and all their time off had been cancelled. The name of the latest victim wasn't included because she didn't yet know it. However, she advised, she would update me later.

I could find little information online other than the victim lived in Igtham – the second from the same small village and I wondered if they might be connected. I checked my notes again and couldn't help thinking I might be missing something vital. Jane and I would put more effort into finding a link between the victims later today, not just the murder victims, but the earlier ones who had just been chased, robbed or hurt.

The clock on the computer told me it was 0742hrs, so I needed to shower, eat, and leave for work. Normally, I eat a healthy diet devoid of processed food, low in unhealthy fats and stodgy white carbs, and I compliment that with plenty of exercise. Now I couldn't exercise and arguably needed to eat less or control my diet just a little bit more stringently, I found myself craving food I wouldn't normally entertain. This morning, I wanted sausages, like a big sausage baguette or something equally filling and satisfying. Thankfully, I didn't have the baguette or the sausages in the house, a deliberate ploy on my part to help me avoid such foods but it was a grumpy version of myself that made a veggie omelette.

The dogs appeared, offering to clean the plate as I was scraping up the last piece of courgette, so I left them licking at it on the floor as I headed for the shower. In the bathroom, I inspected my ribs in the big mirror that dominated the wall above the bath. The bruising was starting to colour, so where it had just been dark red across an area of about fourteen inches diameter it was now tinged with yellow at the edges. Washing my hair was still a task I had to manage one-handed, but it reminded me of the many servicemen I had witnessed without limbs who got up every day and just got on with life. I kept my mouth shut rather than whine about how hard some tasks were currently. Instead, I attempted to emulate their attitude.

The air outside was dry but cold this morning, barely more than a few degrees by my estimate. I put coats on the dogs and took them for a brisk stroll around the village to ensure the lazy creatures got some exercise. They had been reluctant to leave the warmth of the house but tugged willingly at their leads to drag me forward once they accepted the inevitability of it.

Soon enough, they were getting back into their bed in the lounge, and I was going out the door to work. My car warmed itself up and scared away the frost while I grabbed my bag from the house.

Twenty minutes later, I pulled up next to Jane's car. She had beaten me to work as she often did but she was sitting in the car still so must have just arrived. Getting out of my car, I spotted a fresh dent and a two-foot-long scrape along the front left wing and passenger's door. The leading edge of the passenger's door had been peeled back slightly, and I could see mud and bits of grass stuck in her wheel arches. I rounded her car to the driver's side to check she was okay since she had obviously been in an accident of some kind. Then I found a further scrape along the right rear quarter; also fresh. The car looked like it had been savaged by a bear. Possibly one made of rocks.

'Are you okay?' I asked, opening the driver's door. Her face swung towards me, her expression all shock and bewilderment. There was mascara on her cheeks where tears had carried it south and her blonde wig was on a bit skew-whiff. I offered her my hand as I said, 'I think tea is required. Come along.' I hauled her out of the car, opened the office and got her to sit in the office chair upstairs where the trauma of whatever had happened would be far less present and memorable. I busied myself with the kettle and mugs.

'It was the Klowns,' Jane said in a quiet voice. I stiffened.

I handed her a hot mug of tea and pulled a chair up to sit right in front of her. 'Tell me.'

Jane sipped the drink and clasped it between her hands as if needing to warm them. Then she started telling me about her journey to work.

While I was at home getting ready for work, Jane was kissing her boyfriend and leaving her flat to get to work. The pair of them rented a small flat in West Farleigh on the banks of the river Medway. I had never been there but had a vague idea where their apartment was, plus Jane had once shown me a picture of the view from their bedroom window. Their view was the river Medway winding through the countryside not far from the local park. Okay, they didn't own the place, but it looked like a very nice place to live.

The route to Rochester from West Farleigh was about twelve miles and took about half an hour most days. Jane slid behind the wheel of her 2009 Ford Fiesta and wished, yet again, that she had a garage. The car was cold this morning and she hated scraping frost from the windscreen. By the time the task was done, her right hand was thoroughly frozen, and the steering wheel was as cold as ice to touch.

She turned the heating up to full blast, now it was starting to show signs of producing some warmth, and pulled away. The inside of the windscreen was misted up, the blowers inside just beginning to clear the bottom portion so she had to duck her head to see out, but she got to the end of the street she lived on and turned onto The Hunt. By then, enough of the screen had cleared that she could sit up in her seat again. As she moved to turn left onto Smith's Hill, she thought she saw someone move in the trees on the other side of the road. She paused and looked again but there was nothing there. Had she looked up she might have seen the red balloon floating away but she decided she must have been mistaken and pulled out from the junction.

Driving along Smith's Hill and down towards the junction where the road joined the B2163 at the Tickled Trout public-house, she saw a car in her rear-view mirror. She noticed it mostly because it was going so fast. The car was a battered looking Land Rover which seemed oblivious to the frosty conditions, the driver unconcerned about ice on the road.

Slowing as she reached the junction to check for traffic; it was apparent the Land Rover wasn't slowing down behind her. It closed the last fifty yards in no time at all but recalling it later she would say it also seemed to take forever. The certainty of the crash made her heart rate spike but when it came, she had already taken her foot off the brake and was moving forward.

The impact forced her head back into the headrest, violently whipping her neck backward as the force transferred forward again. Then before she could consider what to do or whether she was injured, the Land Rover was forcing her car forward across the street. Looking now in the rear-view mirror, Jane saw a Klown at the wheel, its unmistakable, twisted makeup stretching the mouth into an awful permanent grin. In the passenger seat was another Klown and between them, leaning through from the rear seat, was yet another.

Panicked, Jane stamped on her brake, but the small car was unable to arrest the forward motion being caused by the large four-wheel drive car pushing from behind. She tutted at her stupidity, threw the gearstick into first gear and dropped the clutch to leap forward and away from the menacing car.

She had to twist the steering wheel savagely to avoid the trees on the far side of the road as she shot forward but succeeded and barrelled off down the road toward the Teston bridge with the Land Rover full of Klowns chasing hard behind. She turned toward the Teston bridge and realised her error with a growing dread. The bridge could only accommodate one car going in one direction at a time. If there was anything coming the other way she would be in real trouble.

The Land Rover took the hard-left-hand corner on two wheels and careened after her. As she turned the next corner, she held her breath, waiting to see if the bridge was clear. It wasn't. A car was on it and a Luton van was coming down the hill on the opposite side of the river.

Could she make it? A half second of hesitation as she calculated the variables, then she gunned the accelerator and threw the gearstick into third. Working the little engine far beyond its intended limits, she shot past the back end of the oncoming car just as it cleared the narrow bridge, clipping her paintwork on the right-hand side as it caught against the stone. The bridge was centuries old and thus built in an era when a mode of transport more advanced than a horse was inconceivable. It was also medieval stonework and as solid as can be, plus humped in the middle to create an apex for taller boats to slip under. As she hit the apex, her wheels left the ground, and she lost all ability to control where she landed.

The driver of the van coming down the hill hadn't been paying attention and didn't slow to allow her to pass. Only now, as it was about to reach the entrance to the narrow bridge, did the driver see the approaching danger. The wheels of Jane's tiny Ford bit into the road as it came back to earth and smacked a glancing blow against the stonework on the left-hand side of the bridge before Jane could wrestle the wheel back under control. The poor car was battered but she knew then that she had escaped.

The van couldn't stop in time, but she was at the exit from the narrow portion of the bridge, so swept past it without touching either it or the widening stonework. It wasn't her the van was trying to avoid though for the crazed Land Rover full of Klowns was still right on her back bumper. It slammed headfirst into the Luton van as she sped away up the hill to safety.

A hundred yards after the bridge the road reached a tee junction where traffic forced her to stop. Glancing in her rear-view mirror, she could see the Luton van reversing out of the way. The crash looked to have been convincing, but she wasn't going to hang around to find out whether the Klowns could continue their pursuit. She pulled into traffic at a more normal pace and the Land Rover was soon lost from sight.

By the time she arrived at the office in Rochester, her heart rate had almost returned to normal, and she had finally stopped shaking. The adrenalin had diffused back into her bloodstream and left her feeling spent. She stopped the car and turned off the engine but remained in the driver's seat trying to gather herself.

That was when I turned up. She hadn't called the police, so I did that next. However, I called Amanda rather than dialling 999.

'Tempest,' she answered. 'I'm working. Will this be quick?' I could hear voices in the background – she was working on the dispatch desk.

'This is work actually. Jane was attacked by some Klowns.' I heard Amanda make a shocked noise, her breath being drawn in quickly, so I added quickly, 'She's fine, just a little shaken. They tried to run her off the road and had they succeeded I'm not sure what they might then have done. Her car is a bit trashed, but I was really calling to see if there had been a report of an accident on the Teston bridge?'

'Hold on, I'll check.' The line went dead for a minute. 'Yes, we have two cars there now,' she said when she came back on the line.

'The Land Rover was used by the Klowns. I'm going to guess they didn't stay at the scene to exchange insurance details.'

'No, it was reported as stolen just a few minutes ago. I guess they nicked it during the night, and the owner came out this morning to find it gone.'

'Where was it stolen from?' I asked, suddenly curious.

'Ah. Hold on. It was a farm in Pluckley.'

'Pluckley. Okay. Look, Jane is not injured. I don't think there is any mileage in her making a statement but with two attacks on me, my friends getting injured and now them going after Jane specifically, I cannot help wondering if I'm somehow connected. Are the two Klowns who attacked us yesterday still at the station?'

'I don't know, but it's a fairly safe bet they will be. We will not have processed them to go anywhere else yet although that might happen today.'

'Is there any chance Chief Inspector Quinn will let me see them? I asked yesterday but he refused point blank. I only want to ask them a couple of questions. If I'm somehow connected, my presence might cause them to gloat or reveal something worthwhile.' I was asking Amanda what she could do, even though I knew I needed to speak with Quinn himself. The problem was that I couldn't just call CI Quinn, and he would most likely ignore me if I went to the station front desk and asked for him.

He's a bit of a tit.

'I can't predict what he might say, but I will find him and ask the question,' she replied.

'Well, I can ask no more than that.' We disconnected, and I turned my attention back to Jane. Her tea was finished but the empty mug remained clutched in her hands as she stared at the floor. I had seen this many times before, the after effect of an intense situation. The brain tries to process what occurred and rationalise it. Usually, the person focuses on asking themselves what they could have done differently, running the event over and over in their head to work out how they could have avoided what happened. The answer was always nothing, but quite often counselling was required for the truth of it to take permanent root.

The best I could do for her right now was keep her busy.

'There was something about the Klown in the passenger's seat,' Jane said suddenly, still staring at the floor. I sat myself down again, expecting there to be more. A few seconds later, I was starting to wonder if that was all she had to say on the matter. 'Something familiar about the eyes,' she added before I could prompt more from her.

I nodded mentally. Whatever disguise a person wore the eyes remained the same. One could tackle that with coloured or patterned contact lenses, but few ever did in my experience.

'I know him,' she blurted. 'I just don't know who he is. Like I know that I know him, but I can't work out where from.' Jane was looking at me now, the sense of frustration clear on her face.

'Give it time. It will come,' I said to reassure her. Experience with my own swiss cheese memory was that the piece of information I was searching for would generally surface only once I stopped trying to find it.

Abruptly, Jane stood up. She took her mug to the sink, moving as if she had purpose suddenly. 'Is it okay if I take some time off to get my car sorted out? I gave it a pretty good thrashing this morning and worry it might be more than the bodywork that needs attention.'

'Of course. Take the day if you need to.'

'My brother works at a garage in Chatham. He will fix it and make sure I pay a sensible rate for the work.' She was already shrugging on her coat and checking herself in the mirror. She spotted that her wig was out of place and fixed it with a tut and a sigh.

'Before you go, there is the small matter that the Klowns specifically targeted you this morning. They have targeted me twice, so I think it wise to start thinking in terms of defence. I see no reason to believe they will not come after us again.'

'What are you proposing?' she asked.

I drummed my fingers on the desk. 'Basic should be here soon. I don't want you moving around alone. It's a cliché, but we need to be lucky every time, they only need to be lucky once. Until we can work out why we are targets and do something about it, we need to keep together.'

'Okay,' she conceded, putting her bag down again. 'What about work? What about the caseload?'

'A valid point, but I feel the need to keep ourselves safe must be given a higher priority. What if I go out and the Klowns come to the office and find you here alone?' It wasn't really my intention to scare her, but I clearly had that effect. She was staring at me now, standing by the door with her eyes as wide as saucers.

'Do you think they will?' she asked, a tremor in her voice.

'I guess my point is that I don't know what they might do next. No one knows who they are, or what is motivating them, so since they appear to be coming after me and mine, I intend to focus all effort on finding them.'

'How will you do that?' she asked me directly.

It was a good question. The police were getting nowhere, which wasn't exactly their fault; the crimes the Klowns were perpetrating seemed to have no connection to each other and no visible motive. What I said was, 'Through sheer force of will, Jane. Sheer force of will.' I meant it. What would they do next if I didn't stop them? Would they kill someone I know? Would they have killed Jane this morning? I felt the answer to that particular question was probably yes. Would they come after my parents? My sister and her kids? The police might get lucky and find them, but I wasn't going to use hope as my success strategy, I was going to pull all the available information together, lean on whomever I needed to, and I was going to find the guy at the centre of this and slap his painted-on grin clean off his face.

'I could do with a coffee,' Jane said, breaking my train of thought. It sounded like a good idea, so I grabbed my coat and took Jane to the coffee shop around the corner. It was a place I had been avoiding for more than a week – ever since Hayley, the rather lovely barista there, had slapped my face in public.

It was time to face her.

The Coffee Shop

My stomach was threatening to betray me as I held open the door for Jane. I had been avoiding the coffee shop because the effort of dealing with Hayley, and the potential for another entirely unnecessary fight, seemed worth avoiding. I hadn't done anything wrong, other than failing to give Hayley sufficient attention after our night together, albeit on her instruction that she wanted something super casual. The fight occurred because I erroneously sent Hayley a text which was addressed to Jane. It was yet another example of my brain betraying me and had happened because I was talking to Jane at the time. It had been days before I saw my mistake. That I was nervous about speaking with her again was annoying me; I faced tougher challenges on a daily basis, so why was facing the girl that weighed less than I could bicep curl such a scary proposition?

Because I was rubbish at handling, dealing with or even generally talking to women. That's why.

Maybe she will not be in today. I thought.

135

'Good morning, Tempest,' she said from my right elbow where she had been clearing a table in the bay window.

Nuts.

'Good morning, Hayley,' I replied, wondering what I was supposed to do next. Ahead of me, Jane joined the back of the short queue at the counter.

'Who is that?' Hayley asked, indicating toward Jane with her head. 'I keep seeing her in here recently.'

'That is my assistant, Jane.'

'Aaaah,' Hayley drawled. 'The infamous Jane.' Hayley gave the table a final, angry wipe with her cloth and picked up the tray she had placed the dirty cups on. I was in her way, so I stepped to the side to let her go by, but she stopped in front of me and looked up to make eye contact. 'Look, Tempest. We had a fun night together. I misread the cues, that's all. Please don't feel you need to avoid coming in here and I'm sorry I slapped you. I had no right.'

'Errr. Okay.' This wasn't what I expected. I was thankful for her revised attitude though. The coffee shop had been a working-day haven for me since I opened my business back in the Spring.

'I hope you and Jane are ... I don't know. I don't know what I'm trying to say. She's very pretty.'

I suddenly realised that Hayley didn't know. Could it be that she had never spoken to Jane or heard her speak? This made her actions make more sense. To me, it was obvious that Jane was a man beneath the cute lady clothes, but he did make himself look convincingly girl-like until one heard him speak or paid close attention, whereupon one would notice the hairy knuckles, Adam's apple, and stubble.

'Um, Hayley. Just to clear something up, I really need you to meet Jane.'

'I would rather not, thank you, Tempest,' she replied

over her shoulder as she went to the kitchen with her dirty crockery.

I caught up with Jane at the counter. I really wanted to show Hayley that Jane was somewhat over-endowed in the penis department when compared to the average girl, but I had given my word to Jane that I wouldn't play on her dual personality/cross-dresser thing, so I was stuck with having to stay quiet. It seemed inevitable that Hayley would find out sooner or later and when she did, I would at least then be recast as a gentleman instead of the player she clearly now thought I was.

I paid for the coffees and the jam doughnut Jane selected, then settled into a comfortable armchair while we waited for Basic. I had sent him a text already to tell him where we were and got the standard single word reply from him in return.

Jane and I chatted about property prices and her plans for a summer holiday while we sipped our coffee. She had endured quite a shock this morning and was either handling it well or ignoring it completely. The latter would most likely result in the trauma resurfacing later, but for now, she seemed disinclined to deal with it, and I was no psychologist, so I kept the conversation topics light until Basic wandered in fifteen minutes later.

During that time, my phone had pinged with an incoming text message which advised me the flowers I bought for Sophie had been delivered. I stared at the phone, daring it to receive a text from Sophie. Silently, it defied me.

We saw Basic wandering by the window at the front of the coffee shop and watched as he pushed open the door, poked his head inside and looked about hesitantly as if unsure if he was allowed in. I waved to get his attention, getting a broad smile in return. 'Good morning, Basic,' I said as he arrived at our table.

Jane said, 'Good morning, James.' She always addressed him by his name.

'Hi,' replied Basic.

'Can I get you a drink?' I asked.

He pulled a thoughtful face, and I waited for him to make a decision. 'No, fank you, Tempest,' he replied after a while. 'I just had my breakfast and mum made me a cup of tea.'

'Fair enough, buddy.' My coffee cup was empty, and I was ready to go. 'We are taking Jane to a garage in Chatham. Can you travel with her, and I will follow? If you then stay with her, I'm going to Maidstone police station.'

'Amanda said I was to stay with you no matter what you said.' He was very good at following instructions, so good in fact that were he to be told to dig a hole he would probably keep going until a different instruction came along or perhaps forever, whichever one occurred first.

'Good man. But Amanda will be at the police station. If I'm with her, I will be safe, yes? So, please stay with Jane while they sort out her car and we can catch up later today.' He looked uncertain, as if he would be failing in his task if he let me head off on my own. 'I promise I will go straight to the station and nowhere else.'

'Ok, Tempest,' he conceded.

Maidstone Police Station

I followed Jane and Basic to the garage in Chatham as planned. It wasn't far from where we started out in Rochester as it sits near the river at the Rochester end of the city. They went inside and seemed to have everything in hand, so I left them there and left Chatham via the Maidstone Road, passing the turnoff for my house on the way to the police station. I briefly debated pulling off the main road to check on my house and to take the dogs out for a walk. However, I was heading to Maidstone to follow up on my earlier request to Amanda and I was fairly certain CI Quinn would refuse my request, so I would go home after that and most likely get there right on lunch time.

I was wrong though. CI Quinn thought that having the Klowns see me might provoke them to break their silence. I was going to be allowed access to interview them after all.

'We were able to identify them from their fingerprints, but they have not spoken to anyone other than their lawyer since we arrested them,' he said while doing his best to look down at me. We were almost exactly the same height though, so if that was the effect he was going for, it wasn't really working. CI Quinn and I had an issue, I just didn't know what it was. We first met a few weeks ago when I was looking into *the Vampire* serial killer case. I had managed to get myself arrested a couple of times in a week mostly by being in the wrong place at the right time. CI Quinn had been leading the investigation for the police and had decided I was interfering.

Whatever the issue was, he made it quite clear he didn't like me, and he wasn't about to trust me. Most of all, he abhorred my profession. I thought he was insignificant, so I mostly ignored him, but I was concerned that Amanda didn't like him and that it might be because he was either a misogynist or he had at some point abused his rank. I had no details about it though as Amanda wasn't the sort who shared problems she wished to handle herself.

All in all, CI Quinn and I stepped around one another quite carefully.

'Show me where they are, please. I will let you know how I get on,' I said, ready to get on and grill them.

'Good grief, man. You don't think I'm letting you go in to speak with them alone do you?' CI Quinn gave me a derisory laugh. He could be such a dick. 'You will be accompanied by me at all times. When you speak with the Klowns, you will do so one at a time; I'm not letting them see each other, and you will have all your questions vetted first. Their lawyer will be present, and I'm running out of time to hold them here. Soon I will have to have them charged and processed.'

I gritted my teeth invisibly against his attitude, his need to be dominant. Of course, I wasn't going in alone. I hadn't for one-minute thought I would be. I simply hadn't expected it to be CI Quinn himself who was with me. I was escorted into a small room where he and I were joined by a legal counsel who explained what I could and couldn't say. I had to write down my questions, commit that I wouldn't deviate from them, and sign to agree with those terms.

Eventually, after a half hour of being messed around, CI Quinn finally led me from that room to another room where I finally got to see a Klown without said Klown trying to kill me. The Klown was now devoid of make-up and looked like an ordinary man. He was in his late thirties and there were tattoos on his neck and hands which were the only bits of flesh I could see other than his face, though I felt it likely there was a lot more ink elsewhere. He had short, brown hair, which was beginning to recede, and he was ugly. There was a small scar on his face next to his top lip. It pulled the skin of his face slightly which accented the clearly broken nose. He smiled at me when I came in, revealing teeth that were misaligned, broken, and tobacco stained: Max Travers hadn't taken care of himself.

I knew his name because CI Quinn had given me a rundown on what they had already been able to find out. It wasn't a lot as Max had steadfastly refused to speak since his arrest. He had a criminal record though, so they were able to identify him once they took his fingerprints. He lived in Margate, was unmarried but had several children with a number of different women. His list of known crimes included sexual assault, GBH and attempted bank robbery. He was thirty-seven years old, five years of which he had already spent behind bars. A lawyer had turned up within an hour of his arrest and the man was sitting opposite me now, right next to Max. Both of them were looking at me. Max was still smiling.

I had my list of approved questions in front of me. I ignored them completely. 'What do you wish to say to me?' I asked him. Next to me, CI Quinn stiffened, looked down at my piece of paper to confirm what he already knew and tapped the paper twice to get my attention. I ignored him as well. The Klown might have kept silent so far, but he looked ready to talk now.

He was leering at me from across the table. Then he leaned forward in his chair. 'Tempest friggin' Michaels.'

Not my actual middle name.

'How are you still alive? I was sure someone else would have got to you by now.' His lawyer grabbed his arm and whispered something urgently in his ear. Probably telling him to shut up, however, it had no effect, and Max didn't even bother to glance at him as he said, 'Oh, well. Second chance I guess.' With that, he launched himself out of his chair and across the table at me.

The move shocked me. I was totally unprepared for it as was CI Quinn and the lawyer who both looked equally stunned. I propelled my chair backward to find I only had a couple of feet before I hit a wall. CI Quinn was up and moving as I brought my arms up to defend myself. Max had overstretched himself to get across the table, giving away any secure footing he might have. His top half was now hanging over the table, so even in my injured state, I was able to lunge forward with my right leg and stamp on the back of his head which pushed him down and off the table where CI Quinn grabbed him. Arms and legs were going all over the place. My ribs were hurting again, so I watched rather than getting stuck in but before I had to consider whether I would need to, two uniforms came through the door.

As they wrestled Max, I stood up and took myself out of the room, following the lawyer a few paces down the corridor. I looked at him for the first time. I had often wondered about courtroom lawyers, the ones who are paid to defend a person they knew to be guilty. How do they sleep at night knowing it was their savvy argument that allowed the criminal to return to freedom and be able to commit more crime? I had heard the arguments and acknowledged that everyone deserved to be tried and proved guilty if they were, but the system seemed flawed, and the lawyer earned good money to keep guilty people out of jail. Perhaps my view on the subject was juvenile or innocent. The man I was looking at had a familiar face though. That was the predominant thought in my mind, nothing to do with his ability to sleep peacefully. His chin, his eyes... something about them.

Five minutes later, I was led back into the room where a less lively and far more handcuffed version of Max was sitting in his chair once more. The two uniforms remained in the room in case he decided to try anything adventurous again. CI Quinn had a graze to his chin and a cut to his lip. I wondered when a man of his rank last had to get on the floor for a brawl.

He advised me again that I had to stick to the script with the added threat that he would terminate the interview if I didn't. I saw no option but to agree to his terms this time while also pointing out that my technique had got the man to speak. I felt it more likely it was just my presence that had affected the change but left that point unspoken.

CI Quinn restarted the interview. 'Mr. Travers please tell us why you attempted to attack Mr. Michaels while held in custody inside a police station.'

Mr. Travers said nothing. I was still staring at the lawyer. He had noticed me doing so now and was trying to ignore me. Human nature dictated that he would have to glance at me every few seconds though just to see if I was still looking at him.

CI Quinn spoke again. 'Max, the charges against you are quite serious. Given your record, you're unlikely to see freedom for some time, so it would work to your advantage if you cooperate.'

Still nothing. There was a small vein beginning to pulse in CI Quinn's forehead. I put a hand on his forearm.

Let me try.

He nodded in acquiescence. I turned to face Max more fully and made it clear I was going to speak. He didn't need to shift his gaze as he had been looking directly at me the whole time. 'Max, I'm curious. Why are you such a complete dick?'

He shot out of his chair again only to find a hand on each shoulder forcing him back down; the two uniforms were very useful. Back in his chair, he glared at me, then as I watched, he forcibly relaxed his face and began smiling again.

'Clearly, it will not be me that claims the reward. It's a shame, but I doubt you will see out the week, our numbers are too many.'

'You have me at a loss, Max. What reward?' The obvious inference was that someone had posted a reward for my death. It was a little unnerving.

'You upset Deadface. He wants you dead. Anyone he wants dead doesn't have long to live but he wanted to make extra sure with you, so he offered us a sizeable payment for the task, even more if we could deliver you to him alive so he could kill you himself.' He delivered his news with the relaxed tone of someone talking about their dinner plans.

'Deadface. Is that a person?' CI Quinn asked. The

Klown didn't answer nor show any sign he had heard him speak.

I repeated the question myself.

'You know who Deadface is,' Max replied. 'You created him.' The lawyer whispered insistently in his ear.

I created him?

'All of this is your fault. That is why you must die,' Max continued. I, of course, hadn't the slightest idea what he was talking about, but I was starting to feel thoroughly creeped out. I had to squash those thoughts though and press this idiot for information before his lawyers animated whispering took hold.

'How did you become involved, Max? You have not been out of jail long and there is no mention of Klown-like make-up in your file before now.'

'I answered the call, Tempest Michaels. Just like all my brothers did. Deadface called and we answered. Our victory will be glorious.' The lawyer grabbed Max's arm. He clearly wanted Max to stop talking. I really didn't, so I pressed on.

'What victory?'

'Hah! You can't go spoiling the surprise, Tempest. You will bear witness soon enough.'

The lawyer spoke audibly then for the first time. 'Max, you utter one more word and you will be cut off. Try doing this without his support.'

'Shut the hell up, Adrian. You ain't one of us,' Max spat back at him.

Wait a second.

'Adrian? You're Adrian Plumber.' The lawyer swung to face me looking like a rabbit caught in headlights. I said it as a statement. He shared facial features with his sister, my client. CI Quinn's eyes were boring a hole in the side of my head. He had no idea what was going on. Which I rather liked.

No one said anything for a few seconds. Adrian was especially quiet.

I figured I might as well be the one who broke the silence. Without looking at him, I explained to Quinn, 'I was hired by Adrian's sister to find him. He ran away to join the Klowns. She was worried. She hired me.' All eyes were on me. 'Adrian and I actually spoke a few days ago. Didn't we, Adrian?'

No response.

'You told me you weren't coming home and that you were going to get rich,' I continued.

Still nothing, as if he had learned it from Max.

'I have to wonder what rich means to a man who practised tax law in London. Surely you were already earning more than everyone else in the room added together.'

Stunned silence.

I asked him a series of questions without getting another word from him. Both he and Max were great at not speaking. Fifteen minutes later, CI Quinn called a halt to proceedings, terminated the interview and had Max Travers escorted away, still smiling at me as he went. When Adrian attempted to get up and leave also, he was invited to, "Sit his arse back down." At that point, he went all lawyerly again, citing they had no reason to hold him and nothing to charge him with. CI Quinn disagreed and arrested him on the spot. The two officers who led Max away returned for Adrian. I was enjoying myself even if no one else was. I had solved a case while sitting on my backside. I could call Mrs. Plumber when I left the office and tell her I not only knew exactly where her brother was but that I could guarantee he wasn't going to move on for some time.

I turned to CI Quinn once the room was empty of everyone but the two of us. 'What do you make of all that?'

'I have to say, Mr. Michaels that you are very good at upsetting people. Other than that, we learned nothing of value.'

'Really? We learned the Klowns have a leader. We now know his name. We learned they have a goal, although we have yet to define what it is. We also learned this all revolves around me and thus we have a new perspective from which to view the case, and from which we might glean a correlation of some kind between the crimes committed thus far.'

CI Quinn's face was full of mock humour. 'The whole case revolves around you? Could your ego be any more inflated, Mr. Michaels?' he scoffed. 'That fool was throwing us a red herring, and you bought it. You're the centre of nothing. That you have been targeted by Mr. Travers and his partners and by the previous group on Saturday night proves nothing other than coincidence. Do you know any of the other victims? The men and women who have been attacked?' He watched my face, knowing it was a rhetorical question. 'No? Well then, Mr. Michaels, I suppose you would have me believe the other crimes were committed simply to throw the police off the scent and disguise you as the true target then.'

'Perhaps we should interview the second man from the attack outside my office. He will corroborate the theory one way or the other,' I said, rather than rise to his goading.

'How will we do that now their lawyer is under arrest?' My goodness, he was an annoying tit.

'Are you able to hold him?' I asked.

CI Quinn got out of his chair rather than answer my question. 'Mr. Michaels you're clearly quite badly injured, my advice, as always, is for you to give up pursuing your ridiculous paranormal cases and find a new career. This one does not suit you.' He turned and walked away through a door before I could respond, leaving me to fume silently. Moments later, a uniform turned up to escort me back to the reception area whereupon I was dismissed. In all, it had been a mixed couple of hours. I had learned some things about the Klowns, I had found the missing Adrian Plumber and I had accepted that I probably needed to be really worried.

Outside the station, walking to my car, I retrieved my phone from my bag and called Jane.

She answered on the third ring. 'Hi, Tempest. Where are you?'

'Just outside Maidstone police station. Where are you?'

'We just left Chatham. My brother arranged a loan car for me while he's getting mine fixed. He's very good like that. Very generous. Shall we come to you?'

'No. You should head home. It's long after your working hours and you should be safe enough there. You're no longer in your car, so chances are they will not recognise you now. Just watch for cars following you and can you drop Basic off at the office first please?'

'Of course. See you there.' She disconnected.

I arrived at my car but didn't get in it. Calling Mrs Plumber to inform her about her brother was top of my to-do list. She was pleased to hear from me and very excited to hear I had found her brother. The news that he was in custody and had been representing the Klowns as their legal counsel didn't go down so well though. There was a signifi-cant amount of swearing at the other end of the phone and I found myself listening politely to a monologue about what she was going to do to him when she got hold of him. Eventually, she realised I was still there, briefly apologised and thanked me. We disconnected, and I got in my car.

The Blue Moon Office

I went home via my house as I needed to make sure the dogs were okay. I used to worry I didn't walk them often enough when I was tied up with work but had since learned they were really quite lazy and preferred to stay asleep. Back when I was in the Army, I would take them to work with me most days. They had fun barking at soldiers, chasing squirrels on the rugby pitch and consistently got lots of exercise as I was always going somewhere. Now though, like me, they had settled into civilian life and the reduced level of activity.

Nevertheless, I kicked them out of the house for a run around the garden, gave them a piece of carrot to crunch on and settled them back on the sofa before I headed to the office.

I found I was checking my rear-view mirror far more than I would usually. After two Klown attacks in a few days, followed by them chasing Jane this morning, I was being sensibly wary. Would they target my house? I couldn't come up with a reason why they wouldn't, and the thought worried me. What if they set fire to it while I slept? What if they set fire to it while I was away? How would the dogs get out? Ever more disturbing derivations along the same depressing line surfaced in my consciousness. It was freaking me out. I turned the car around and went back for the dogs.

'Dogs,' I called going through the door. I had only been gone a few minutes, so I got the usual response in such circumstances which was no response at all. I found them on the sofa still pretending to be asleep in the hope that I might go away. They had undoubtedly heard me pick up their leads and collars as I came through the house. 'Boys, is it really necessary to be this lazy?' I asked them as I threaded their collars over their heads.

Reluctantly, they plopped off the sofa and came with me to the car where I deposited them both on the passenger seat. The trip to work was only a few minutes' drive but I got there after Jane and found both her and Basic in the office. The dogs charged ahead of me to get to the top of the stairs as they could tell there were people up there and people meant fuss and possibly treats.

'Doggies. Hur hur.' I heard Basic talking to the dogs and when I got to the top of the stairs, he was kneeling on the floor to tickle their bellies. He was a gentle soul, loving and giving and he liked the dogs. Most people did.

'Hi, Jane. Thank you for staying with Basic. What is your plan now?' I asked her.

'Actually, I think I would like to hang on here, maybe help out with whatever you have planned. If I go home now, I will just be at home by myself and I think I would rather stay with you pair until my boyfriend is home. Is that okay?' she asked the question carefully as if I might say no and send her away.

'Of course, Jane. Our next task is going to be to sift as

much of the available information on the Klown crimes as possible and see what we can add up. The police are wilfully ignoring the possibility that I'm somehow at the centre of the whole thing, so we are going to use that as our start point, and see if we can't make the crimes make sense using me as a motive.' I looked at Jane and Basic for their opinion, then realised they were looking for me to lead them and were ready to follow whatever daft idea I might have.

I grabbed my bag from the desk where I had placed it and fished out my wallet. 'Let's start with some lunch, shall we?'

Twenty minutes later the scent of warm pizza floated up the stairs to herald Basic's arrival back at the office. I had suggested pizza and the others were only too happy to fall in line, especially since I was buying. I was wondering whether I should be worried about my food choice. I eat pizza, who doesn't? But it was the sort of thing I would allow myself as a rare treat if I was out for food, not something I would order from a second-rate takeaway joint. Since my injury on Saturday night, I was displaying a worrying trend towards eating food that would expand my waistline, which since I couldn't exercise to combat the unnecessary calories, was the most likely end result. I shrugged mentally, telling myself to worry about it later; I had bigger problems right now, so I selected a slice of glistening, gooey meat feast and went back to the whiteboard I was beginning to make notes on.

Basic was sitting at the table by the window eating a piece of pizza, but I noticed he had gone quiet. As I looked across at him, I saw why. He was in a standoff with Bull who had managed to jump onto the spare chair and then the table and was threatening to dive onto the plate Basic had stacked several slices of pizza on. Basic had a piece of pizza in his mouth and both hands on it, but his eyes were on the dog. Dozer was trying to distract him by climbing his leg, dividing Basic's attention and making the likelihood of pizza theft more probable.

I walked across the room, nudged Dozer's bum with my foot to knock him off balance and scooped Bull from the table. He grumped his displeasure at me as I placed him on the floor. I gave them each a very small piece of pizza as compensation for spoiling their endeavour and instructed them to leave Basic alone.

Satisfied they might now give up on their quest for food, but with one eye on them, I went back to what I had been doing. On the wall opposite the desk was a map of Kent. I used to have a map of the local area, but I had bought this one just a week or so ago when I had seen it in a shop and it was proving useful now because the Klowns had targeted people all over the County. I had small, coloured push pins dotted into towns and villages from Pluckley to Pizien Well, Tonbridge to Tankerton. The pins had a white sticker on their heads, on which I had written numbers which corresponded to my notes on the whiteboard. The crimes on the whiteboard were in chronological order, listing the place the person was attacked and the nature of the crime. I had written the recent murders in red ink – the escalation to murder demanded it.

The crimes had all been restricted to Kent apart from one. Was it just coincidence or were all the people they wish to terrorise simply living in Kent? The only time they had appeared outside of the County had been more than a week ago towards the start of their campaign when they attacked a woman in Scunthorpe. Marion Lloyd had been attacked outside her house early on the morning on Tuesday 17th. Four Klowns had kicked and beaten her, leaving her with multiple internal injuries and broken bones. They sprayed their calling card on the side of her car, but the attack had been dismissed by the police as a copycat attack and thus not perpetrated by the same Klowns at all. I wondered about that.

At the desktop PC, Jane was cross-referencing data, looking into the history of the victims, their lives and careers etcetera, and trying to find patterns, links, anything that might tie them to me. The problem was I didn't know any of them. Not one name was familiar and only one name was missing – the murder victim from last night had still not been named. It was quite possible, probable even, that there were other victims who hadn't yet come forward. There was no point including that possibility in my considerations though.

I had marked on the board the one connection we had found – the two women who went to school together in Charing, a small village just outside of Ashford. They appeared to have no other connection, and Jane couldn't see that there were any other victims who had also gone to that school. There was most certainly no connection to me that I could perceive.

'I have something,' Jane said, putting her hand up but not taking her eyes off the screen. I went around to join her behind the desk, pushing a plate with a couple of pizza crusts out of the way with my fingertips so I could put my hand down and lean in to inspect the screen myself. She said, 'These two, Mark Tanner and Erica Carpenter, worked at the same business a few years ago. I had to dig right back into their work histories to find it. They both worked at Inspirations Web Developers in the late nineties. Their time at the firm overlapped by about two years.'

'Okay,' I said staring now at the whiteboard for their

names. I spotted Erica first. She had been attacked quite early on, almost a month ago now but hadn't been hurt. The Klowns had chased and harassed her but nothing more than that. This had occurred near her house in Ramsgate. She was fifty-eight and the second oldest person on the list. Mark Tanner had been mugged by three Klowns in broad daylight less than a week ago. It had happened as he came away from an ATM during his lunch break in Rainham. The mugging had been violent in that they knocked him to the ground and kicked him a few times. 'So, they worked together. Anything else?'

'Not yet. I was going to pull up employment records for the firm, which might not be the easiest thing to get hold of, but maybe there is a link between them and someone they worked with.'

'Exactly what I was thinking.' My very loose theory had been that I was somehow linked to all the victims so their injuries, murders, attacks were designed to affect me on some increasing level. Was I being egocentric like CI Quinn had claimed? Was this not about me at all? If so, what was all the nonsense about a reward? And why had the Klowns come after me twice now, attacked my friends and tried to run my assistant off the road? 'Dig up whatever you can, Jane, and see if you can get a list of the kids who went to school with the two girls.'

I went back to the board and drew in a link between Mark Tanner and Erica Carpenter. Then on the map, I linked the two pins that represented their crimes with a piece of coloured string. This could all just be coincidence, and I was wasting my time exploring a theory that would prove to be a dead end. So far, I had nothing else to work with.

At the table by the window, Basic was colouring in a

book he had brought with him in his backpack. I guess his mum packed it for him every day as it contained tissues, a can of coke, a wagon wheel in case he needed a snack and a pencil case of felt-tipped pens to go with the colouring book. He wasn't inclined, nor possibly able to add much to our deliberations but he had made tea and was quite content to just hang out with us at the office. He smiled and gave me a thumbs-up when he felt me looking across at him. Then he showed me the picture he was colouring. it was the *Little Mermaid* who he'd elected to give bright blue hair. She was having a punk phase it seemed.

A couple of hours ticked by as Jane and I worked separately on the research, she on the PC and I on the laptop, but we uncovered nothing else of use. There was a lot of information to process, so many victims already and for each one, we needed to examine their work history, relationships, family tree and on and on as far as we could go.

I felt Jane moving behind me and glanced up to see her stretching in place. I checked my watch: 1603hrs. I opened my mouth to speak, and the phone rang.

I answered the call in my usual professional manner. 'Blue Moon Investigations. Tempest Michaels speaking. How may I help?'

'Hello,' the voice at the other end said.

'Hello,' I replied. 'This is Tempest Michaels. Do you have a paranormal enquiry I can assist you with?' I heard audible relief at the other end of the phone.

'Oh, thank goodness. Mr. Michaels, I really need your help. My son has been possessed by a demon called Fonteneseque. He's speaking in tongues and saying the most awful things. Can you help me?' the voice wailed.

The voice was that of a middle-aged woman if I was any good at guessing ages. I knew of course that she was a mother, which put her age almost certainly above twenty, but I was guessing at closer to forty. Other than that, I didn't know anything at all, so it was time to press for information.

'Can you tell me your name please?'

'Oh. Oh, yes. Sorry. It's Cheryl Carter.'

'Mrs Carter, thank you. I need to ask you a few more questions, but if I believe I can help I will do so. Can you tell me where you are, please? Your address?' I snagged my notebook and pen and plonked myself back down at my desk. Basic paused to listen. She gave me the address, and I repeated it aloud as I wrote it down.

'Mrs Carter, can you please describe your son's behaviour with as much detail as you can give?' I listened again while she answered and made notes beneath the address. 'Thank you. Now please tell me about your son. His age, his hobbies, what he watches on TV, which football team he supports … all that information, please.'

Once again, Mrs Carter launched into a lengthy description from which I picked little nuggets of information.

'Finally, Mrs Carter can you please tell me when this new behaviour manifested and what it is that you would like me to do.' Mrs Carter answered this question as concisely as she had the others but ended with a surprising piece of detail I had to ask her to repeat.

'I said the parish priest suggest we look for other solutions when the exorcism he performed didn't work,' she said again.

Disbelievingly, I confirmed, 'You're telling me you have an actual priest there and he has attempted an exorcism?' I was struggling to believe her. Priests do not perform exorcisms, except on television. I was fairly certain of that.

'Yes, Mr. Michaels. He came right over when I called him.' I was really curious about this now.

'Mrs Carter, I'm prepared to visit you and can be with you within the hour.'

'Thank the Lord,' she interrupted.

'I must stress though,' I continued unabated, 'that I do not believe your son is possessed. Demonic possession was largely the diagnosis given for mental health problems in a less enlightened age. I believe I can rid you of this issue, but I do not expect to find a demon at the end of my investigation. Is the priest still there?' Mrs Carter said Father McMeadow was still at the house and still chanting incantations. I outlined what I would have to charge her, that I was bringing a colleague with me and gave her a rough time by which I expected to arrive. That done, I put the phone down and looked at my notes again. Like every case I had ever had, I was instantly dismissing the option there could be a paranormal explanation, but the presence of a priest was bothering me. I'm not a church going man, but I respect the belief system and while I consider religious teachers to be deluded, I can't deny that they are also intelligent people.

'Are we going out?' asked Basic.

'Yes, we are.'

'To Margate? I like Margate.' I waited to see if Basic had anything more to say on the subject of the seaside town, but he appeared to have exhausted his repository of comments.

'Well, we need to leave quite soon so if you need the bathroom, now is your chance.' I did a quick mental calculation and decided I didn't need to go myself. Wallet, phone, and keys went in my bag or trouser pocket, and I stood up to put on my coat.

'What time will your boyfriend get home, Jane?'

She checked the time on her phone. 'Soon actually. I should go.'

'Drive carefully, Jane, and watch for the Klowns when you get home. Circle your house and see if you can spot any cars with people in them or cars you do not recognise. Don't stop your car until you believe it's safe.'

Jane promised she would do exactly as I suggested and report back when she was home and safe. Basic and I followed her out to the car just in case there were any Klowns out there, but no one leaped out on us, and we were all able to leave the car park unmolested.

With the dogs balanced on Basic's lap, both of them eyeing him suspiciously as they weren't used to sharing their seat, we shot off to my house. It was already after the dog's dinner time, and I didn't want to leave the dogs in my house while I was out; I was still quite paranoid about Klowns attacking it. Instead, I knocked on my neighbour's door and waited for her to answer with the two dogs sitting obediently at my feet. The light went on inside the porch and the dogs' tails started to wag. I called out so Mrs Comerforth would know it was me. Mrs Comerforth was a widow in her seventies with an abundance of grey hair turning to white. She held it in place with a mass of pins and clips, and it was nice that I had that to look at because her bosom threatened to eclipse her belly button. She was very pleasant and asked little of the strong, young man next door which simply encouraged me to offer her my help whenever she had a use for it. On a weekly basis, I took out her bins, mowed her lawn, performed minor repairs around the house and in return she very willingly looked after my two stupid dogs whenever I needed her to.

As the door opened, the dogs began to leap about in a

desperate bid to get her to fuss them – so much for obedience. We exchanged pleasantries and I explained I had to go out for a few hours. She was only too happy to have them for the evening though, so I left them there and received a text on my way to Margate telling me that she had let herself into my house to feed the dogs and had then taken them for a walk. Oddly she was thanking me for the opportunity while I was thanking her for helping me.

A Possessed Child

In the silence of the car, punctuated only by the noise coming from the Gameboy machine Basic was playing Tetris on, I considered what little I knew about the Klown case and wondered just what I could do to advance my investigation. The client who was coming to see me this morning claimed to have information pertaining to the case, but she had never arrived, so I assumed she was either lying to get some attention, quite why I couldn't fathom, or had perhaps changed her mind. Either way, I had got nothing from her and the excitement of Jane's car chase had caused me to forget about her until now. I couldn't even remember if Jane had told me her name. If she had, then I had forgotten that also. I would check with her later, or in the morning.

Basic had decided he didn't need to go to the toilet before we left and then had changed his mind fifteen minutes down the road, forcing me to pull off for the services at Farthing Corner. While I waited for him, I received a text from Jane to let me know she was safe inside her house. I exhaled a small sigh of relief.

With Basic back in the car, the journey took just under the hour I predicted it would, and the Satnav took me right to her door where, in the window next to it, I saw the curtain twitch as I pulled up. Before I was out of the car, the door to the house was opening and a lady in her early forties was coming down the driveway. 'Mrs. Carter?' I enquired.

'Yes. Mr. Michaels, is it?'

'And my associate, James Burnham.' I motioned towards Basic as he rounded the front of the car to join me on the pavement. Mrs. Carter had naturally blonde hair that was going grey but had been dyed to maintain its original colour. It was a few weeks past needing a refresh on the dying process though and it made her look unkempt. She was wearing dark blue jeans and chestnut, calf-height Ugg boots, a white satin camisole top plus an oversized, brown cardigan and she was bereft of make-up. The overall impression was that she had given up on her appearance a bit, but I could see she had been attractive once and could be again if she decided it was something she wanted.

'I'm so glad you're here,' she said, ushering us into the house. 'He has been like this for hours now.'

'Please show me.'

Mrs. Carter led Basic and me up a narrow staircase that bisected the house. It was a design one found all over England in semi-detached houses of a similar era. At the top, there would be a short landing leading to two rooms. One on the left, at the back of the house, and one on the right, at the front of the house. The reverse would be true of the house next door which formed the other half of the building. As we went up the stairs, I began to hear voices. A low murmur and an intermittent screeching. I couldn't make out what either was saying but then the smell hit me like an uppercut to my nose.

Human Faeces.

We turned left to go to the back of the house as I had expected we would. The room at the back was always smaller and thus usually housed the child or children with the parents in the larger room at the front. Mrs. Carter pushed open the door to reveal candlelight inside. The flickering wicks of maybe one hundred candles of varying sizes adorned every surface of the room including the floor. The carpet had been pulled back so someone could draw symbols on the floorboards with a black marker. The marker itself was abandoned next to one foot of the cast iron bed frame.

'Mrs. Carter, who are these men?' demanded a man in a priest's cassock. In his hands, he held a heavy looking bible. He had been murmuring something when we entered the room but had stopped when he saw us and was now staring incredulously in our direction, his gaze swinging from Mrs. Carter to Basic to me and back again.

'You said we needed to look at alternative solutions, Father,' said Mrs. Carter. 'Mr. Michaels is a paranormal investigator.'

'He's a what?' asked Father McMeadow looking quite flustered.

I ignored him for a moment. On the bed was a man in his early twenties. He was tied to the headboard with what appeared to be the heavily embroidered stole from the priest's uniform. It was the fancy bit that went over the shoulders to fall either side in front. His feet were free but currently tucked underneath his body. He was naked, all bar a cloth of some kind he had wrapped around his junk to form a primitive type of underwear. The smell was coming from him – he was covered in poop. His own I assumed. It was utterly disgusting, and I regretted taking the case.

'Mrs. Carter,' came the priest's voice from behind me as I approached the bed. 'What are these men doing here? When I said alternative solutions, I meant I would bring in help from within the church. I have summoned the priests that train for this...' I silenced him by lifting my hand.

In thirty seconds, I had taken in all there was to see. Kieran Carter was putting on a fantastic act. He had Mrs Carter completely fooled. She was standing by the door next to Basic, staying as far away as she could. Distance seemed like a wise choice given the stench assaulting my olfactory system, but if Kieran could take it, I could too. Kieran continued to mutter obscenities under his breath, most of which I couldn't make out but odd words such as arsehole and lick I could discern. As I leaned towards him, he suddenly locked eyes with me and screamed. The scream was a deep noise rather than a high-pitched screech.

It ended as he started to form words. 'You will die tonight. Begone and never return. Kieran is mine and I will not give him up.' The voice came out singsong with a sense of amusement to it. It was quite creepy until one considered it was all an elaborate ruse.

To what purpose?

'Mrs. Carter, I must protest!' said Father McMeadow in an authoritative and angry tone. 'I had calmed the demon. Now once again he's agitated and may bring harm to your son. It's imperative we wait for the arbitrators to arrive. This charlatan has to leave.'

'Charlatan?' I repeated, straightening up and turning to face him.

'Do you not plan to extort money from Mrs Carter for

rendering some ridiculous service in a feeble attempt to rid her son of this demon?' asked Father McMeadow. He looked beyond me now. 'Mrs Carter, please ask this man and his friend to leave.'

'Well, I um... I'm sorry, Mr. Michaels. It seems I misunderstood Father McMeadow's instructions.' Poor Mrs Carter looked more flustered yet.

I didn't take my eyes off the priest. I was waiting for something. 'What do the arbitrators cost, Father?'

He looked at me. 'Exorcizing a demon is not something one can put a price on.' I was waiting for him to glance at Kieran for support. It would be an unconscious gesture with his eyes only. I was playing a hunch they were in it together and the whole sham was to get money from Mrs Carter. That the son had to then be in on it was disturbing, but Kieran wouldn't be the first person ever to swindle his parents. The glance didn't come though.

'Mrs Carter if you wish us to leave then we will do so.' I turned to face her with the intention of telling her I thought the whole thing a scam but as I looked at her, I noticed that Basic was absent.

I found him behind me where, despite the smell, he was about to sit on the bed next to Kieran. Saying nothing, I heard him start to sing a nursery rhyme: Half a pound of Tuppeny Rice.

Kieran was staying in character and was trying to bite Basic as he got closer. Restrained by his wrists, he couldn't quite get within biting range though, so was just snapping his teeth in the air.

Basic's childish singing voice was soothing, and I wondered if he was trying to coax the demon into submission – to calm him somehow. I hadn't considered how Basic would perceive such a case. He often seemed confused by the concept of the paranormal and had trouble working out whether what he saw on his television was real or not. Cop show: Real. Vampire cop show: not real? I understood how it might get confusing.

Basic sat on the bed about halfway down its length, leaning toward Kieran. He lifted his left hand as if to stroke Kieran's hair, a move I would advocate against as it too looked to have crap in it, but as Basic reached the end of his verse he punched Kieran in the side of his head with his right fist. 'Pop goes the weasel. Hur hur,' he chuckled.

Kieran was bleeding from the mouth, but the demon act was gone. 'What the hell, man?' he yelled. 'What the hell?

Father McMeadow started up his incantations again. I turned to face him. 'Really?' I asked.

'What's happening?' Mrs Carter wanted to know.

'Hit him again,' I instructed Basic.

'No. No. No, dammit,' protested Kieran as Basic lifted his enormous fist once more. 'Dave, stop messing about and untie me.'

Dave?

Father McMeadow was looking a little panicked. His eyes were darting about. From the doorway, we heard a noise downstairs.

The Arbitrators had arrived.

Mrs Carter looked quite confused, but I believed I knew what was going on. Basic was looking at me with his fist raised towards Kieran, checking whether he should actually hit him again, or not. I shook my head just enough that Basic got the message.

Father McMeadow was beginning to gather up his things. He was bright enough to know the game was over. I darted forward though and snatched his phone from the dresser behind him before he could get to it. 'I'll have that, thank you.'

'Hey!' he protested but I ignored him as I quickly scrolled into his messages. Getting more agitated and trying to take the phone back from me his next utterance was, 'Oi, dickhead!' as he flailed against my outstretched arm.

Not very clergy-like language.

Basic got up and took a step forward in warning. It was sufficient to convince Dave *the fake clergyman* to give up on his phone. There were footsteps on the stairs and Mrs Carter was moving to meet with them.

'Dave,' yelled Kieran from the bed, reminding him of his predicament. It was time to finish this off.

Using Father McMeadow's phone I dialled 999 and was connected just as two men in black cassocks came into the room preceded by Mrs Carter. 'What service? The police, please,' I said smiling at the two new men. They took one look at me, glanced at Kieran on the bed and bolted. As they ran loudly back down the stairs, I covered the mouth-piece of the phone and said, 'Let them go.' I saw no point in Basic giving chase. The police would pick them up soon enough.

'Will somebody please tell me what is going on?' pleaded Mrs Carter.

'Of course,' I replied. 'Give me just one moment, please.' The police dispatch person came on the other end of the line, whereupon I invited him to send a squad car to the address and provided a brief explanation of what they would find there. When he asked for more details, I asked him to wait a moment and sent Basic to take Mrs Carter downstairs where he should assist her in making some tea. Bewildered, she complied and went with him, holding his hand.

Father McMeadow moved to untie Kieran but stopped when I instructed him to do so. I wanted Kieran left where he was until the police arrived. It wouldn't be very long. Kieran was protesting that he needed to pee, which I ignored as he had clearly been content to urinate and defecate on the bed thus far. I did, however, leave the room, quite thankfully, and took Father McMeadow with me.

The police arrived just a few minutes later, by which time I had drunk half my tea and had explained to Mrs Carter that she was being scammed by her son and his friends. She was going to be asked to pay the arbitrators a few thousand pounds to rid her son of the demon. I showed her Father McMeadow's phone on which a series of WhatsApp messages between him and Kieran and another chap named Herbert could be read setting the whole thing up.

Staring disbelievingly at the phone, I watched as the truth of it dawned on her and a mother's rage took over. Yelling that she was going to kill him she headed for the stairs. I had expected something like this from her, so had blocked her route. For her own sake, she needed this to be handled by the police now.

Basic opened the door to them as they came up the driveway and thirty minutes later we were back in my car on our way back to Finchampstead. I couldn't decide though if the smell of human poop was in my head or had permeated into my clothes or was perhaps actually on Basic because he had got quite close to Kieran when he whacked him in the head.

I hoped that it wasn't the latter as it heightened the possibility that there were actual bits of poop on Basic. I didn't want them in my car, stinking it out until I got it valeted, and I didn't want a phone call from Basic's mum asking me what the heck we had been getting up to.

There was nothing I could do about it for now. I swung off the A road, down the ramp and onto the motorway with the car pointed north towards London. It wouldn't take long to get home, but it would be close to 2000hrs by the time we got there and that would effectively be the end of the day.

From the passenger's seat came a gentle snoring noise; Basic was slumped against the window asleep. In the quiet of the car, I thought again about the Klown case. I should call my clients, who I had mentally labelled as the CLITs, and check in with them. It was a standard practice for me to call my clients on a daily basis during a case, to give them an update, answer any questions they might have.

My car had a dial to scroll through my phone list which appeared on a screen in the centre of the dashboard. As I pressed dial on my steering wheel, I realised that I didn't know which of the gentlemen the call would connect to. It was a safe assumption that I had the number for only one of them.

The call clicked in as someone picked up. 'Hello?'

I recognised the voice as belonging to Richard Leva-raugh, otherwise known as Big Dick. 'Mr. Levaraugh, good evening. This is Tempest Michaels. I need to update you on your case.'

'Ah,' he said, hesitation in his voice. 'Ah,' again. 'I, um. I'm afraid there has been a change of plans.'

'How so, Mr Levaraugh?'

'Well, not me of course, but some of the chaps, weren't convinced that the Klowns are actually real men and not demons like you said.' He picked his way around the words carefully.

'I'm listening.' I already knew where this was going. The CLITs wouldn't be the first customer to decide that I had no idea what I was doing when I claimed that their particular case wasn't at all paranormal in nature.

'Well, err. Well, they hired a different investigator and those of us that wanted to stay with you can't afford to do so by ourselves.' He fell silent.

'Mr Levaraugh, thank you for your candour.' I was annoyed, bordering on angry but I was calm. 'I will be solving this case regardless of whether you and your friends are paying me to do so,' I told him through gritted teeth. 'The Klowns are just men, I have met several of them now so there is no doubt whatsoever in my mind.'

'Oh,' he said, sounding surprised.

I pressed on, disinterested in what he might have to say now. 'I will assume that your new investigator is Dr Lyndon Parrish. I'm afraid you will find that he's misleading you, so please be careful what your group commits to pay him for his services. Once I have solved the case, I will let you know. If you change your mind about Dr Parrish please contact me.'

I bid him a good evening and punched the button to disconnect the call. Dr Parrish and I were going to have a conversation soon. It was one thing to set up a rival business under my nose and mere feet from my office but another thing entirely to poach my customers.

Evening Meal

I dropped Basic at home and watched him go into his house. He lived with his mum still and was a necessary part of her life. I had never asked him about his father, so the man may have absconded years ago, be a mystery to his mother or might even have died at some point in the past. Whatever the case was, Basic was the man of the house and took care of his mother just as much as she took care of him.

I lived just around the corner from their house and was home in less than a minute. Just as I had instructed Jane to do, I drove past my house looking for anything that seemed out of place. I took two laps but could see no cars with people in them or cars that I didn't recognise. I parked hesitantly nevertheless, then waited in the car with the lights off for a few minutes looking all around for movement. When I was as satisfied as I could be without sending out a patrol to check the area, I got out, locked my car and went to Mrs Comerforth's.

The dogs heard me coming or perhaps reacted to the

outside light coming on as I neared the house and were both at the door trying to get out to me when Mrs Comerforth opened it. I greeted them with equal enthusiasm, getting on the floor so they could climb on my lap and lick my hands. I thanked Mrs Comerforth once again as she handed me their leads and water bowl, then took them home where they went immediately to the kitchen to stare intently at the cupboard I kept their treats in. I followed them to the cupboard, teased them for a moment with a conversation about their lack of exercise but gave them each a chew stick anyway.

I checked my watch to find it was 2037hrs. I was overdue for my evening meal and my stomach rumbled as if spurred into action by my thoughts. The pizza at lunchtime had undoubtedly carried me further than my usual lunch would have, but now I was hungry, and it was already getting late to start preparing something healthy. I opened the fridge and rooted around a bit looking for a magical low-calorie meal to jump out. When one wasn't forthcoming, I gave in and went to the pub.

The dogs were only too happy to go out again, they still had their collars on when I called them and as usual, they worked out where we were going and dragged me the last hundred yards through the public-house car park. My ribs were starting to hurt again, reminding me that I was due another dose of painkillers. I fished in my bag and popped two out of their blister pack while I waited for the landlord to pour my pint. I swallowed them with the first gulp of amber liquid.

'Shall we take a seat, chaps?' I asked the two dogs. They stared up at me quite intently after they heard the landlord hand a packet of crisps across the bar to me. The crisps were for sharing, although I planned to eat most of them and they were to tide me over until my dinner arrived. I ordered a burger and chips as it was something the landlord assured me wouldn't take long and paid for a second pint in advance as I was fairly sure I would have finished the one in my hand before the food arrived.

As I lowered myself down into the old sagging sofa near the open fire, my phone started buzzing in my pocket. I had to shuffle around a bit to retrieve it. It was in my back pocket, so I was sitting on it, but the simple movement was compounded by the stiffness in my ribs.

The screen identified the caller as Sophie which caused me to swiftly punch the green answer button.

'Sophie.'

'Good evening, Tempest,' she said, her voice guarded and far different from the excited tones in which she had addressed me a few days ago. 'Thank you for my flowers and the note.'

'You're very welcome.' I felt that I had apologised enough and that any more of the same would come across as groveling – not a characteristic I expected a woman would want in a prospective mate.

If she was expecting more grovelling, she didn't pursue it. 'I have decided to give you one more shot at this, Tempest. I like you, but I have to say I didn't expect it to be like this.'

'I understand. It has not gone as I planned, but I will endeavour to make it up to you. Why don't you tell me what your favourite restaurant is, and I will make arrangements to take you there?'

'Hmm… that does sound nice. There is an Italian place in Rochester High Street that I like.'

'Monte Verdi's?'

'Yes, that's the one.' I knew it well. It was one hundred

yards or so from my office, had an excellent and well-deserved reputation and was expensive. Not so expensive that I balked at the idea of taking an attractive woman there though.

'Jolly good. I'm looking forward to it, Sophie. When would like to do this? How about Saturday?' I asked.

'Can we make it Friday instead?' she asked.

'Of course,' I replied without bothering to think. Just like that, I had a dinner date with an attractive, single woman on Friday night. Neither one of us had children to worry about so the evening could take us wherever it fancied. I suggested picking her up, but she answered that she was local so would make her own way. My brain was whispering to me that I would have to let the chaps know I wasn't able to make it for our regular round of drinks on Friday, but I knew they would understand. I then remembered that Jane had invited me and anyone else from my crowd out for birthday drinks tomorrow night. I had failed to contact any of them yet because my brain appeared to be misfiring recently.

I concluded the phone call with Sophie by agreeing a time to meet on Friday. I was yet to book a table but was confident I could sort that out. We said goodnight and disconnected.

I put the phone back on the table in front of me and picked up my pint. Technically I had a third date with Sophie Sheard. Third dates came with certain connotations, although chuckling to myself about how crap I had been this week, I doubted she would be interested in hearing me joke about it.

I sent a group message to Jagjit, Big Ben, and Basic as well as Frank and Poison, telling them that there was a meet for drinks the next evening and encouraging them to come along. Just before I sent it, I added Hilary. Hilary 'Brian' Clinton is a good friend and member of the regular Friday night pub crowd who recently came out on a night-time adventure with me and the others. The event resulted in his arrest and his wife took it badly. So badly that we hadn't seen him since. I thought his attendance was a long shot, so I added that his good lady would be more than welcome and ended the message with an apology for the short notice.

I drained my drink just as the burger and chips were delivered. They were as tasty as the menu claimed. I had eaten at the pub before but only once or twice; it wasn't a habit I wanted to fall into, and I was already berating myself as I mopped up the last of the ketchup with my final chip.

I'm going to get fat; I can feel my waistline expanding.

I told my paranoia to shut up and finished my pint. It was 2127hrs. I needed to get home, get clean and get to bed, so I bid the other patrons goodnight, clipped the dogs back onto their leads and sauntered home with a full belly and slight haze from the beer. Apart from the ache in my ribs, I felt good.

At home, I went upstairs to run a bath and came back down to pour myself a generous rum and coke. It would help take the edge off the pain in my side. At least that's what I told myself. Yawning as I swirled the bathwater, I added a cap-full of my Molten Brown muscle soak. I doubted it would have any real effect on my body, but it sure smelt good, and what is life without a few treats?

I shuffled to my bedroom. Checking my phone, I saw that Jagjit and Big Ben had responded to my earlier group message to say they were coming. Jagjit was bringing a date, the paramedic lady from Saturday night. Big Ben was coming alone but then he always did; he just turned up, flashed his smile and took someone home with him. Basic had also replied but he couldn't attend as he took his mum to bingo at the church hall on a Thursday. No reply yet from anyone else. Sitting on my bed, sipping rum from a Mason jar, I remembered the missing client from this morning, the one with pertinent information about the Klown case. As my bath ran, I sent a text to Jane. It was late, but I was sure she wouldn't mind. Calling would get a more certain response, but it seemed intrusive at this time of day.

Her answered pinged back in less than a minute, answering my question with a name - Angela Barclay.

I stared at the screen on my phone for a while. Angela Barclay was a woman I had met during the Vampire case. She had been dating one of the ringleaders and had been completely blind to the crimes they were committing. At the time, I had coerced her into giving me information which helped me solve the case and now she was trying to give me more information. This time about the Klowns. How did one woman get herself mixed up in so much trouble?

I checked my phone contacts list to find that I did still have her number. I called it and waited for her to answer. She didn't pick up, though. I tapped my phone to my forehead thoughtfully. There was something I was missing here. Why was Angela involved again?

I had alcohol and painkillers in my system now, so my brain was a little fuzzy, plus I was tired, so I shucked my clothes and went for a soak in the bath. As I left the bedroom the dogs were climbing onto the bed.

Late Start

Sunlight woke me which meant I had slept in again. I was turning into a civilian! I was eating unsuitable food, allowing poor excuses like broken ribs to keep me from the gym and I was laying in my bed getting nothing done. All these thoughts rampaged through my mind in the first few seconds of alertness. I glanced across at the clock to find that it was 0812hrs. Well after the time I ought to be out of bed.

I levered myself up onto my elbows and blinked a few times. Was I feeling better? Did my ribs hurt less? The painkillers I had taken last night would be out of my system by now. I gingerly prodded my ribs with the fingers of my left hand. It was still sore, but five days after the injury it was also not as sore as it had been. Was I healing more quickly than predicted or was the Molton Brown muscle soak imbued with magical powers?

There was a knock at my door and an instantaneous episode of barking from the dogs, both of whom were still beneath the duvet revelling in the warmth it provided. They emerged at speed, still barking a warning to the intruder outside. I already knew it was Basic or was most likely to be Basic, as I had offered him a lift in with me this morning. Yawning, I struggled into my clothes and stumbled downstairs carrying the Dachshunds. Their little tails were wagging madly as they tried to evade my grip and get to the front door. Instead, I deposited them by the back door and forced them outside to do their business in the garden, then I went to let Basic in.

'Good morning, Basic. My apologies, I'm not yet ready,' I said around another yawn.

'That's okay, Tempest,' he replied coming through the door.

'Would you like a cup of tea? I'm having one.' He nodded yes and took a seat at the breakfast bar in my kitchen as I set the kettle to boil. The dogs barked to be let back in. They wanted their breakfast.

At the breakfast bar, Basic pulled a Gameboy from his coat, it was already playing a tune to accompany whatever game he had on. I recognised the music but couldn't tell which game it was just by listening.

I left him there to let the dogs back in, the pair scrambling around me to get to the kitchen as soon as I opened the patio door. That they needed to wait for me to serve their breakfast and thus running ahead of me achieved nothing, failed to deter them from doing so every morning. I made them wait impatiently for their breakfast while I made the tea, then scooped them each a half cup of kibble which they attacked before I could even get the bowls to the floor.

I turned on the news expecting to hear of more Klown attacks last night. However, the two anchors went through a half hour cycle of national news while I made breakfast. There was nothing about the Klowns at all. As they finished their set, it switched to local news where I felt certain there would be reports of murder and mayhem, but again it was as if the Klowns had never been.

Was it incongruous that there was no report of Klown activity, or had there been other days in the last couple of weeks when they had been inactive? I dismissed it, left Basic playing with the dogs and went upstairs to get showered and dressed. My ribs were definitely not as sore as they had been, and I was able to wash my hair with only minimal wincing.

It was just before 1000hrs when we finally left the house, the dogs dragging me out of the door and over to the car. I had already called Jane to let her know I was running late. Again. She was fine about it, of course and was pleased I remembered to wish her a happy birthday. It wasn't a keenly attuned brain that remembered though, I had set a reminder on my phone, so it pinged and flashed a message before I left the house.

There are a number of different routes I could take to get to my office. I usually let my mood dictate which direction I pointed the car but this morning I went through Borstal to bring me down to Rochester via the Maidstone Road. There was a good florist in a short parade of shops about halfway down where I stopped to get birthday flowers.

I was such a caring boss.

When we pulled back out into traffic, the two dogs were displaced by a large bunch of Gerberas on Basic's lap. They were unhappy about this as they felt the passenger's seat was only there for their purposes anyway, now they had flowers to contend with as well. However, they selected an alternative solution to just laying down for the last mile; they climbed across the centre console and onto my lap instead, making it far more adventurous for me to drive the car. I quickly checked there were no police about to see the Dachshunds on my lap and as I did so I noted that the silver Mondeo I spotted earlier was still there. There were two cars between us so despite trying to see the occupants, I couldn't. Was I being tailed by Klowns? Was this to be attack number three?

They trailed me all the way around the back of the castle but vanished from sight as I pulled into my parking space. Cautiously, I told Basic to leave the flowers and the dogs in the car and stay alert.

The car park behind my office was contained by walls on all sides. The only gaps were the one I had driven in through and one at the front which allowed pedestrian access to Rochester High Street. I went on foot back to where I had entered the car park. I peered around the corner of the brickwork but of the silver Mondeo there was no sign.

Paranoia?

I turned around and bumped into Basic. He was standing right behind me looking massive and ready to kill if required.

'Klowns?' he asked.

'Not this time. False alarm, I think. Let's get to the office.'

I retrieved the flowers from the car and fished out my keys. I tried the bottom door to my office, pleased to find that Jane had locked it once inside as I instructed.

Basic was waiting behind me. 'Hey, Tempest. What happened when the lion ate the clown? He felt funny.'

His jokes were getting worse, but I smiled anyway. I called out to Jane as we went up the stairs. It threw me a little that it was James sitting behind the desk when I got to the top; he came dressed as a man so rarely that I had almost stopped bothering to think of him as one. Yet here he was wearing what looked like a fresh from the box Le Coste navy-blue polo shirt, dark blue jeans and a pair of tan Caterpilla boots. He was over by the window at the small table leafing through a wad of A4 sheets and drinking coffee. The office stank of freshly brewed espresso instantly making me want one.

'There is a freshly brewed pot,' James said, without looking up. He knew me well enough, I guess.

'Happy birthday, James., I brandished my bunch of flowers. 'These do not seem as appropriate now. I was expecting Jane.'

'They are lovely. Thank you,' he said, getting up to take them. 'I like flowers regardless of how I dress.'

'What are you reading there?' I indicated the printed pages he held.

'Some online theories about the Klowns. I printed it off at home last night to read when I needed a screen break. It's all utter rubbish though.'

I nodded. I often read online forums about the cases I was investigating, the bigger cases attracted them some-times, or if I was looking into something generic like a were-wolf, I would read generic forums on the subject. Mostly it was garbage but sometimes the garbage led me to consider something, some tenet of the case that I might otherwise overlook.

'Okay,' I said, cracking my knuckles. 'Time to figure this thing out.' With no better option, I intended to spend the day going over and over the available facts and theories until I found out who the Klowns were and what they were doing. We had managed to find a couple of connections thus far which was more than the police had, so far as I knew. It wasn't something I took pride in; it was just how things seemed to work sometimes.

I set Basic up at the table by the window. He had a Gameboy and a dinosaur colouring book and was humming quietly to himself while I wrote on three different whiteboards.

'James, do we have any interview notes from the victims?' I asked.

'Not really. I think the police have largely kept them under wraps but there are some uncorroborated quotes in the media. Why?'

'I want to ask the victims about the attacks. What they heard, what the Klowns said, why they believe they were targeted.'

'Didn't you already try that when you were contracted by Mrs. Plumber?'

'Yup. There have been a lot more attacks since then though. Some of them really stand out. Take this one.' I tapped the board, more for my own purposes than to bring his attention to it. 'Edna Wilkins, seventy-three years old, a retired infant-school teacher. If the attack was deliberate, then what on earth was the motivation behind it?'

James got up from the table and came to join me in front of the whiteboard I was poking. Basic noticed and followed him.

'Then there is Marion Lloyd. The only attack to occur outside of the County. Why?' I asked, not that I was expecting an answer.

'The police said it was a copycat crime. Someone taking advantage of an easy to replicate M.O.'

'But what if it wasn't? What if the Klowns deliberately drove two-hundred miles north to attack a woman? The victim is an ordinary middle-aged woman. Nothing special about her. If this was a copycat attack, there needed to be something significant to motivate it.

'Surely the same is true of the Klowns? If they had to drive all that way, there must have been something significant to motivate them,' James pointed out.

'Indeed,' I agreed. 'I just don't know what it is yet. It's the same problem we have with all the Klown attacks. I still think there is one thing linking all this together.'

'So … phone numbers?' James asked.

'Phone numbers,' I agreed.

It took James almost no time at all to find a number for Marion Lloyd. I left him tracking down contact details for Edna while I went over by the window to place the call. The phone rang for some time and went to the answering service. I clicked off then tried again. This time it was answered but it was a man's voice I heard at the other end.

'Hello?' the voice said in a tone that was treading a line between bored and angry.

'Good afternoon, sir. My name is Tempest Michaels…'

'And you're another damned reporter after an interview,' he snapped at me and hung up.

I tried calling back, but I got no answer and after a few attempts it was clear he had turned the phone off. My guess was that it was Mr Lloyd that had answered the phone and that he was probably justified in his annoyance after being pestered by the press; they could be persistent.

'I have a number for Edna,' announced James from the desk. 'It's at an old person's home though. Sheltered living, if that is the right expression. So, it's a number for the warden, I guess.' He looked up finally having been reading from the screen. 'You want it?'

'Might as well give it a go.'

I had a little more luck this time, which is to say that I

wasn't immediately hung up on. My call wasn't welcome though, yet again they had received several already. I was able to convince the lady at the other end of the line that I wasn't a reporter or journalist, but she still wouldn't allow me to speak with Mrs. Wilkins.

I couldn't blame her, but I felt no choice but to the push the issue. If I was going to make headway, I was going to have to take steps I might otherwise not. The area code was one I recognised. James gave me the address – Tonbridge. I could be there in little more than thirty minutes.

I thought about it for a few seconds, the choice was obvious though. There was something connecting the attacks. There had to be. I had considered the possibility that they were all completely random and just didn't buy it.

'James, I'm taking a road trip. Going to see Mrs Wilkins.' At the tone of my voice, the dogs lifted their heads in interest. They always knew when there was something to be awake for. Looking at the two cute, stupid dogs sitting beneath Basic's chair, I saw how I was going to get in to see Edna.

'Okay,' James replied. 'Will you be coming back here afterward?'

I checked my watch: 1107hrs. 'Yes, most definitely, but it will be a couple of hours at least. Will you be okay here by yourself?' I asked.

'I will lock the door after you leave. If the Klowns turn up looking to kill me, I will escape through the travel agents while they are busy breaking down the door.' He sounded calm and confident, so I kept quiet about how easy it would be to throw an explosive device through one of the old glass windows.

'We going out, Tempest?' asked Basic.

'We sure are. We are taking the doggies to see some nice

old ladies.' I convinced Basic to use the bathroom before we left the office, then we walked the dogs for ten minutes on their leads around the corner to the grounds between the castle and cathedral. It was tranquil and pleasant there as if the world, in general, had no thought of the Klowns.

Old Dears' Home, Tonbridge

The address was easy to find. I had a rough idea where it was from checking the map on the wall before I left, and the satnav did the rest. I found myself checking my rear-view mirror far more regularly than usual, searching for a car that might be tailing me. I saw a Silver Mondeo at one point, but no sooner had I spotted it than it pulled into a petrol station.

We arrived at the destination which advertised parking around the back, so I followed the signs, putting the car in a space with room either side of it. The Dachshunds were up and excited, climbing all over Basic in the passenger's seat to look out the windows. They knew they had arrived somewhere.

I was fairly confident that I would be able to find and quiz Mrs Wilkins provided I could bluff my way beyond whoever they had on the front desk. There was a voice entry system attached to a buzzer at the front door, which made getting inside more difficult since I wouldn't be able to see who I was talking to. Luck was on my side though. It was the kind of assisted living where the old dears got to come and go as they pleased. They had separate accommodation inside, much like living in an army barracks where the rooms were private but joined by central interior corridors. Each had a kitchenette, and they were able to cater for themselves. Two of the residents were returning from a nearby shop as Basic and I approached the front door being led by the two Dachshunds.

'Ooh look, Mavis. Look at the sausages,' said the first, trying to nudge the second with an arm weighed down by her bags.

Hearing her, the two dogs instantly diverted their route to intercept hers. I was holding the dog leads, but Basic, the wonderful soul that he was, darted forward, offering to carry their bags the rest of the way to their accommodation.

They appeared to be deliberating. Basic, while harmless and good-natured was also hulking and a little scruffy. 'Good afternoon, ladies,' I greeted them as the dogs closed the final few feet. I held them back as they were ready to climb the ladies' legs for attention. 'We are just popping in to see Edna Wilkins. My friend will carry your bags to your rooms if you wish.'

Mavis was too interested in the dogs to give it any further consideration, perhaps she judged that we were unlikely to be there to steal her fruit loaf and tea bags. Whatever the case, she handed her bags to Basic without looking at him and bent her knees as far as they would go, so she could reach down and pat the dogs. Her friend, the one that had spoken first, did likewise.

It was an old ploy of mine, old ladies liked little dogs, they were easily swayed by them. Before they knew what they were doing, they had entered the door code and walked us inside the building. We chatted amiably as we followed them to their rooms, talking about the dogs – Mavis had owned a Dachshund as a child, and about Edna and how we knew her. I had to lie at that point. Sticking to vagaries, I claimed I had grown up with her as a neighbour and that she had been kind to me. My tactic avoided the potential pitfall of claiming I was her grandson only to discover that her friends knew that she had no children; it hadn't occurred to me to look up such facts before setting off.

Mavis and Coleen, we learned the other lady's name when Mavis addressed her, led us to a day room where they said we would most likely find Edna watching TV with some of the other residents. They were right, although I had a brief moment of panic when we went in as I realised I didn't know what she looked like. Thankfully, Coleen called out to bring Edna's attention to her visitors.

'Hi, Edna,' I tried hopefully. My hope was based quite cruelly on the concept that there might be some memory issues going on. All the residents looked to be in their eighties or beyond. The youngest might be in her late seventies.

'Oh, hello,' replied Edna, not even looking up at me. The dogs were far too interesting as they buzzed around her feet. I selected Dozer as the dopier and more cuddly choice, picked him up and deposited him upside down on her lap. He stayed there with her tickling his belly, his head back and his eyes closed.

It took a while, but in the end, one by one, the other ladies drifted away. Bargain Hunt was about to start, it was lunchtime; various reasons to be elsewhere. Now that it was just Edna and me, since Basic had found a Smurfs jigsaw puzzle to play with, I figured it was time to come clean and tell her why I was there.

'So, young man. Would you like to tell me why you are here?' she asked. The old bird was as sharp as a tack. She had pegged me right from the start. 'Nice move bringing the dogs. Are they yours or did you hire them? I assume you are a reporter of some kind.' She fixed me with a stare that demanded I tell the truth. I remembered then that she had been a schoolteacher for most of her life.

'Mrs. Wilkins, my apologies for the subterfuge. My name is Tempest Michaels. I'm an investigator looking into the Klown case.' I omitted the paranormal bit; it tends to just confuse people. 'I hoped to ask you a few questions about the attack. Would that be acceptable?'

'To what end, Mr. Michaels?'

'I intend to stop the Klowns. I think the police are looking in the wrong place and I have been targeted twice myself, so I have a vested interest in finding out who they are and what they are up to.'

'Well, Mr. Michaels, I will tell you what I know. I already told the police everything though, so I'm not sure what help I can be.'

'Specifically, I want to know why they would target you.'

'The police said it was random.'

'That is the bit I think they have wrong. I believe it's not random, which means they came after you as part of a plan. The question is why? Why are you linked to them? I asked. Edna stared at me blank-faced. 'What did they say to you? I know it must be awful to think about it, I apologise for bringing up the memory.'

'What did they say while they were kicking me?' I felt awful pressing her to consider it again in detail. 'They didn't say much at all. One of them though. He said... he said,

"Today's lesson is pain, Mrs Wilkins." I hadn't given it any consideration until now, but now that I think about it, I would always start my lessons by saying "Today's lesson is..." and then telling them what we were going to learn.

'You think maybe this Klown, the one that spoke, was one of your students once?'

She shrugged. 'I guess that makes sense.'

I pressed on with the next question, feeling like I was getting somewhere. 'Was there a boy that sticks out as being one that would hold a grudge against you?'

She frowned at me as if the question was unacceptable. 'Mr Michaels, I was a teacher for fifty-seven years with thirty or so new students every year. Regrettably, when I started, way back in the late fifties, it was perfectly acceptable, even expected, for the teacher to whack a child if they stepped out of line. It was the late eighties before this really changed so there will be hundreds of children that might hold a grudge.'

Dozer was still upside down on her lap, snoring gently. She scratched his chest a little, her face thoughtful. I kept silent, waiting for her to coalesce her thoughts into... something. A name would be useful.

Nothing came though and soon I realised she had fallen asleep. I collected Dozer gently from her lap and clipped him back to his lead as he blearily came awake. Tapping Basic gently on the shoulder and with a finger to my lips, we left Edna sleeping peacefully in her chair and let ourselves out.

That the Klowns had delivered a message, even if she hadn't comprehended its meaning, had to mean something. The messages the Klowns delivered to me had felt personal. I didn't understand them, but now I wanted to know how many others had been given similar messages as they were stabbed or beaten or robbed? It was a question I intended to have answered.

As we pulled out of the car park, my phone was ringing. The screen in my car claimed it was Big Ben calling.

'Hey, buddy,' I said as the call connected.

'Tempest. Get me out of here,' he whispered.

'Ben? What going on?'

'I've escaped. They are probably looking for me. I need you to come to the hospital and get me now.' His whispering voice was still able to convey a tone of desperation.

Confused by his change of heart, I said, 'I thought you were enjoying yourself there, working through all the lady staff.'

'Yeah, well, I was. Now they are starting to fight over me, arguing about whose turn it is. I think they have a roster up somewhere. The food is awful, even on the private plan they have put me on and I'm getting so much action I actually think that my dick is starting to erode.' I was finding it hard to feel sorry for him.

'I'm in the car with Basic. I can't collect you – only two seats. Get a taxi?' I tried, helpfully.

'No money. I had to leave without getting my things. I don't know where they are and when I asked for them yesterday, they became suspicious.' The trials of being a sex god. How difficult it must be.

'Just grab a cab to my office. I'll sort the bill out there.'

He thought about that for a second. 'Okay, Tempest. I think that will work... hold on... oh, nuts! I think they spotted me. Gotta go.' The line went dead.

'Is Ben okay?' asked Basic from the passenger seat.

'I believe that depends on one's perspective,' I answered with a cruel grin on my face. I wasn't going to be able to feel sorry for him.

'Perspexitive?'

'Yes, Basic, Ben will be fine. I expect we shall see him shortly. He was just being dramatic.'

The short conversation had taken us out of Tonbridge. It was very much lunchtime according to my belly, so I aimed the car at my house rather than the office.

The Blue Moon Office

THURSDAY, OCTOBER 27TH 1512HRS

Basic was quiet in the car on the way back to Rochester apart from when he yelled out "High score!" causing me to swerve the car as I jumped. I had been deep in thought, working through the problem I faced.

'Sorry, Tempest,' he said, thumbs twirling on his Gameboy.

I let my heart rate return to normal and went back to the Klown conundrum. I called James from the car as we were setting off from Tonbridge and tasked him with digging out a list of every student Mrs Wilkins had ever taught. I just hoped it wasn't going to be a wild goose chase. He had been about to leave the office, heading to a salon before his evening out in Rochester for his birthday tonight.

I kept checking my mirrors for the silver Mondeo or any other car that might be shadowing me. The road I was on though was a straight line that wound through all the villages between Tonbridge and the Motorway and then did the same thing once it crossed over the motorway all the way to Rochester. Conceivably, a car could sit behind me all the way from A to B with no evil plan being hatched. Furthermore, silver Ford Mondeos were common as muck. There was one behind me now about five cars back, but I couldn't see the occupants, and it was gone the next time I checked.

Despite the possibility that Big Ben was on his way to the office, I needed to eat, and I wanted to drop the dogs off with my neighbour since I was going to be out this evening and really couldn't have them with me.

There was some deliberation over lunch as Basic didn't want the spinach and courgette omelette I intended to eat. He pulled a disgusted face when I suggested it, so we settled on grilled ham and cheese sandwiches with pickled onions on the side. While they were heating through in my pan I popped around to see the lady next door.

As expected, Mrs. Comerforth was once again only too pleased to have my dogs come to stay with her. I wouldn't be out late so would collect them from her house before she went to bed. I gave her their food and bowls and dropped them off after Basic and I ate our sandwiches.

On our way from my house to the office in Rochester, we went via his house to check on his mum. She came to the door and gave me a wave as I sat in my car. Basic went inside but came out just a few moments later carrying a Tupperware box that looked to be suspiciously full of cake, which, it transpired, it was. His mum had baked a Victoria sponge for us, just in case we got hungry. He cracked the lid to show me as he settled into his seat, instantly filling the interior with the sublime smell of freshly baked goodness. My stomach growled at me despite the lunch I had just eaten.

Zipping along the tight country lanes that led through the villages close to the river, the phone rang again. I had taken the scenic route back to the office, partly this was because years of living as a theoretically attractive target for terrorists had drummed into me the need to vary my route and avoid predictability and partly it was because I was in no particular rush. Sometimes I was and would take the motorway, today I wasn't, so I was cruising.

I jabbed the answer button on my steering wheel as the screen identified Big Ben as the caller.

'Ben? Did you escape yet?' I asked with amusement in my voice.

'Damned right I did. I'm nearly at your office. Have you got some cash?'

'How close are you? I'm about ten minutes away.'

'Nuts. I'm about two-hundred yards away. Just coming around the back of the castle.'

'I'll call James. He can bring some money down from the office.'

'I need some clothes too.'

'You're naked in the cab? Does the driver have wipe clean seats?' I heard a woman laugh in the background.

Was he naked in a cab with a woman?

'I managed to snag a gown and some pants but that's about it. The first three cab drivers refused to pick me up. Fortunately, Shelley was good enough to understand my plight. We are going out this weekend.'

Naturally, he had picked up the cab driver and arranged to have sex this weekend while escaping from his hospital sex prison. What else would Big Ben do?

Big Ben and Shelley were now giggling about something in sexy, flirting tones. I said I would see him at the office and disconnected.

Ten minutes later I pulled into my parking space behind the office just as Big Ben was finishing up paying Shelley for the ride. His stupid, great-big head was shoved through the driver's side window where he was probably kissing her. He was indeed wearing only a hospital gown and some pants. In typical Big Ben style, he hadn't really bothered to do the gown up, so leaning forward it was hanging around his neck by a single spaghetti strap leaving him almost naked in the street. People were looking, which was, of course, the general idea.

He withdrew his head, beaming a big naughty smile and waved her off.

'Hey, guys,' he said, seeing Basic and I approach.

'Doofus.'

'Hardly fair,' he countered.

'Naked in the street in October, been held captive for five days,' I was fairly certain I had a point.

'Held captive by women in nurse uniforms so that they could have sex with me. It wasn't exactly torture,' he argued.

I smiled and shook my head. He was entertaining to know, if nothing else. His behaviour begged a question though. 'Why did you escape then?'

'I appeared that I had gone through the list of willing ladies and some of them were coming back for seconds. There are too many women in this world to sleep with the same one twice.' He actually seemed saddened by the prospect.

'What about Patience? Is she a special case?' I asked.

'Actually, maybe. That lady knows her way around the bedroom. I tell you…'

'NO!' I cut him off. 'Basic and I have no desire to hear about your exploits in detail. Come on, I have a job for you since you're here.' I started moving towards the pedestrian exit from the car park onto Rochester High Street.

Big Ben made a show of hugging himself. 'I'm a bit cold, mate. I could do with some clothes and a tidy up. I was hoping to borrow your car to get home.'

I stalled my forward momentum for a second, considering whether he had a point. 'In a bit,' I decided. 'You're perfect as you are for the task at hand.'

The task at hand was to visit Dr. Parrish and his make-believe Paranormal Investigation Agency. I didn't take kindly to having my customers poached. Since I had Basic with me, who looks like an evil villain's henchman and now had an unkempt, mostly naked and slightly deranged looking Big Ben to accompany me, I felt it set the right tone for the conversation.

We drew a few stares walking along the High Street, mostly from women checking out Big Ben, so I was glad his office is less than a hundred yards from mine. I pushed open the spotlessly clean glass front door, making sure I pressed my hand to the glass and missed the chrome inset panel designed to keep people's handprints from marking it.

Inside, I was met by the same tall, attractive woman behind the reception desk. Today she had on a different suit but looked equally well groomed. She looked up as I came in so I could see her eyes widening with the arrival of Basic and then Big Ben.

Scanning the room, there was no sign of Dr. Parrish but a closed door and muted voices coming from behind it told me where he was. I walked in a direct line towards his office ignoring the lady waiting at the reception desk.

'Excuse me.' The reception lady jumped from her stool to intercept me. Her face was cool and impassive.

'I got this,' said Big Ben from behind me.

Just as I was reaching the door, it opened and there was

Dr. Parrish, holding open the door for an older couple. They looked troubled.

Lyndon spotted me. 'Mr. Michaels. Always a pleasure. Won't be a moment.' I allowed him to slip by me to show the old couple out.

'Oh, my,' said the old lady. 'Come along, Herbert.'

Turning around to watch him revealed what the lady had reacted to. Big Ben had the reception lady bent over in his arms, hanging from his embrace like a willing ragdoll. He was kissing her deeply. I still had no idea how he did it. He was good looking admittedly, but women just look at him and throw their knickers away.

At the door, Dr. Parrish went ahead of the older couple to hold the door open and bid them a good day, at least that was what I assumed his intention was. Instead, he glanced back at me, then legged it down the High Street. He checked over his shoulder once before he was lost from view in the crowd.

I guess I will deal with Dr. Parrish later then.

Left standing in his shop, I couldn't decide if we had just appeared too threatening, or if his guilty conscience had forced him to flee.

Big Ben looked up. 'We done?'

'Yup.'

He simply let go of the woman and stood up. She crashed to the floor at his feet, looking shocked and hurt. Walking away he blew her a kiss, 'If you want more you know where to find me, naughty girl.' Instead of hurling insults, which I'm quite certain would have happened to me, or anyone else, the woman smiled to herself. Big Ben was unbelievable.

We wandered back to the office with Big Ben attracting yet more appreciative looks from female pedestrians. A young lady on a bicycle rode it into a raised flower bed while staring at him. He went to aid her, so Basic and I waited while he picked her out of the flower bed, dusted the dirt from her clothing and handed her bike back to her. All the while he was chatting amiably with her and complimenting her outfit. Then he handed her a business card.

He was wearing pants and a hospital gown!

I didn't wish to dwell on where the card had been, but I had seen them before, he kept a supply of them to hand out to girls when he was short on time to chat them up. The card was little more than a "get it here" token with a phone number. Again, I wondered how he got away with it. Back upright and back on her bike she wobbled off down the High Street with a grin on her face and almost crashed again as she checked him out over her shoulder one more time.

'Come on, walking penis.'

'Tut, tut, Tempest,' he mockingly chided. 'You should be observing and learning, not getting envious.'

I rolled my eyes, went inside and up to my office with Basic and Big Ben following behind. It was warmer inside, making me realise just how cool it was outside and thus what a convincing job Big Ben had done of ignoring it.

'Hi, guys,' James said as we came in. 'Anyone for coffee?'

We all nodded. 'James, have you been able to find any victim or witness statements that refer to the Klowns delivering messages during their attacks?' I asked him as he headed over to the kettle and cups. I went to the window and looked out.

'Err, one or two, I think. It's not a detail I have been looking for.'

'I'm going to spend some time on that now. Are you

staying for the afternoon?' I asked as I looked at something across the street.

'If you need me to. I was heading to a salon to get my hair done and then meeting Simon for a little food before drinks tonight, so I might as well just stay here rather than go home first.'

'Perfect. We can tackle it together,' I said, still looking out of the window.

'Is everything alright?' James asked.

'There are two chaps on a bench across the street.' Big Ben, Basic and Jane came to look with me.

'Yes, there are,' Big Ben acknowledged.

'They look like cops to you?' I asked. They were in their late twenties probably, wearing cheap suits and had functional haircuts. They were talking between themselves, but they weren't eating lunch, they weren't eyeing up passing girls, and they didn't fit in.

'Maybe.'

'Hey, Fellas!' I called out loudly. They both raised their faces to see where the shout had come from, and I memorised their faces so I would know if I saw them again. I had a distinct feeling I was being tailed.

'I could do with going home to get clean and maybe find some clothes,' said Big Ben.

'Sure thing, just take the car and leave it at my place once you're done.' I stepped down from the window and handed Big Ben my keys.

'Are you coming tonight?' asked James.

'Most certainly,' he replied. 'I'll get a taxi back from Tempest's when I drop the car off later.' Big Ben departed, leaving us to the task of yet more research.

I left James trying to find any record of the Klowns saying cryptic things to the victims and called Amanda.

While I waited for it to connect, I went back to the window. The two men were gone.

Then the call connected, the sound of Amanda's wonderful voice reaching my ear, bypassing my brain and whispering thoughts directly to Mr Wriggly. 'Hi, Tempest. You're lucky you caught me. I'm just going out on patrol.'

'Have they got you working crazy hours?' I asked, ignoring the ideas about her uniform and cuffs coming from my pants.

'Pretty much. They have trebled the police presence in towns and villages, in shopping centres and at any event that is taking place. Lots of overtime pay, which is nice for a while and most of the chaps want it, but it will get tedious soon enough. I'm telling myself this is the last time I will ever do any of this, but it has meant that my shift count-down clock went out the window. I only had eight shifts left and suddenly they have shoehorned in another four, plus each one of them is more hours. What can I do for you, anyway?'

'I have a sneaking suspicion about the Klowns motive. Can you get me whatever information there is in the victim and witness statements about the Klowns saying things to them?'

'What sort of things?' she asked.

'Well, I don't really know. The old schoolteacher that was attacked...' I went on to explain the message they delivered to her and how I wondered if there was some personal connection. She agreed that my theory made a kind of twisted sense. I got a feeling there was something she wanted to tell me, but that she was holding back. When I pressed her for it, she clammed up. She had to go, so we said goodbye, I wished her a quiet patrol, and I got back to the task at hand. As always, James had found something.

'There is a fellow here that was chased and robbed and given a beating two weeks ago in Borough Green. He was interviewed by the Weald Word in which he is reported to have said, "They told me I had earned it. I was a know-it-all bossy git and had it coming." He goes on to say that he had no idea what they were talking about.'

The statement fit the pattern I was looking for – it was a personal message delivered by the Klowns to an individual that I believed they had deliberately, not randomly targeted. But why? For the next hour, James kept on at the computer while I looked up numbers for the victims. These weren't easy to come by as most people are unlisted now, the era of the mobile had killed the home phone market, but I was able to find a handful and that was enough. A young woman in Dover had been attacked leaving work in the car park behind her office. The Klowns hadn't hurt her exactly, it had been one of the very early attacks, but they had certainly scared her and had told her she should have said yes when he asked her out. They hadn't elaborated on who *he* was.

Then I found another woman who the Klowns had slapped on the face repeatedly all the while asking her how she liked it and why did she think she had the right to slap *his* face?

James found another report in an online news feed. They all pointed to the same thing – the Klowns were targeting people with pinpoint accuracy. Everyone they had gone after was for a specific reason.

My whiteboards were filling up with information, getting to the point where I could barely understand them myself. I stepped back and looked at the list again. Could I call it a pattern? Or was I forcing the pattern into existence because it suited my theory? I asked James, but he just shrugged.

'I really need to think about going, Tempest. Simon has a table booked for six o'clock.' I resisted asking him if he meant 1800hrs because I would just sound like a dick if I did. My watch claimed it was 1747hrs, so it was indeed time for James to go.

'Basic, can I get you a taxi home?' I asked. He was taking his mum to bingo. He had been quiet all the while we were going over the case, sitting at the table adding hues of greens and browns to a complex scene where herbivores were coming out of a swamp and eating the trees that lined the water's edge. In the background was a carnivore watching them. He had done a good job.

'Manda said I was to stick with you,' he replied simply while continuing to colour. His tongue was sticking out of the corner of his mouth in concentration.

'I'm going out tonight with Big Ben and the others. I will have lots of protection.' He thought about that for a moment but agreed that I would be safe with Big Ben and Jagjit and Hilary.

Ten minutes later James was gone, and I was watching out the window for the taxi to appear. When it did, Basic and I descended the stairs together. I gave the driver sufficient to get him back to Finchampstead plus a tip and gave him the address. 'Hey, Tempest.' Basic was leaning out the taxi window. 'What did the egg say to the clown? You crack me up!'

The Warren, Rochester

I had considered inviting Sophie out tonight. We had a date tomorrow and there were going to be other ladies out with us tonight not including James, who was dressed as a boy for once. In the end, I theorised that a first date where she met more than half the people I knew was probably not a clever move.

Thinking about ladies reminded me that Hilary was coming and was bringing his wife. I had never actually met Anthea Clinton. She had glared at me once when I came to pick Hilary up from his house some months ago, but we had never exchanged words. Speaking with Hilary, who I might have to actually call Brian for the night, I got the distinct impression that she did not approve of me, or my business or of my friends or of her husband's involvement in any of it. Thus, I was suspicious that I might spend a portion of the evening giving her a good listening to. I wasn't however of a mind to be talked down to at length, so my bigger concern was whether I could successfully navigate a truce with her before it became a problem for Hilary/Brian. I would find out soon enough.

I pushed open the door and went inside. A bored-looking doorman gave me a once over when I stepped inside. Looking around the bar I couldn't see any of my group. Was I really the first to arrive? I went to the bar to get myself a drink.

'Tempest,' called a voice I didn't recognise. It came from an ordinary looking, slightly pudgy guy with a beard. I was looking at him, trying to work out where he knew me from, but he left the post he had been keeping at the bar and came to me before I could do the maths. 'Simon,' he said, offering me his hand. He saw my confused expression and laughed. 'Sorry, I hear so much about you that I feel like we know each other. I'm James's boyfriend.'

Of course.

I shook his hand and said it was a pleasure to meet him. Behind him, Big Ben was coming through the door with Jagjit and his date. I hadn't exactly been paying attention to the paramedic Jagjit had been flirting with on Saturday night but what little I remembered was a pleasant enough looking woman. Accompanying him now though, with her arm looped through his and a laugh on her lips was a lady that I would challenge others to not describe as stunning. Simon saw my gaze and followed it, although he managed to miss the lady I was looking at and spotted the larger-than-life man holding the door for her.

'Is that Big Ben?' he asked in a hushed and reverent tone and watched as I nodded. 'Boy, I really wish he was gay. I would leave James in a heartbeat.' Big Ben's appeal was universal.

Big Ben was wearing a pair of skinny jeans that made his

thighs look muscular and his waist small. Beneath his jacket he had on a Ralph Lauren polo shirt, which he favoured because they had a cuff to the sleeve that would cut into his biceps, accenting just how big they were. As he came into the warmth of the bar, he shucked his jacket and made sure the veins on his arms were visible. There were girls in the bar, so for him, this was probably a target rich environment.

'Hey, guys,' I said in greeting as they came to the bar. 'This is James's boyfriend, Simon.'

As they all shook hands I introduced each of my friends in turn until I got to Jagjit's date.

'Alice,' she provided helpfully.

'Good to meet you, Alice.' I meant it. Jagjit had been single for a while and deserved some fun.

'So, um. Where is the birthday girl or boy?' asked Big Ben. Like me, he struggled to work out how to refer to Jane/James when they/them wasn't present because one could never tell what way they/them had elected to dress that day. Big Ben isn't known for his political correctness, though. In fact, he would often play upon it in an attempt to get laughs or shock people.

'James went to the gents,' answered Simon. 'Here he comes now, in fact.' Sure enough, James was weaving through the people gathered at the far end of the bar to get back to us.

So, Simon. Do you cross-dress at all?' asked Big Ben. The question wasn't one that I would have considered polite to ask but he managed to ask it engagingly as if he was truly interested.

'No. No, I don't. I'm strictly just gay. James is LGBT. It makes his wardrobe hard to fit into our bedroom, so it spills into the guest bedroom.'

Big Ben chuckled, which drew a quizzical expression

from Simon as if perhaps Big Ben was mocking him. 'Sorry. I was laughing at myself,' he said quickly, seeing his rudeness. 'I only just learned what LGBT stands for.'

'Really? It's hardly a new term,' said James as he joined us.

'No. But I thought it stood for Lingerie, Grub, Booze, and Tits. Like a bro code thing for a great night in. Make sure she's set up for LGBT. Hey, buddy my girlfriend totally went LGBT on me last night. Score! That sort of thing.'

James was just staring at him.

'Shall we move to a table?' Simon asked, trying to change the subject. 'I reserved one in the back.'

There was a consensus of agreement. I stayed at the bar to get drinks as the others shuffled off. Seconds later, there was a hand on my shoulder. In the mirror, I saw that Hilary and his wife had just come through the door and were behind me now. The barman had just addressed me, so I placed my order then turned smiling to greet them and ask if I could add their drinks to my order.

Hilary shook my hand, as did his wife, but if I needed any ice for my drink, I could just take it from her expression. Despite her obvious desire to remove my testicles and make earrings from them, she allowed me to buy her a Malibu and diet coke.

With a tray of drinks and with Hilary clearing a route for me, I made my way to the back of the bar. At the table, the chaps were engaged in a discussion about tattoos.

'I have a couple,' volunteered Alice.

'Do you?' asked Jagjit, failing utterly to hide the interest in his voice. He did manage to resist asking where she had them though. Instead of answering she just smiled cheekily at him.

'It's really not my thing,' I offered, joining in the conversation. 'The permanency of them holds me back. What if I don't like it ten or twenty years from now?'

'I have been thinking I would get one for myself as a birthday present,' said James.

'What sort of thing?' Alice asked.

'I don't know. Something feminine I guess,' he replied, a thoughtful look on his face.

'Something feminine?' Big Ben questioned. 'Like a tampon with petals around it?' His face held genuine mystery.

'No, Benjamin,' answered James with an eye roll.

'Poison,' Jagjit announced with a flick of his eyes. I turned to see the delightful Miss Ivy Wong with some friends at the bar. Earlier today I sent her a text telling her we would be in here but did not expect to see her. She was still the right side of twenty so had no business hanging out with the old, crusty thirty-somethings. Despite my thoughts on the matter, she was coming our way.

Beyond her, at the bar, I spotted two guys in cheap suits. They weren't the same two I had seen earlier, but they stood out from the crowd as they were paying no attention to the ladies in the bar and were both drinking bottled water. They were not looking my way, and I was having too good of a time to worry about it right now.

'Hi, everyone. Happy birthday, James,' Poison said as she neared our table. She was flanked by three friends, all Chinese, who she introduced as Hatchet, Mistress Mushy and Bob. The names were probably not what was written on their birth certificates. They were dressed in a similar style to Poison which is to say they had colourfully dyed hair and make-up, even the guys, and wore a lot of distressed black clothing. Together they looked like a post-apocalyptic rock group. 'We are not staying. I just wanted to swing past and wish the birthday boy a good night.' Her hand, I noted, was intertwined with that of Hatchet. A boyfriend I assumed. This was welcome news to me as she had for some time been trying to convince me to sleep with her.

We bid her and her friends a good evening as they turned to leave. Just as they were going Poison caught my eye and winked. Maybe I wasn't off the hook just yet.

Anthea had seen it. 'Are you messing with that young girl?' she asked me quite directly. I felt that she had been looking for an opening from which to launch an attack and here it was.

Thankfully, I didn't have to get into an argument with her as almost everyone sitting around the table leapt to my defence. I ended up feeling almost sorry for Anthea. She clearly wanted to dislike me, yet I was being reflected by all those around me in a very positive light.

As an awkward silence fell, Big Ben waded in with an anecdote to change the tone. 'Chaps, you know the old fella that is always sitting at the end of the bar in the Dirty Habit?'

'Roger?' asked Jagjit before I could.

'That's the fella,' confirmed Big Ben. 'Would you believe he was a porn star back in the seventies?'

We all considered that for a moment.

'No. No, I wouldn't believe that,' said Hilary.

Big Ben was fiddling with his phone. 'Well, here's the evidence. His stage name was Roger Ring and here are some of the movies he made.' He passed his phone across for everyone to crowd around and look at.

It was a Wikipedia page showing a black and white of a man in his early thirties. He had a shock of wavy black hair and a mustache so bushy it would have scared Tom Selleck. His shirt was unbuttoned to his waist, revealing a mat of black chest hair supporting a huge gold medallion. I couldn't tell if it was the old fella at the pub or not but there was some resemblance around the eyes. Jagjit reached out with a finger to scroll down the page a bit. His movies were listed beneath his bio: Damned Good Roger Ring, Good old Roger Ring, Well, Roger me!

The list was quite extensive.

'So, what is it that you do, Ben?' asked Simon. 'You clearly keep yourself in great shape.' James cut his eyes at his boyfriend. 'Are you a gym instructor?'

'No, dear chap,' smiled Big Ben. 'I'm however responsible for helping ladies burn calories. As often as I can.'

'Are you unemployed?' asked Anthea, some disdain in her voice.

'I would class myself as retired, actually. I have sufficient funds to avoid paid employment. Besides, not having a job means I can spend more time helping ladies with their pelvic fitness.'

'You mean you just laze about and chase women.' Anthea was being a bit snarky. Hilary had picked up on it and was gently nudging her with his knee. She was happily ignoring her husband though.

'Chase women? Not a bit,' replied Big Ben causing Anthea's face to crinkle in confusion. His answer didn't gel with the picture she had of him. 'They never feel the need to run away,' he finished with a cheeky grin.

Now her face was caught between disbelief and anger. 'Sooo, Big Ben was in the Army with Tempest,' injected Hilary, trying to deflect the slaughter. 'Did you know that?'

Simon saw an opportunity to get involved again, but he had picked up on James's mood and directed his question at me rather than Big Ben. 'How long were you in for?'

'Just shy of eighteen years.'

Simon almost spat out his drink. 'Eighteen years? Surely, you're not old enough. You both look so young.' I got this a lot, although I didn't really understand why.

I shrugged as I replied, 'I joined when I was seventeen and now, I'm in my late thirties and I think I look about right for my age.'

'I stay looking this young and vibrant because I moisturise my face with perspiration collected from the breasts of women in their early twenties,' Big Ben claimed with a smile.

Jagjit snorted his drink. It was a good line and very typical of the sort of thing Big Ben would say. I often wondered how such ideas got into his head but never asked because I was worried that most of them were actually true.

Anthea looked like she wanted to say something, but Alice was laughing, and all the guys were laughing, and it was clear Big Ben didn't care if he offended anyone.

'Let's get shots,' suggested an excited Alice, which received an approving chorus from all but Anthea and me. I avoided shots whenever I could but suspected I would end up with one now.

Shots appeared, a toast was given, and the tiny glasses were upended with a cheer. It was horrible.

'Oh, my word,' said Big Ben with surprising reserve. 'Was that neat vodka?'

Alice nodded. 'I love it. They have the really good stuff here.'

'Good stuff? That was like having a robot ejaculate in my mouth,' he replied, trying to scrape any remaining liquid from his tongue with a fingernail. His analogy brought about another round of laughter and the evening continued.

The gathering was a success. James clearly had a great

night and was quite merry when Simon decided it was time to get him home. The clock believed it was close to midnight, so I needed to get home as well. Mrs. Comerforth had texted at 2200hrs to say that she was off to bed and had put the dogs back in my house and tucked them up. She was a love.

Big Ben had disappeared more than an hour ago when a pair of ginger-haired, buxom twins had approached him looking interested. Of the group, I was the only one leaving alone. Maybe I should have invited Sophie along after all.

I got a lift home with Hilary and Anthea, their insistence winning over my protestations. Anthea had warmed to me a little as the evening progressed, which I was glad for more for Hilary's sake than my own. He might be allowed to come back to the pub now.

Back in my house, I sent a text to Amanda to ask if I was being followed by the police. Her reply came back almost immediately assuring me that she knew of no surveillance operation in place. It was an ambiguous answer and thus out of character for her. I was unsure what to make of it.

I fell asleep with a little more alcohol in me than was usual and a purpose for the day ahead.

A Trip to Scunthorpe

For the first time in days, I was up early, or perhaps up on time if I was being less generous. It didn't happen by accident. It took an alarm, which I had set for the first time in so many years that I couldn't remember the last time I had felt a need to use one. I was driving to Scunthorpe which was a solid two hundred miles directly north and required that I bypassed London to the East via the Dartford crossing. There was no alternative route, and I knew from experience and anecdote that leaving after 0600hrs meant adding at least an hour to my journey as the traffic level rose and clogged the route as it funnelled over the Thames.

In something of a sleepy haze and with a rather dry mouth from the drinking last night, I made myself a cup of tea in a thermos mug and packed the dogs into the car. They looked quite confused, not only with the fact that they were out of bed but also that they were awake, and that I was refusing to give them their breakfast. I knew that if I fed them now, they would become more alert and would want their dinner all the earlier. Instead, they rather grumpily went back to sleep in the car after only being awake for a couple of minutes.

Hours of research yesterday hadn't quashed my belief that the Klowns were deliberately and carefully selecting their victims. If that was the case, then they had gone to Scunthorpe, not on a whim, but because they really wanted to hurt Marion Lloyd. I intended to find out why and since she wouldn't speak to me on the phone I was going to drive there and ring her doorbell. I had no good reason to believe that my trip would result in the opportunity to speak with Marion Lloyd. However, I was in a mood that suggested I was going to be hard to deflect, so if she didn't wish to speak with me, she was going to have a hard time of it.

An hour north of Dartford, I was on the A1(M). The early traffic had been light, so the miles had ticked past, and we were almost halfway there. The dogs were becoming restless, probably wanting their breakfast now that it was time for it. I concurred with their opinion.

On a grassy bank at the edge of the car park in a large motorway service station, I gave them a breakfast to share from a single bowl. They shared by eating at exactly the same extraordinarily fast speed rather than by agreeing to split the food evenly. When they were fed and had thoroughly explored the undergrowth, I locked them back in the car and went into the service station to find myself something to eat.

I checked my rear-view mirror more than a few times on the way up; paranoia demanding it. There had been no crazed Klown faces filling it, trying to run me off the road. I hadn't expected them. More to the point, all my theories were based on them never leaving Kent again but the niggling doubt in my mind reminded me that I probably had no idea what I was doing.

A further twenty miles up the road, I was already regretting the full English I had allowed myself to be tempted by. I felt heavy and fat and sluggish and worse than that I felt tired, and I still had a long way to go.

The dogs slept most of the way, however, Bull took it upon himself to check my navigation periodically by climbing on to my lap, placing his front paws on the steering wheel and looking out the window. I found it entertaining, wondering just what was actually going through his doggy brain but also checked my mirrors for the police as I suspected they would frown on such canine activities. I also considered that it would be fun to scooch down into my seat as I passed other cars so that they might look across and see only a Dachshund at the wheel. For safety's sake, I abstained from such self-indulgent behaviour.

At 1037hrs, I drove slowly by the address I had for Mrs. Lloyd. There was a car on the driveway suggesting someone was in. I parked a street away, let the dogs out and went for a walk. As we walked by her house, I glanced at it and the street around me several times, then mimed stopping to pick up poop so I could check around a bit more and not look like I was doing so. The dogs continued to snuffle, ignorant of the subterfuge. I completed a circuit, arriving back at the car where I then left the dogs peering out the passenger window at me once again. It was cool, but just in case I cracked the windows before I left them. Mostly I had been scanning the street to make sure the house wasn't being watched by anyone. I didn't want to deal with reporters or police, but I was fairly confident that the house wasn't under surveillance.

The big question that remained unanswered, was whether Marion Lloyd was even in the house, which was really just the first hurdle of many in finding out any worthwhile information. As it turned out she wasn't.

Her husband was.

I introduced myself but that only warranted a stony glare. I elected to wait until he got bored enough to speak.

'What is it that you want, Mr Michaels?'

'Like I said, I'm not a reporter. I'm not the police. I'm a person threatened by the Klowns and wanting to know what is going on. My survival and that of my family (I didn't elaborate) might depend on getting some answers.'

He slumped slightly at that. My embellished answer wasn't what he expected, and he had no prepared defence for it. He retreated into the house with a defeated nod of his head to indicate that I should follow.

'Sorry, Mr Michaels,' he apologised. 'There have been so many people here already dredging up Marion's past.'

'What past? Sorry. I have to ask.'

Mr Lloyd ignored me for a minute, tapping at a laptop that he had collected from a countertop as we went through the house. I indulged him and watched his face. He was looking me up. At least that was my guess. I would have done the same.

He nodded to himself. Satisfied. 'Blue Moon Investigations? Google has quite a bit on you. Sorry, I needed to check that you were who you say you are.'

'No offence taken. It makes me sad that your experience since the attack has made you feel the need.' He was looking directly at me now. 'How is Mrs Lloyd?'

'You see? That right there. That is how I know you are what you say you are. Everyone else has called her Marion, as if they were trying to be knowledgeable or as if they knew her or we were old friends. It made me hate them.'

Apparently, my simple, honest approach worked. For today at least.

Mr Lloyd told me everything he could think of to tell me. He gave me so much detail and kept me so long that I started to worry about the dogs. My concern was unwarranted though. When I got back to the car, they were still fast asleep on the passenger's seat. I insisted they get up and come for a walk anyway as we had another three-hour ride home, which I would do in one hit if they gave no indication that they needed to get out. Key to that was making sure their bladders were empty.

No Friggin' Clue

What I had learned from Mr Lloyd was that his wife Marion had taken a hard beating that had landed her in hospital, and it had happened right outside their house. Mr Lloyd heard the commotion, ran outside to intervene and got a beating of his own. He said that it would have been far more severe, but serendipity sent a random police patrol car into their street and the Klowns had fled. The Klowns that had perpetrated it may or may not have been the same ones that were causing all the trouble in Kent. I might never know or never be able to prove it, but they had delivered a message just as I had hoped they might.

One of them, while kneeling on her back and grabbing her hair had shouted, "You shouldn't have given him up for adoption." Or words to that effect. I felt it likely Mr Lloyd had deleted some expletives in his retelling.

Marion had returned to work just this morning. She was a barrister, an intelligent lady and the breadwinner of the house, leaving her husband at home to raise and care for their children. The message made no sense to him at the time, but they had talked about the incident while she was still in the hospital. He hadn't asked her about it, he assured me, she had volunteered the information as if glad to finally be able to tell him.

She had been fourteen when she got pregnant, fifteen when she gave birth and had given the baby up at the insistence of her parents though she told him she hadn't resisted. Doing so allowed her to continue on the path she mapped out for her. Marion Lloyd had lived in Scunthorpe all her life. The baby had been born there but the adoption service had removed the child just days after the birth and she had no idea, or way of finding out, where it went.

Her maiden name was Hargreaves. The child's name was Sebastian.

Sebastian Hargreaves. It meant nothing. It wasn't a name I had ever heard. I spent the entire trip home running through variables and derivatives in my head, wondering if it was a guy I had known in the Army or someone I had dealt with since at some point. Was it just a dead end? A red herring? Was Marion Lloyd not connected at all? Was it just a copycat attack? My gut told me that it couldn't be.

The taste of blood made its way into my consciousness. I was biting my lip. I had no idea what was going on and it was really pissing me off.

Over and over I ran the few connections I had, trying to tie them to me, to Edna Wilkins and her school children, to Marion Lloyd, to anyone. Nothing made sense. There was no connection between the crimes or between the victims. It made me angry as if it made a difference if the Klowns had a reason for their reign of terror rather than no reason at all.

The anger I felt had dissipated only slightly by the time I arrived home at 1521hrs. Parked on my driveway, I slowly relaxed my grip on the steering wheel, unaware that my knuckles had been white with tension until I let go. My hands hurt. I shot a sorrowful but loving look at the two dogs now awake and excited to leave the car. They were both standing on their back legs looking out the passenger's window. They knew where they were, either by smell or sight and they wanted to get out and run around. I couldn't blame them; it had been a long period for two dogs to be in a car.

My phone rang. We were still in the car, but the engine was off, so it didn't transfer to the car hands-free system. I checked the screen on my phone to see that the caller was Sophie.

I had to deal with the dog's needs ahead of my own, so rejected the call, leaned across and opened their door. They vanished from view, reappearing a few seconds later beyond the bonnet of the car as they shot under a bush at the front of the house. I followed them, then convinced them to leave whatever they had found of interest under the bush and come through the house to the back garden where they could explore in safety.

With the danger of them wandering off averted, I turned my attention back to my phone and returned the missed call. Little more than a minute had passed since I rejected it, filling me with a hope that she would still be on a work break or something into which she had shoehorned her call to me.

She picked up straight away. 'Tempest?'

'Yes. Hello, Sophie.'

'Hi. Err. I just wanted to check that we are still on for tonight. You know… after that last couple of times.'

Fair point.

'Yes, Sophie. I fully intend to meet my commitment to dine you in an appropriate style, as promised.'

'McDonald's will do, Tempest. Just so long as you actually turn up.' I had nothing I could say to defend myself. 'Look, I will meet you there at eight o'clock as planned. If you're not there it's okay, just please do not ever call me again. Okay?'

'I understand.' I was going to be there, and I was going to be the most charming dinner companion she had ever heard about.

'Okay, well... I hope you are. I'm looking forward to it. Bye for now.' We disconnected. I checked my watch: 1457hrs. I had five hours before my date with Sophie. I wanted to use them wisely to pursue the Klown case but still had no idea what I was doing.

The large breakfast I foolishly allowed myself was hours ago now, the bloating I had felt after eating it forgotten and all I had eaten since was an apple I had taken in the car with me. My stomach lightly rumbling, I headed into the kitchen to find a late lunch. Being healthy for the first time in what felt like days, I grilled a piece of fish and paired it with some brown rice and green veg. I ate it in front of my computer while trying to find information on Sebastian Hargreaves.

As usual, I found lots of men called by that name; both social media and Google are great for that, so I spent an hour sifting through them to filter out those that were too old, too young, too geographically displaced or, in one case, too dead. In the end, I had two possible candidates, but neither of them looked likely to be the guy.

I made a fresh tea in my thermos mug and took the dogs for a walk through the vineyards to clear my mind. It was breezy out, with a little moisture being carried on the air. There was a distinct smell of autumn to it. Oblivious to my concerns, the dogs scampered ahead of me, sniffing where other dogs had marked, adding their own scent, then moving on to the next smell. It was a pleasant way to erode thirty minutes of my life, but it didn't get me any closer to the Klowns. Giving myself time to think wasn't helping. My thoughts strayed to my date with Sophie. I had booked a table online since such things were easy to do now, but I wanted to demonstrate to her that I had put a little more thought into it than that, so when we arrived back at the house, I popped the dogs into the car and drove to the restaurant.

A crisp twenty pound note pressed into the hands of the Maître d', ensured we would be positioned near to the open fire and well away from the cool breeze coming through the door as it opened and closed. It also meant we had a more intimate two-seater table which had a great view. Furthermore, the table was close to a wall so that it was a little more separate from other tables than most locations in the restaurant – correct table selection is essential. Not that I planned or expected to be talking about subjects that others should not overhear but providing a romantic setting for an evening with a charming female companion simply felt like it was the right thing to do.

All the better to charm her knickers off.

I ignored the voice coming from below my belt, his counsel could be pertinent at times but was mostly predictable. I hadn't given any thought to the concept that Sophie and I might get beyond a first date or that at some point Mr Wriggly might get to enact some of the plans he was making.

Satisfied that I had made all the appropriate arrangements I could without going over the top, I left the restaurant. The dogs were where I left them tied to a post outside, but they were not alone. Another Dachshund had joined them, a little girly one if the pink harness and lead were any indication.

'Hello,' I said to the lady holding the lead. She was crouching down to fuss my dogs, who were, in turn, taking great interest in the new dog and her back end.

'Hello,' she said looking up. 'Are they yours? They are lovely. I'm so jealous that you have two.'

I nodded that they were indeed mine while marvelling at how wholesomely pretty she was. She had on muddy wellies and tan jodhpurs and a wax jacket to keep her warm. Her hair was yanked into a rough ponytail that was already mostly unwound so that wisps were escaping. She had on no make-up but was nice to look at, nevertheless. Staring at her, I wondered if she really was as pretty as I thought or if I just needed to get laid.

'Err, are you okay?' she asked.

I had been looking at her rather than speaking. 'Err, yes. Sorry. And yes, the dogs are mine. Bull on the left and the squidgy looking one is Dozer. I'm Tempest.'

'This little princess is Lula,' she said stroking her dog affectionately. 'Are the boys done?'

'Done? You mean castrated? No. I couldn't bring myself to do that to them.' At the thought of it, my testicles tried to make themselves smaller.

'Hmm, this little one is about to come into season. It's probably why your boys are so interested in her. Would you be interested in breeding with me?'

Mr Wriggly woke up instantly.

I wanted to smirk at her turn of phrase – like a boy would. I was actually finding it quite hard not to, but I maintained my straight face. 'I have never given any thought to having the dogs breed. I don't see any reason why I shouldn't though.

'Can I get your number then, Tempest?' She stood up finally. I was glad of it. I had found it a little hard to concentrate with a pretty girl crouching with her head at my groin height and asking if I wanted to breed with her. 'I'm Elizabeth,' she said, sticking out her hand for me to shake.

I smiled, shook her hand and gave her my business card so that she had my mobile number and email. The three dogs were still circling each other, the boys very keen on Lula, Lula very keen on the boys. There was a lot of butt investigation going on.

'Come along, Talula,' instructed Elizabeth, giving a tug at her lead. Reluctantly, the little dog allowed herself to be pulled away from the boys who I had to hold in place as they were trying hard to follow her. I guess she was giving off a scent they were finding hard to resist. I knew how that was.

Walking back to the car I wondered if they would get some action before me. It seemed very possible that they would. But hold on; would it be both the boys with little Lula? I didn't know what was normal. Well, I might never hear from Elizabeth again anyway.

A Date with Sophie

I had arrived home at 1816hrs, well after the dogs' appointed dinner time, so wasn't surprised to watch them run to the cupboard that housed their food and bowls. Dinner might be a little late, but they were well exercised and would be no trouble for Mrs. Comerforth tonight. I would drop them off just as I was going out, although I was certain my neighbour would happily have them right now.

I was already hungry, so I took an apple from my fruit bowl and headed upstairs to shave, floss and make myself as clean and presentable as I could.

In Rochester, I parked the car in its usual spot behind my office. I considered popping up to my office as there was a stack of information on the Klowns that I wanted to check, but I worried that I would become engrossed in it, forget the time and arrive late for my date with Sophie. I couldn't risk that, so I bypassed my office door and headed along the High Street. I noticed the two guys in suits from Wednesday once again. They were dressed in casual clothing this time and walking along the High Street

towards me. I thought about approaching them but reasoned that if I made it clear their cover was blown, they would just get replaced by someone I wouldn't recognise and who might be better at the job of staying out of sight. Besides, if the Klowns did attack me and these guys were police, it would help to have them around.

Walking back through the door of the restaurant, I was pleased to see a little plastic sign claiming my chosen table as reserved. A lady at the door took my coat and escorted me to the table where I made sure everything was to my liking. I gave the lady a description of Sophie so that she would be able to act as if she were expected and instinctively bring her across.

Sat idly waiting at the table, I considered the Klown case again. No one had tried to kill me or anyone I knew for almost forty-eight hours, and no crimes had been reported at all. Why? Were they planning something big and that meant they were too distracted to commit other crimes? It was a worrying thought. That the Klowns had simply disbanded and gone back to their previous lives seemed implausible. That there appeared to be no reason for the crimes in the first place didn't help me to rationalise why they might stop.

So, if I ignore that the Klowns have stopped and go back to the one person at the centre theory…

What if the person at the centre isn't me? What if it's one of the Klowns instead. Who is Deadface? My brain went around in a circle trying to work out how the people that had been attacked were linked and why. Were they just not linked at all and the whole crime wave perpetrated by the Klowns was sporadic and random? How do you get a group of people to dress as Klowns and then convince them to maim and kill random people?

What if each of them was somehow linked to Dead-face? As always, there was a piece of the puzzle that I could perceive but couldn't actually see. Something tantalising, hiding just out of sight.

'Good evening, Tempest,' Sophie said, speaking from right next to me. It made me jump. I was so deep in thought I not only failed to hear her approach but had totally forgotten I was waiting for her. My reaction caused her to jump in turn.

'My Lord, you gave me a scare, Tempest,' she laughed, one hand on the table to support herself as if the shock had made her legs weak.

'Sorry, Sophie. I was deep in thought and didn't hear you.' My pulse was returning to normal thankfully. I got out of my chair and went around behind her to the other side of the table. 'Good evening, Sophie. Thank you for joining me,' I said as I pulled out her chair.

'Thank you, Tempest,' she replied, manoeuvring to the chair but instead of sitting down she turned to face me, leaned in and kissed me gently on the lips. Pulling away again she smiled at my surprised expression. 'I always get so nervous on dates, wondering if the boy will want to kiss me, whether I should try to kiss him, trying to work out when I should do that. I thought that maybe if we got a kiss out of the way early on it would make it easier.'

Sophie was being really sweet, it was most endearing, and I liked it a lot. She turned around again and allowed me to push in her chair. I tried very hard to not hear what Mr Wriggly had to say about her delightfully toned bottom. He was right though.

The Maître d' himself came across to deliver water and menus and ask about wine then returned a few minutes later with a bottle of 2014 Châteauneuf Du Pape Les

Cornalines. I planned to have one glass and see how the evening went. If I felt inclined, I could always get a taxi home and come back for the car in the morning.

Sophie looked at me, a serious expression on her face. 'Tempest, I would like to set just one ground rule for tonight, if that is okay?' she asked.

'Go ahead,' I replied. I was fairly sure I knew what she was going to say. Doubtless, the lady had been forced to calm the amorous advances of men hoping for first date action many times in the past.

'No talking about exes,' she said, surprising me.

'Oh. Okay.' I tried to suppress the surprise in my voice and the cheer that came from beneath the table. It wasn't what I had been expecting at all.

'There is nothing worse than hearing about the ex-wife and I know that I can be guilty of bringing up my ex-husband. There you go, I did it already,' she laughed at herself.

I smiled at her. 'I wasn't aware that you had been married.'

'Unfortunately, yes,' she sighed. 'For three long years. The first thing I did when I got the paperwork through was change my name back rather than have the permanent reminder there every time I signed my name.'

He changed his name.

I stood up immediately. There was a look of confusion on Sophie's face. As usual, all the information had been right there in front of me the whole time and I had been unable to see it. How had I been so blind?

I started moving towards the door, oblivious to everything around me. Her voice arrested my forward motion. 'Tempest?'

I turned, twitching with indecision. 'Sorry, I have to go,'

I blurted and left her sitting there looking bewildered. I rushed from the restaurant with my brain whirling. I had just glimpsed the answer, and I didn't like it. I needed to head back to my office so I could cross-reference with the information there. I knew I was going to be right though. He had changed his name and now that I knew what I was looking for, I could tell that I had already seen it. It made everything make sense. Why I was at the centre of it, why the victims seemed to have so little in common. I was certain that they all had one specific thing in common. I just needed to prove it to myself.

'Hey!' I heard Sophie's voice behind me, and I almost paused, but I had to deal with the Klowns first. Sophie would either forgive me, or she would not. I would find out later.

The restaurant was less than half a mile from my office so only a few minutes later I was opening the bottom door and going inside. In my office were the whiteboards and map and a ream of information that Jane had printed off and sorted into piles. I went directly to the pile that listed all the school children Edna Wilkins had taught. On page six, halfway down, I spotted his name. I had read the page earlier but while I had seen the name, it didn't register until I considered that it might not have been the one originally on his birth certificate.

He had been given up for adoption at birth by a fifteen-year-old girl. Somewhere along the way, he had assumed a different name. It was so ridiculously obvious.

I dropped my bag on the desk and swung myself around and into the chair. A quick flick of the mouse brought the screen to life. I typed his name into google and had results a nanosecond later. There were a number of options, yet none of them were what I wanted. I tried again with a cross-reference for work history and opened a separate window for social media feed to see what I could find out about the person's friend group.

The work history listed a dozen firms going back over twenty years. Some periods of employment had been quite brief, but I spotted what I had hoped to see instantly. I already knew the name of the firm because two of the victims had worked there. Mark Tanner and Erica Carpenter both worked at Inspirations Web Developers in the early nineties and so had Nigel Havers. It was enough to convince me I was right although I checked for more connections anyway. Ten minutes later I had found a link between him and more than half the people that had been targeted by the Klowns.

Nigel Havers. Better known as Obsidian Dark. The man who had been most closely involved with the Vampire serial killer had escaped the police and justice and was still on the run. Except he wasn't running, he was attacking.

Back then he had been dating Angela Barclay. Now she was dead and so was the man she had started seeing after Nigel fled. She had been coming to see me. Had she known? Or just suspected? The victims were girls he had gone to school with, people he had worked with. People, who given the comparative ages were most likely in supervisory positions and had thus somehow caused the anger fuelling his determined spree of retribution. Was it really that simple? He was going after everyone that had ever upset him, or gotten away with some injustice in his eyes? No wonder I was high up on the list. He had been setting the Klowns to hurt girls that had spurned his advances, or dumped him years ago, targeting old bosses that had made him work, or pulled him up for being lazy. I was guessing, but between the lines, I knew I was right.

When the Vampire ran into a stake in the dark and died, I had wondered for days afterward whether any of the disbanded Brotherhood of the Dead would come after me, pay me a visit in the night but none had, and I had all but forgotten about them and about Obsidian Dark. I had allowed myself to believe that he had left the area, if not the Country. It was what I would have done in his position. Yet he had recruited an army of maniacs that were coming after everyone that he perceived might have wronged him and I was high on that list as were Big Ben, Jagjit, Basic, Amanda, Frank, and Poison plus very possibly my parents. All of us had been involved in taking the serial killer and the wannabe vampires down.

Obsidian had reinvented himself, given himself a new name and had enough resource or money or whatever it took to stay out of police custody for the last month. Where was he now though?

I turned the chair away from the desk and stood up. Then I remembered Sophie.

Oh, Lord. I had walked out on her, just abandoned her at a restaurant. She was unlikely to forgive me this time, but I had to call her and apologise, nevertheless. I had earned a good shouting at if nothing else. I needed to call the police, but they could wait two minutes.

I walked over to the mini fridge by the window. I kept milk and a couple of bottles of sparkling mineral water in it (plus two cans of ready-made G&T just in case). As I opened a bottle of water to quench my thirst, I called Sophie.

While I waited for it to connect, I took a long draft of the water. It was the first water I had drunk all day, most unusual for me as my normal routine involved several litres a day.

I heard the phone connect and Sophie's voice. She sounded angry. 'This had better be good, Tempest.'

I was staring out the window over Rochester High Street. The Blood Fest Halloween Festival was getting underway in the grounds of the castle just around the corner. It had attracted a crowd that was beginning to build in numbers. People were going by in both directions, shops were open late, expecting a boost to their trade from the extra visitors. On the other side of the street was a figure half in and half out of the shadows. He stood out because in contrast to everyone else he wasn't moving, and I was staring because I could see enough of him to tell that he had on bright red trousers. On the top half was a grey hoody, the man's hands tucked into the large pocket at the front. He was moving forward, coming into the light.

'Tempest!' yelled Sophie, trying to get my attention. I disconnected. Staring up at me was a Klown's face shrouded in the hood of his top. From street level, no one would be able to see his make-up unless they looked directly at him. To avoid detection, all he need do is keep his head down and his hood up.

He grinned at me. Even beneath the crazy, garish Klown makeup, I could see it was Obsidian or Nigel or Deadface. Pick a name, he was going to jail regardless. I started moving but stopped. He was holding something up to show me. From the pocket of his hoody, he removed a pair of dog collars. They were mine.

I hit the door at the top of my stairs running full speed, nearly taking it off its hinges as I ripped it open. The stairs were a blur beneath my feet as I flew down them in two bounds and exploded out of the bottom door.

I skidded into the busy High Street having to dodge between people. Many of them paused to look at the crazy man. Obsidian was nowhere to be seen, exactly as I had expected, so I jumped onto one of the many benches that line Rochester High Street. However, the improved view over the heads of the crowd did nothing to reveal his position. I swung my head in every direction, checking the entrances to the many dark alleyways that led from the main road but there was no grey hood heading away from me in any direction that I could see.

I stepped down from the bench, my teeth gritted. I was mad now. If he had the dog collars then he had the dogs, which also meant he had most likely done something to my neighbour Mrs Comerforth. I was going to push his teeth out with my foot. Or someone else's foot, or if I could find a way to do it, his own foot. If he had hurt my dogs I couldn't guarantee I would stop hitting him if I started.

I was by myself though and it was likely that Obsidian/Deadface wasn't. Basic was at home with his mum, Big Ben would be out shagging somewhere, Amanda was on duty... then I remembered that Frank and Poison were here. I had to find them. The crowd of people was thick and getting thicker. I wanted to run but the best I could achieve was a hasty shoving/slipping action to get between the families and groups of friends or couples holding hands. I was heading back to the office, which wasn't what I wanted to do but I had a spare set of body armour there and a feeling I would need it. I also had a stash of weapons that I badly wanted to get my hands on.

As I reached the bottom door to my office three seconds later, I saw that I had left the damned door open. Looking back, I should have anticipated what happened next, but at the time it came as a complete surprise. I charged up the first few stairs then felt the presence ahead of me. As I looked up, our eyes connected, it was a Klown, but not Deadface. I heard a guttural growl escape my lips as I charged for him. He had the high ground, and my attack made no sense, but I was beyond rational thought, and I deserved what I got.

He grabbed both sides of the doorframe and raised both his huge Doc Martin boots to kick me. I feigned left then lunged right and caught both his legs on my shoulder. I was still coming up the stairs with all the speed I could muster which tipped him backward and onto the floor in my office.

He was down, and I was up.

But he wasn't alone.

Three more Klowns were in the office but that wasn't the first thing I noticed. The prominent feature of my office was the stench of petrol fumes.

'Too late, Tempest Michaels,' said the one to my right. I turned to him thinking murderous thoughts. Brainless murderous thoughts of course because it was four on one and I had no chance. The first punch landed on the left-hand side of my face. It knocked me off balance more than it hurt me, but the next hit was on my jaw and probably from someone different to the person that delivered the first punch. I tasted blood and I went down to the floor, only holding myself up with one hand.

'Survive this, dickhead.' I heard from behind me. They were going down the stairs, all of them. Fast.

Then there was no air in my lungs and the air all around me was on fire. I hadn't seen the match they threw, but the fuel they had thrown about the place had caught as one and my whole office was on fire.

I was low to the ground, thankfully still close to the stairs. If I had wanted to do anything about the flames eating the walls of my office I couldn't have. The heat was instantly oppressive, and I needed to breathe – all the oxygen in the office was long gone. Survival meant escape. With no alternative, I propelled myself toward the stairs and in my confusion, I slipped and fell down the length of them.

I hit the bottom door with my head and fell through it and onto the cold pavement outside.

'Crikey! Are you alright, mister?' asked a young voice from a few feet away.

It was followed by, 'Come away, Tommy.' The voice undoubtedly that of the boy's mother.

I must look like a drunk rolling in the street. I forced myself to turn the right way up. Tommy was still looking back over his shoulder from between his parents as they guided him away.

'Are you okay?' asked a voice by my ear. I turned my head to see a set of men's feet and looked up. He offered me his hand and helped me off the floor.

'Thank you.' I looked back up at my office on the first floor just as one of the windows cracked and flames licked out and upwards.

'Fire!' shouted a woman's voice from somewhere behind me.

The crowd had spotted it now. People drawn by the spectacle were gathering at a safe distance. The man that had helped me to my feet was now tugging at my jacket, trying to pull me back as if he was concerned I might try to go back into the burning building. I pulled away but offered him my hand to shake in thanks.

The office was gone. Nothing would escape the fire, but I had bigger issues. I needed to find Deadface and the rest of the Klowns and beat them to death. I started towards the castle with the man calling me back and asking where I thought I was going. I rudely ignored him.

I pulled my phone from my pocket, thankful that I hadn't lost it in the scuffle upstairs. Who should I call? I hadn't the time or patience to explain this to the police, so I called Amanda. As I did so, I was jogging through the crowd, sticking to the buildings where there were less people. I wanted to get to Frank and Poison. If they were here, they were in danger and were probably oblivious to it.

Amanda's phone continued to ring with no answer. I rounded the corner by the North Gate, so the cathedral was now to my left and the castle dead ahead of me. There were stalls set out all over. Frank and Poison were here somewhere, but there must be a hundred stalls and at least ten thousand people. I cut the phone off and shoved it back in my pocket. Then I pulled it out again, there was someone else I wanted to call.

He answered immediately. I had to cut him off as he started talking and I had no time to listen. I explained what I needed, listened as he promised to do what he could, and I disconnected.

Frank's shop was behind me now as I came into the castle grounds. I was betting they were at this end of the event. The cathedral bell tower chimed for 2000hrs just as a PA from the stage delivered a short burst of feedback and an announcer started talking, welcoming one and all to the first annual Rochester Blood Fest.

The Big Fight

I spotted Poison's blue hair through the crowd. An overhead light caught it for a split second. She was serving a customer, handing over a bag and smiling at them. Probably wishing them a horror-filled night or something. Their stall was facing towards me, comic books and memorabilia adorning the canvas rear wall and all over the tabletop front counter. It was sandwiched between a stall selling t-shirts and clothing, where I could see a pair of heavily tattooed and pierced ladies making a killing and a stall selling hospital blood bags that contained some kind of vodka cocktail. I barged through a small gap, heading directly towards Poison, then saw the grey hood step through the back of the stall where the canvas overlapped.

Back in the street, I could hear a fire engine making its way towards my office. The sound of its siren was bouncing off the walls of the old town's buildings, making its location hard to pinpoint but it was there somewhere.

'Poison!' I bellowed at the top of my lungs. The sound was absorbed by the crowd around me. In my haste, I shoved a man over and left him behind me as I moved to the next obstacle. Ahead of me, Deadface lifted both hands above his head, a knife gleaming in each of them. The customer she was serving pointed to behind Poison, laughing just as the blades began to descend.

She thought it was all part of the evening's entertainment!

Poison turned, screamed and ducked out of the way. I was nearly there. The twin blades dug into comic books on the front on the stall, piercing several of them which then came away attached to the knives when he yanked them back out of the wood.

Poison darted under his arms, kicking him in his side as she went. The customer, a young woman with her boyfriend was watching and enjoying the show. With three paces left until I would reach the stall, a gap in the crowd finally appeared. Deadface was chasing Poison and didn't see me coming. I took two fast strides and leapt across the counter to tackle him around the waist.

I collided as much with Frank as I did Deadface though as he beat Deadface back with a shield he produced from beneath the counter. The three of us went down to the floor which was about as dangerous as it could get. I had no idea where the knives were in relation to my body, but I had hold of something, so I hit it as hard as I could and in return I received a kick to the face that shoved me to one side. There was light above my face suddenly.

I looked up to see an arm with a cruel knife in it swinging towards me. Then the shield came over my eyes to deflect the blade with an audible clang. Frank had saved me! The shield swung up again smacking into Deadface's head. He went backward with the blow, following the motion and falling out through the back of the stall.

My phone started ringing.

I could hear clapping also. The damned crowd still thought it was a show! There were calls of bravo as Frank pulled me off the floor. I darted after Deadface but there was no sign of him, he had slipped away into the crowd. I couldn't pursue him alone and I knew he was after my friends. Back inside the stall, I pulled Frank into a bro hug and patted him hard on the back. We were hip deep in trouble again. Behind Frank, Poison was kneeling on the grass, straining hard to pull something out from underneath the counter. Whatever it was had some size and weight to it.

'A hand here?' she asked, shooting a look at Frank and me.

The crowd that had been standing in front of the stall were now beginning to disperse since there was no more street theatre to watch. Frank leaned down and together with Poison hauled out a large, solid oak-looking chest. It had a convincing padlock on the front hasp.

My phone rang again. I pulled it from my pocket while in front of me Frank was patting his pockets, he finally produced a large key from one of them.

Amanda's name was displayed on my caller ID. 'Amanda, we have Klowns at the castle in Rochester. I need units here as soon as you can mobilize them. Deadface is here.'

'I know, Tempest. I'm on my way there already. The Klowns have attacked the police that were assigned to you and all the others in uniform that were on duty at the event.'

'The ones assigned...? Hold on. What are you talking about Amanda?' There had been police following me? For what purpose?

'Look, Tempest. I don't have time to argue. Quinn thought you were the most likely target for the Klowns and has been having you watched and tailed for the last few days. The two plain-clothes guys were found fifteen minutes ago in an alleyway near your office. Both had been stabbed.'

That idiot Quinn. He had lied to me and set me up.

'Amanda, you knew about this didn't you?' I demanded. I was already angry. Klowns had tried to kill me or someone I knew twice in the last few minutes, my office was destroyed, my dogs had been taken goodness knows where and now I find out that Amanda and the police have been using me as bait. She hadn't answered. 'Tell me the damned truth,' I shouted down the phone.

'Tempest...' she trailed off. I disconnected. I had other things to focus on.

A scream lit the air. A few feet away a woman laughed having jumped at the sound of the scream. Her boyfriend was laughing at her. Oh yeah, this is all very funny.

At my feet, Frank got the chest opened and showed me what he had inside. It was an arsenal. There were swords. There were knives of all sizes and shapes. There was a crossbow. There was a double-headed axe! Knuckle dusters, a taser or two. No firearms, but there was one item I was quite familiar with. I had used it just last weekend when dealing with the zombie hoard.

'I threw that in at the last minute,' Frank said. 'I thought you might be pleased to see it again.'

I grinned as he handed it to me. I hefted it again, feeling the familiar weight. All I needed now was a Klown to hit with it. 'My question, Frank, has to be, why do you have a chest full of medieval weapons under the counter of your stall?'

'It seemed like a good idea,' he answered with a shrug. 'There have been so many Klown attacks, and they have come after you twice already...'

There was another scream and then another and suddenly the crowd woke up to the Klowns in their midst and started trying to get away. I heard a chainsaw somewhere. The screams were everywhere now, the crowd shoving each other in a bid to be somewhere else. The herd mentality was knocking over stalls, and I saw opportunistic thieves grabbing things as they ran.

The people would be gone soon, they were running away from the castle grounds and disappearing through the ancient North Gate in front of me. 'Guys this is not a safe position.' Frank and Poison were listening. 'We need to keep the Klowns here until the people have escaped. They are after us.'

'Why?' asked Poison.

'Yeah, why?' echoed Frank.

'Remember Obsidian the vampire-wannabe?' The colour drained from Poison's face as she remembered being kidnapped and drugged by him.

'He reinvented himself as the head Klown and has been systematically going after everyone that has ever done him any wrong. At least that is what I think is happening. I'm right at the top of his kill list and by association so are you two and all my other friends.'

They were both quiet for a moment, then Poison fixed me with her eyes. 'So, what is your plan, Tempest. You always have a plan. There are a ton of them and three of us and I do not feel like getting carved up with a chainsaw tonight. Do we run?'

I looked up and around us at the crowd of people fleeing the castle grounds. It was oddly comic to watch in that everyone was going as fast as they could but there were so many people that they mostly had to walk... so they were screaming... and not running away. Through a gap in the press of people, I saw a face I recognised. Deadface was fifty yards away and staring directly at me. He had shucked the grey hood, but it was that fact that he was motionless that made him stand out, not the garish clothing and face paint he wore. I spotted another Klown and, now that I was looking, yet another. They were forming a perimeter around us. We needed to get away from the stall. It had poor fields of vision over what I had to now consider as the battlefield and provided zero as a defensive position. We were armed, but I had to expect the Klowns would be also, and they outnumbered us. Badly.

'If we run, they will chase us and most likely hurt more innocent people as they try to get to us. We need to wait for the crowd to thin, then lead them away from here and into somewhere that we can defend ourselves a little better. The police will be here soon enough and will send armed units, I'm sure. This is what we need to do...' I outlined a rough plan that I hoped would keep all of us alive.

From just behind me I heard a voice. 'Need a hand, fellas?' asked Big Ben nonchalantly. Poison, Frank and I turned as one to find him leaning against the upright of the stall. He was grinning and had on his black combat gear. 'I thought I might find you here.'

'Ben, where did you come from?' I asked, disbelief that he was here in my voice.

'I was on a date with a couple of girls.' A couple of girls. Obviously. 'The bar we were in was evacuated because of a fire a couple of doors along, which turned out to be your office. I guessed that you would be here somewhere and most likely in trouble, so I sent the girls home, grabbed my gear from the boot of my car and grabbed an extra set of armour for you.' He lifted his right arm and chucked a set of black Kevlar body armour over to me.

'You, my friend. Are a sight for sore eyes.' Big Ben. Six feet seven inches of well trained, muscular, barely suppressed violence. 'How's the wound?'

'For now, it's insignificant,' he replied. I knew what he meant, I felt the same way about my ribs. We were in a fight whether we liked it or not. The Klowns would use our injuries against us if they knew about them so we might as well ignore them and get on with the job.

'Hey, that's Jagjit,' said Frank, pointing.

We followed his indication. Sure enough, Jagjit was hurriedly escorting Alice away from all the danger. She had a large fluffy toy tucked under her right arm. Big Ben went after him, calling that he would be back in a minute.

The crowd of people was almost gone. Thankfully, the Klowns, visible here and there, were mostly ignoring everyone else. They were here for us. A few bewildered souls, those less mobile or less able were still heading away from the area we were in. Soon it would be just us and the Klowns, which meant they were contained. The police would be here soon enough, so all we had to do was hold them off or keep them here for a short while.

'We should move, yes?' asked Poison. She was dressed in her usual style of black, tight, distressed clothing with layers to keep her warm. The fringe of her black hair was cut at an improbable angle to sweep from left to right over her eyes with a band of bright blue running beneath the upper layer so that it peeked out here and there as her hair moved. It looked to be a costly effect to achieve. She looked good though. Tough and athletic and somehow at home with the short swords she had in each hand. Next to her, Frank was still rooting through the chest of weapons trying to find something he liked. The shield he had used was strapped to his left forearm already like a knight. I half expected him to pull out some chain mail and a giant mace. Instead, he selected a double-headed axe.

'Yes, Poison,' I replied. 'We should move. Get one of the buildings to our backs.'

I could hear sirens in the distance. Lots of them.

Good.

'Hold on, Tempest,' called Frank from the floor. 'This might be useful.' I looked down and sure enough Frank was hauling several sets of chain mail from the bottom of the chest, and he had a couple of steel helmets to go with it. The helmets looked to have been designed in the twelfth century with the steel extending down over the cheeks and neck and a bar that came down over the nose. They looked heavy.

Poison took a chain mail and slipped it over her head and arms.

'Tempest Michaels,' Deadface called out loudly to me. Frank, Poison and I all looked in the same direction. He had our attention. 'It's time to die,' he called in a mockingly sing song voice.

Then the Klowns came. The police or anyone else who might have been able to help us were somewhere else still. I heard a chainsaw, it might even be two chainsaws, coming towards us and could see at least twenty Klowns. The numbers weren't good.

I threw the front counter of the stall out of our way. It clattered upside-down, scattering comic books which flapped in the light breeze as we stepped over them. The Klowns were walking slowly towards us, closing the circle. We were in the middle of it. Time to change that.

With a battle cry, I ran to my right dragging Poison and Frank with me. There were alleyways all over the old part of Rochester. If we could just get to the cathedral, we could get into a position that was at least defendable.

Ahead of us were Klowns. They had formed a circle of sorts so no matter which direction we went there would be some of them in our way. Their intention had most likely been to corral us and close the circle so that Deadface could either kill us himself or watch us being killed. By attacking them instead, we changed the game. The Klowns were starting to react though. We were running straight towards one of them but to his left and right were two more that were less than ten yards away. All of them were moving in our direction but it was only these three that I needed to get through to escape the circle. What we couldn't afford was to get caught up fighting them for more than a few seconds or the horde would descend on us.

I had covered twenty yards and was almost upon the first Klown. He looked familiar, like maybe he was one of those that had attacked me last Saturday night. He was about my height and weight though and he was just standing his ground trying to look tough when he should have been backing off. Had he done so, the two Klowns from his left and right would converge on us as we reached him. Instead, I closed the distance with Poison and Frank on my heels and watched with glee as Big Ben and Jagjit hit him over the head with a steel trash bin. He had been raising his arm to swing at me with the machete he was holding, unaware of the chaps coming from behind him at a run with the bin, their timing perfect as we were able to continue running with no break in our pace at all as the Klown crumpled unconscious on the floor.

There was yelling behind us. I risked a glance over my shoulder. The Klowns were all converging on us, but the circle they had tried to trap us in had placed those on the far side almost fifty yards away from where we now were. They were running but we had several seconds before we would be outnumbered.

I changed the tactic again: I wanted to attack.

'Ben. Go right!' I shouted, grabbing Frank and Poison and pushing them along with me. The five of us suddenly had Klowns to our front all coming our way one at a time. The Klowns behind us would be a problem soon enough but not so soon that we couldn't pick a few off.

It was time to even the numbers a little.

The first Klown had his face painted into a cruel and twisted expression that looked like someone had roughly sewn his mouth and eyes shut. He had a blade in each hand and heavy workman's boots on. He was a big man, heavy around the shoulders and chest and he was running at us. Our change in direction caught him off guard though as without warning the gap he was trying to close disappeared. Big Ben punched him in the face before he could even raise his knives, then barrelled through him with a hard shoulder, sending him to the ground where Jagjit kicked him square in the side of his head.

The next Klown saw what had happened and came to a halt, but it was far too late to avoid the blunt force trauma of Big Ben. The Klown had a baseball bat that he managed to swing, only to find that Big Ben caught it with one massive hand. Right on his shoulder, I will admit that I took great pleasure in trying to remove the Klown's head with my own weapon.

'Wow,' said Big Ben. 'What is that?'

'This little thing?' I asked hefting the three-foot rounded bat. I turned it over in my hands to reveal the words running down the length of it.

Zombie Twatting Stick.

'Frank had it in his apocalypse survival kit,' I explained. Big Ben nodded his approval, and it was time to deal with the next Klown.

They appeared content to continue running into us despite what had already happened to three of their number. The next was no different but the gaps were now closing so this would have to be the last one. I heard a war-cry from behind and glanced to see two more Klowns finally converging on our position from the other direction.

I slapped Big Ben on the shoulder and peeled off to deal with them. We had a few seconds before we needed to change direction once more and leave the remaining Klowns to follow behind us. As I turned around, I found Frank and Poison ahead of me with their weapons up. The two Klowns, one with a stupid blue wig, one completely bald, both had bats which they were holding above their heads to smash down. They were also out of shape and out of breath and easy pickings. Not that I got to do anything to them. There was a blur of motion as the tiny, yet graceful, Poison, spun her short swords in a series of arcs before their oncoming faces. Perhaps realising they were about to be turned into mincemeat and no longer imbued with the bravado they felt when they had lots of their brethren around them, they screeched to a halt. Both were looking at Poison who was still swishing her swords and failed to see Frank and Jagjit. The pair of them hit the Klowns in the face, Frank with the end of his battle-axe and Jagjit with a discarded bat he had collected from one of the other fallen Klowns. Both men went down with a spray of blood from their faces. The team was being remarkably polite about whacking the Klowns. We would have been well within our rights to maim or kill them as they would most probably do to us if we allowed ourselves to be caught. Real violence like that though leaves a mental scar and overcoming the natural urge to not cut chunks from people takes quite a bit of motivation. Plus, it would make our explanation to the police far more complicated, so it was for the best that we left them injured or unconscious but alive.

The once spread-out circle of Klowns was now nearly upon us as one converging hoard. We had taken care of half a dozen or more, but it still left us outnumbered by better than two to one. All the time we had been running, I had been directing us towards the North Gate where we would exit the castle grounds and be back where there were alleys to slip down. The tightness of the alleyways meant that the Klowns would only be able to get to us one or two at a time. The general area was also where I was certain the police would come from. The Klowns were only a few yards behind us as we turned right onto the High Street. Frank's shop was just to our left around the corner. My office was dead ahead and I could see light from the flames playing off the white walls of the Elizabethan buildings as ahead there were firefighters tackling it.

Then, as we ran through the dark shadow of the stone gate, a flare went off just to our left, then a half heartbeat later another to our right.

'Quickly, all of you get behind me,' instructed Lyndon Parrish. He was standing in our path wearing a robe and looking surprisingly calm, as if oblivious or unconcerned about the madness chasing us. In his right hand was another flare which he lit as we reached him. 'Quick, Frank. Get them beyond the circle markings.'

We hadn't broken our pace and would be behind him in a second. The Klowns were right on our heels though and would carve this fool into pieces. I was sure of it.

'Lyndon, they are just men, and they are armed,' I yelled grabbing his arm.

He shook me off and I wasn't going to hang around. Frank looked like he might though until I grabbed his sleeve and pulled him with me. He had too little body weight to resist. We left Lyndon behind us as we turned onto the High Street.

Lyndon was bellowing Latin incantations at the top of his lungs. As I watched, he took a few steps backward, allowing the Klowns to come at him then stuck the flare's burning end to the floor. A brief explosion followed which hurt my eyes with its brightness. Something on the floor had ignited in an elaborate pattern all around and between where the Klowns were.

The flash stunned the Klowns, leaving them stationary and looking bewildered. In front of them, Lyndon had his hands held aloft still screaming indecipherable phrases. But he ended with, 'You're trapped, foul hell-spawn. Now I will banish you.' With a flourish of his arms, he opened his mouth to speak, but a claw hammer sailed out from the midst of the Klowns and hit him square in the forehead. He went over backward and lay still.

It broke the spell for us and for the Klowns. Everyone started running again as one. Them trying to catch us, me trying to lead my friends away.

'There, on the left,' I yelled as we ran. The others saw what I was pointing to and one by one ducked down a tiny gap between two buildings. It was barely wide enough for Big Ben's shoulders so would most certainly stop the Klowns from coming at us as a mob. Equally, it meant that we were only able to fight them pretty much one to one. I was last to enter the alleyway, thankful for the refuge it offered. Only then did I realise my awful mistake. The alley was a dead end.

Emphasis on dead.

I squashed my panic down. If the Klowns had any guns they would have used them by now, so we just had blunt weapons and knives to fend off until the police came. The sirens were getting closer, the sound difficult to pinpoint in the confines of the alley. Then it sounded as if they had driven passed us and were going away, because the sound was getting quieter.

'Did I just hear the police drive straight by?' asked Frank, expressing the worry the rest of us felt.

I had no time to be concerned about that now though as the first Klown came around the edge of the building at speed. He was moving so fast he careened into the wall of the building on the far side as he entered and bounced off - directly into my bat which I swung upwards to connect under his chin. I had been expecting the first one to be caught off guard so had waited right at the entrance to the alley and suckered him as he appeared.

He fell out of the alley and into the street as a warning to the next in line who slammed on the brakes. Two, then three, then multiple faces appeared to block off the end of the alley. We were trapped. Pinned in by my poor judgement.

The Klowns were not attacking, and I wondered why for a very short moment until I heard the reason. From just out of sight, a chainsaw started up, and then another. The Klowns at the front parted to let the two chainsaw-wielding maniacs enter. They came at me slowly. I hefted the bat, genuinely scared. Between us, we had no weapon that was long enough to hit the Klowns without getting too close to the chainsaws. If I threw my bat at either one of them it might hit but was unlikely to do enough damage and would then be lost. I took an involuntary step back. They were grinning.

Behind me, I could hear my team looking for a way out. Big Ben had found a small door and was smashing into it with his shoulder. I glanced over my shoulder as I backed away. Big Ben had no run up so was throwing himself off the opposite wall of the alley. As I watched, he slammed into the door with all his might and weight.

He bounced off. 'That was about as pointless as dating a flat-chested woman,' he observed. 'Okay. Plan B is I take the chainsaws and shove them up your arses. Who's first?' he asked the Klowns by leaning over my shoulder.

They just grinned again. 'No way out this time, Mr Michaels,' taunted Deadface from behind them.

Angry, I swung my bat hard, hoping to knock the chainsaw from their hands. They both moved to intercept with their chainsaws which gripped my bat and snatched it from my hands. It was gone in a flurry of wood chips.

Deadface laughed.

Then from above, came a familiar voice. 'Why did the Klowns lie down in the street?' A solid oak park bench flew over our heads to land on the two Klowns in front of me. It bounced once and knocked Deadface over. 'Because they had a bench on their heads! Hur, hur. Skittles!' As one we all turned to look up. Above us on the flat roof of the shop to our rear, was Basic. Looking like Quasimodo silhouetted against the night sky, he had come to our rescue.

'How did you get that thing up there?' Jagjit asked.

'Wasn't easy,' came his simple reply. The park bench must weigh at least two hundred pounds. I could ask him about it later. For now, Deadface was still on the floor trying to get up and the chainsaws had automatically switched off when the operators released the triggers.

I took two purposeful paces forward, stepping onto and then over the bench and the other Klowns beneath it to grab Deadface by his hair. At the mouth of the alley, the remaining Klowns were looking far less confident than they had a few seconds ago. I pulled Deadface up but as usual, I had underestimated him. In his right hand, which had been tucked beneath his body he held a wicked looking knife.

With my hand holding his hair he spun and thrust it at me. It came right for my heart, thankfully ending in a dull clang as it hit the Kevlar plate in my armour. He followed it up with a fist to my injured ribs though. I should have seen it coming but anger had clouded my senses. I let go as the pain hit and threatened to overwhelm me.

He slipped away from me, got to his feet and dived back along the alleyway towards the Klowns and safety. I dived, slipped and crashed to the floor still wobbly from the burst of pain in my side.

I heard sirens again, the blissfully welcome noise dopplering off the tall buildings of the High Street. Big Ben hauled me to my feet.

'Let's get them, Tempest.' Big Ben had a full head of steam and was looking for something or someone to smash. I had seen it before. I wouldn't want to be on the receiving end, but it was great to have by my side.

'Yeah. Let's do that,' I replied, my teeth gritted against the pain I felt and my face set with resolute determination.

Ahead of us, the Klowns were no longer looking at us but were glancing around in all directions as they tried to find an escape route. The police had cut them off from both ends of the High Street. I could see flashing lights in both directions. The sirens we had heard going by us was them circling around to trap them. Deadface was out there some-where. I had to find him and force him to tell me what he had done with my dogs and Mrs Comerforth.

I got to my feet and started back down the alley towards its exit onto the High Street and the confusion of Klowns still there. Right on my shoulder were Frank, Poison, Jagjit, and Big Ben. Basic was most likely circling back around to join us.

In a complete reversal, the Klowns ran and now we were chasing them. On the opposite side of the street, there was another alleyway. It looked like nothing more than a dark hole between two shops that was eating light rather than allow it to penetrate the gloom. But it went somewhere and once the first Klown had disappeared down it, the rest were swift to follow. The Klowns were heading back towards the castle. This was going to work in my favour.

As I ran, I grabbed my phone from my pocket and dialled. As it picked up, I started talking. Big Ben glanced at me but left his question unasked. The alley ended at the back of the two buildings forming it. We had now run three sides of a square and were crossing College Yard which would bring us back out next to the cathedral.

Perfect.

Ahead of us, the Klowns skidded to a stop. There was roughly a dozen of them, all armed still and dangerous. We were behind them, but it was what faced them that had brought them to a halt.

In the clearing, just in front of the cathedral, was a sea of clowns. The call I had made had been to Big Dick and the CLITs. I promised I would keep him informed of my progress and I had. My earlier call had been received when he and his cohort were meeting with Dr Parrish again, right here in Rochester High Street. Dr Parrish had recruited dozens of them, all at the same rate rather than for one fixed fee, so had he been able to banish the Klowns back to hell he would get a big payday for it. My simple advice to Richard had been that the Klowns were here and we could end the whole thing tonight if they showed up in force.

Now they were fanned out in a semi-circle, three deep in places, all of them hefting bats and looking angry despite the painted-on smiles.

The Klowns had nowhere to go. From the midst of the clowns, a lone horn honked to break the standoff. Deadface screamed a banshee cry and charged them, the other Klowns followed him. It was the only tactic that could work. They would try to punch a hole through the line. There was no way I was going to let him escape but chasing after them yet again I realised that I could no longer tell who was who.

In front of us was a melee of Klowns and clowns.

Then, finally, the police arrived. Someone was shouting instructions through a loudhailer, telling the disorganised riot of men to drop their weapons and lie down. No one paid him any heed.

With a battle cry that started in the pit of my stomach, I charged. My ribs did their best to remind me I was still broken but I ignored their advice and ran, my head down to collide with what I hoped was a Klown. It wasn't though. I let him go and tried another, grabbing him and spinning him around so I could work out whether to punch him or not. Wrong again.

Where on earth was Deadface?

'Tempest!' A cry split the air in Amanda's familiar voice.

There she was, on the other side of the open space by a

dark gap between buildings. A few paces to her left, CI Quinn directed the black uniforms as they met with the Klowns and clowns. In his hand was the loud hailer. He lifted it to his lips and bellowed out another command, drowning out what she was trying to tell me.

I separated myself from the battle. Big Ben was behind me, visible above everyone else, smacking heads together and enjoying himself. Somewhere in the muddle of fighting bodies, would be Frank and Poison, but both were so short I couldn't see them, and I had no idea where Jagjit was. The police were converging on the whole lot of them now, so I felt hopeful that the fight was over, and my friends would be safe.

I jogged quickly across the street to Amanda, saying, 'I lost Deadface,' as I got to her.

'I saw two Klowns slip away from the fight. They were heading in the direction of the castle. The Chief Inspector sent a team after them but if Deadface is not over there,' she said indicating the pile of people now with their hands in the air surrendering or already on the floor in cuffs. 'Then he must be this way instead.'

'Amanda, I keep Tempest safe,' claimed a slightly out of breath Basic as he arrived by my side.

'Yes, you did, buddy,' I called back over my shoulder as I started down the dark path. If Deadface went this way, then I needed to catch up with him. 'Amanda, I need you,' I shouted as she wasn't following me. I had no clue where they had gone and little chance of tracking them without radio contact, which Amanda had.

She hesitated, looking at CI Quinn, then tore after me and Basic, speaking into her lapel mike as she ran.

A muffled reply came back over her radio. 'Go right, Tempest. They are heading towards the river,' she shouted.

We were all getting out of breath now. My pulse was hammering from adrenalin anyway, fighting is hard on the body even without getting hurt.

We came out from between two buildings onto Epaul Lane and were back in the castle grounds, but further away from the cathedral than we had been. The scene ahead of us was one of desolation. Abandoned stalls, discarded clothing, food and general detritus from the event was strewn all over. Smaller, lighter items were being blown about by the chilly breeze. Several stalls had been knocked over and I could smell a fire somewhere, probably an untended food truck with food now burning on the hot plate. There were no people in sight, but I was sure they would return soon, the stall holders at least would want to get back to make sure their source of livelihood was intact.

We cut down Castle Hill then had to run up the steep incline to get inside the castle's outer wall. Basic stopped before we reached the top; he was out of breath. Amanda glanced at him and may have stopped had she then not heard a call for help over her radio.

Someone was hurt.

'Oh, God,' she swore. 'It's Brad.' She was talking into the radio to get their position. We had paused as we needed a direction to head in. I wanted to find Deadface, but casualties had to take priority. Basic caught up with us just as Amanda yelled and ran off again, across the castle grounds in the dark towards the exit onto the esplanade and the river.

At the steps that led down to the road from the castle, we saw two forms on the ground, both in uniform. I recognised Brad Hardacre immediately. I didn't know the other officer, but they were both clearly hurt and were leaking blood onto the cold stone.

Amanda swore again and called for assistance at our location. Then we were both attending to the wounded, each using our training to stem the blood flow.

'Hey, buddy. What's your name?' I asked the officer. He was conscious, and I wanted to keep him that way. I hadn't seen blood like this since I was in the army.

'Ian,' he said. He wasn't very talkative and had given me his name through gritted teeth. I reassured him while I checked the wound. It was a stab to his abdomen and was spilling enough blood that it must have nicked his artery there.

CI Quinn's voice came over the radio. 'Harper. Report. What is your location and situation?' he sounded cool, calm and in control. Part of me wanted to throttle him, the rational part of my brain observed that he had most likely risen to his position because of such attributes.

Equally controlled, Amanda replied, 'At the north side of the castle grounds, on the steps leading down to the esplanade. Hardacre and Bloomwell are injured. Stabbed, and need urgent medical attention.'

He acknowledged her message, and the line went dead again.

'What happened?' I asked, then listened as Brad started speaking from his prone position. A team of six had gone after a pair of Klowns they had seen escape the police net but had lost them and split up into three pairs. Brad and Ian had been attacked and stabbed as they came level with a stall that the two Klowns had been hiding in. They escaped down the stairs, but the Klowns had made no attempt to pursue them anyway. The last thing Brad had seen was the Klowns disappearing back towards the castle itself.

I didn't think that Ian or Brad was losing enough blood that their lives were in danger, provided of course that they were treated and taken to the hospital fairly soon. I wanted to go. I wanted to find Deadface.

'Basic,' I called him over to me.

'Yur?'

'I need you to hold this in position here and keep pressure on it until the paramedics arrive?' I said, showing him the clean handkerchief I had stuffed into Ian's wound. It was now soaked with his blood, of course, but it was doing its best to slow down the blood leaking out of him.

'Tempest, what are you doing?' asked Amanda. She was a few feet away from me on the floor tending to Brad and his similar wound.

'Ian is fine, Amanda. Deadface is out there. We catch him now or he slips away and...'

'Don't you dare leave, Tempest. That man needs you,' she snapped at me.

'Amanda, the man needs proper medical attention. Until then he will be just fine being looked after by Basic. I'm going to find the Klown. When I get back, we can discuss how you and Quinn were using me as bait.' My words were angry and harsh. I doubted she had been complicit in the concept of using me as bait to draw the Klowns in, but she had known about it or had become aware of it at some point and hadn't told me. It compromised the trust I expected to exist between us as work partners. It was something I would have to address with her soon, but not now. Now I was filled with rage, and I planned to use it as fuel to finish this.

I stood up as Basic manoeuvred himself into the position I had occupied. I patted my pockets and set off.

'Tempest!' Amanda shouted from behind me. 'Tempest, damn you!'

She was right to be upset about me leaving Ian to bleed

while I went after Deadface, but I needed to do this. Back up the ancient stone steps, I re-entered the castle grounds. It was still devoid of people. The only noise I could hear was from the items being blown about by the wind. I stood still and listened.

Nothing.

I was certain the police would have blocked off all access roads by now, making escape by car improbable. On foot, they might manage to slip through, but I knew there were police officers looking for them.

The castle grounds were too vast though, with too many shadows for me to believe the Klowns couldn't slip through whatever net the police might try to cast. I had to guess where Deadface would go if I wanted to catch him.

So where would he be trying to get to, which route would provide the greatest chance to slip away? I spun in place, my eyes closed and my mouth open to amplify any noise that might be available to hear. I had no way of applying intelligence to determine a likely direction to head in. There were so many possible streets that led away from the castle. To the north and just beyond the outer castle wall was the river.

The river?

I stopped trying to work it out and started running. I would be right or wrong.

It turned out I was both. Deadface wasn't trying to run. He was waiting for me. I ran through the castle grounds heading towards the castle itself. To the right of it was a door in the wall that led to a set of steps down to street level. As I went through the door, he hit me. The blow came full in the chest, his bat swinging hard. It might have killed me had I not been wearing armour and been fortunate enough that the blow landed squarely on the Kevlar plate.

I was shocked more than hurt although there was enough force to drive the air from my lungs. I fell, tucking into a roll to get some distance. He was alone, or at least I couldn't see another Klown with him. Perhaps the other guy had seen the sense in making good his escape.

Deadface came at me with the bat. I was still on the ground, in pain and short of breath and he was going to try to kill me, I was certain of that. He raised it above his head as he came running forward. I kicked him in his knees before he could complete the downswing and ruined his aim. The bat struck the ground next to me and was momentarily motionless. I wrapped my right arm around it, ignoring the pain in my ribs and rolled my whole body over to wrest it from his grasp.

Now I span my legs around to get them under me and came up fast with an uppercut to his chin delivered courtesy of the top of my head. I heard the connection of bone on bone reverberate through my skull. I didn't have much fight left in me and I was alone, so I either ended this quickly or I would lose.

He stumbled back holding his face, blood coming from his mouth.

'Where are my dogs?' I demanded.

'Dead,' he sneered, pulling out the wicked knife he had been brandishing earlier. 'Why don't you join them?'

I had to dive out of the way as he lunged for me. I came up against the outer wall of the castle grounds. It was a low wall, perhaps no more than five feet tall. He slashed at me again, I parried as his arm went past me, but he kept hold of the knife. On the backswing I timed his movement, allowing him to get closer. The blade nicked my arm as I ducked back but with the knife passed me and travelling away from my body, I pushed off the wall and hit him with my left fist as hard as I could in the side of his head. It changed his trajectory, causing him to topple. The knife was still in his right hand until I kicked his forearm. The blade flew away into the dark.

I was drawing ragged breaths against my broken ribs. I needed to throw myself on him and pin him, get a sleeper hold in place or something but I felt that I must look like an exhausted boxer in the fifteenth round, barely able to keep my fists up and constantly stumbling.

Deadface was little better than I. The police had finally spotted us, though they were all the way across the castle grounds, more than a hundred yards distant so even though we were running, it would take them twenty seconds of more to reach us. I spotted CI Quinn and Amanda among the twenty or so coming our way.

Deadface saw them too and I gave him new energy. He got to his feet and climbed onto the castle wall; he was trying to escape over it. I tried to stop him but a backhanded swing from him pushed me away. I knew there was a drop on the other side of the wall that was over one hundred feet. He noticed it just before he jumped, clearly changing his mind to then attempt to run along the wall to the door and steps he had ambushed me from just a minute ago.

I snagged his foot as he went by which tripped him. As he fell, he lost his balance and fell to the outer edge of the wall. I caught a flailing arm, not because I wanted to save him but from instinct. He was hanging mostly off the wall; his left hand locked in my right. His eyes locked on mine, showing anger more than fear.

I glanced to my right, the police were still fifty yards away; close enough that they could all see the drama playing out before their eyes, but too far away to help.

Holding his weight with my right arm, my ribs were on fire, I couldn't breathe from the searing agony and lights were starting to dance in front of my eyes.

'This is your fault,' Deadface squeaked at me.

I opened my hand and let him go.

The Aftermath

I sat in the back of the ambulance hugging my knees and staring at nothing. I had been reunited with Big Ben, Jagjit, Frank, Poison, and Basic. To my great relief, they were all uninjured. The clowns had been separated from the Klowns and the Klowns had been arrested and taken away. I would have to catch up with Big Dick later. For now, I was content with the report that they were also all alive.

The CLITs had been in Rochester receiving instruction from Dr Lyndon Parrish on how to cast a circle of protection when I had called Big Dick. When he had announced to the group that I was going to fight the Klowns and that they were also in Rochester, Lyndon had decided he could take them all down in one go. He had all the right ingredients to set a huge banishing circle. It hadn't worked, of course, so now Dr Parrish was in the hospital with a concussion from the blow to his head. I figured he would probably make a full recovery and had got off very lightly. The CLITs had followed Big Dick's lead and, having seen the Klowns ignore Dr Parrish's attempt to magically bind them,

263

had agreed to try it his way. There had been forty-three angry clowns to spring the trap. It was a little ruthless of me to use them like that; I could have easily got someone killed, but I hadn't, and they all had tales of heroic effort to tell now.

Deadface was... well, he was dead. He had fallen from the castle wall onto the street below, but it was too far to drop and survive. The police weren't holding me responsible for his death, but I knew that I was. I had only needed to hang on for another four or five seconds. Had I done so, the police would have been upon us and could have pulled him back.

I had let go because I wanted to. I wondered how long that would haunt me.

For his part, CI Quinn had seen that I was administered to. When he came to check on me, I threatened to kill him. My words were not well received. I accused him of using me as bait, of getting two or more of his own officers hurt and of cowardly subterfuge. He would most likely get a glowing report for his handling of the case. When he departed, Amanda had appeared looking sheepish.

'Why did you not tell me?' I asked her. 'What if they had killed Big Ben, or Jagjit, or anyone? What about my dogs?'

'What about the dogs?' she asked worriedly.

'Deadface took them. He showed me their collars as a taunt and told me they were dead.'

Mrs. Comerforth!

'Amanda, you have to get a car to my neighbour's house right now. She's looking after the dogs. She might still be alive but hurt.' I gave her the house number to be sure she got the right place and sent her away without another word. I wasn't in a talking mood.

Presently the paramedics told me they were taking me to A&E. I refused though. I was going home. I was bloody and beaten but they had sutured the knife cut to my arm so there was nothing else they could do for me in hospital.

I trudged slowly across the castle grounds. It was full of police officers. Stallholders were being kept at bay behind crime scene tape. One stall had caught fire and burnt to a charred crisp. It was a wet mess now and I wondered if the same fire team now packing away their gear had tackled the blaze in my office.

I felt like I had lost, even though I would be told I had won.

'Tempest,' called Amanda from behind me. I still didn't want to talk to her, but I turned anyway. I was at the edge of the grounds now, about to leave the area and all the drama behind me. 'A squad car is at your neighbour's house. She's fine. The dogs are fine. No one went there tonight.'

He had bluffed me.

I let out a breath that I didn't know I'd been holding. I mumbled my thanks, turned, and gritting my teeth against the pain I felt, slowly ducked under the tape.

'Tempest?' she called me again. She wanted to talk, to clear the air perhaps. I wasn't ready to hear what she had to say, so I just kept on walking. Mostly, I didn't want her to see the anger and betrayal in my face.

My car was in the car park behind my office. At least that was where I had left it earlier this evening. I was genuinely surprised to find it still sitting there, its shiny red paintwork unmolested. As I dug around in my pocket for my keys, I looked up at my office. It was a burnt-out shell. Even the roof was gone, the supporting timbers reduced to blackened stubby fingers. There was nothing precious in it, but I once read that most businesses do not survive a fire.

Too much is lost, even if all the people survive, for the business to reopen again elsewhere quickly enough to not be supplanted by a competitor. Well, I had a competitor now even if he was in the hospital with a dent to his face.

I shut the door to my car and went home.

Postscript

I told myself that I was overdue a break, that the business would function perfectly well without me and that I absolutely wasn't running away. I had been telling myself that for the past day since I made the decision to run away.

Amanda had betrayed my trust. I was still not sure how I felt about it or about her and I didn't want to be here tomorrow to deal with it. I had no live case that I was in the middle of, and the cases the business did have could be tackled by Amanda in between her final few shifts as a police officer. Or they could just be left until I returned. I was telling myself it didn't matter, and on that matter, I was probably correct.

I was going away for the week. I was taking the dogs and the three of us were going to have a holiday. It was a bit cold for a break by the sea but that was what I was going to do anyway. We would have long walks along the coastal pathways and venture into the surrounding countryside and have cream teas by warm open fires in quaint, time-forgotten alehouses. I was genuinely looking forward to it, even if I did worry that what I was actually doing was running away.

Yesterday, I had met with Jane and gave her the task of setting up the new office. We had gone shopping for a new computer and other office-essential equipment, then I set her up in my home office so that she could work from there. New stationary was ordered, and I was confident the business would tick over for a week without me directly at the helm. All Jane had to do was handle calls and emails, set Amanda up to tackle anything she felt like dealing with and maintain a presence for the firm.

My Landlord, Tony Jarvis, had called yesterday morning. The building we both occupied was well insured and would be rebuilt. He had a meeting on Monday to sign some paperwork but expected to have work started within a week. I imagined it might take a good deal longer than that but would be pleased to be proven wrong.

I had barely slept the last two nights. The memory of choosing to let Deadface go still too fresh in my mind. It wasn't the first time in my life that a traumatic event had stolen my sleep. I had been in the army for too many years and deployed to too many war zones to have avoided such things. One never gets used to it, but coping mechanisms do develop I suppose.

Lying in bed last night, two snoring dogs in the otherwise empty other half of the bed and with sleep cruelly evading me, I had avoided thinking about the death of Nigel Havers by piecing together the final parts of the Klown case.

The Klown spree of assault, battery, theft, and murder really had been all about me in a way. Nigel Havers was a broken man, beaten down by a poor start in life and an enormous chip on his shoulder that he could never get beyond. During his life, he had endured the same amount of disappointments as anyone else might have; he had been dumped, been fired, had lost when he thought he would win, but unlike the rest of us who just move on, he had amassed a list of people to exact retribution upon.

When I spoiled his plan to be turned into a vampire, I had cut off his intended method of revenge. Once supposedly made immortal, he would have gone after all the people on his list of hate and bitten out their throats. That was my working theory anyway.

Instead, he had formed a cult of Klowns. It was a testament to what he could have achieved with his life had he been sane. Attracted by the promise of revenge on everyone that had ever done them wrong, with a side order of making money through robbery, he had recruited criminals and set them tasks to perform. He had lured Adrian Plumber in by the expedient of adventure and excitement, two things that were missing from his life. The same sad story was probably true of many of the Klowns. The police would undoubtedly uncover some of the details by interviewing the Klowns they had in custody but much of his motivation, his reason behind the Klowns had gone with him to his grave.

Amanda had wisely given me some space after apologising yet again. Rather than call me or just come to my house, as she had been doing since we met, she had emailed me the news that the Klown I had knocked out in the Lockmeadow car park, the one with the green wig, had finally woken up. He had missed the whole thing. His injuries weren't permanent thankfully, but he was off to jail to join his friends.

The press was having a field day with the story. There had been a local journalist at the Blood Fest, probably thinking it was a rubbish event to be assigned to cover.

However, he was savvy enough to continue taking pictures as the crowd fled the castle grounds and hung around in the shadows after that catching the action in still and video formats. Pictures of Poison in chainmail and helmet, twirling twin swords had made it onto the cover of two national papers. The nimble little minx had caused Frank's shop to be inundated with new customers apparently. I doubted he would be upset at the rush of business as he probably lost a lot of stock on Friday night. The chap had also captured images of Big Dick and the clowns. His tiny stature and clown outfit made him stand out, so footage of the fight between clowns and Klowns was going viral on YouTube. My involvement had made no more than a by-line. I had no problem with that. At least, I didn't until CI Quinn swept in and claimed to have stopped the Klowns through his department's great detective work and uncompromising bravery in facing the menace. He had been allowed to make a statement to a swarm of TV cameras on Friday night while the dust was still settling, and I was at home drinking my fifth rum and coke and wondering if my ribs would ever heal.

On the subject of my ribs, I had found myself forced to go to the hospital on Saturday morning to get some painkillers. Over the counter at the pharmacy ones weren't going to do it. I had been healing; on Friday morning I had felt much improved, but if anything, the wound now was worse than when first inflicted. It was another reason to take myself away. I needed to find a place of solitude and quiet where I could properly relax. It was a necessary thing.

Nevertheless, I was running away on some level and trying to ignore it as an inconvenient fact. The dogs were playing in the garden while I slowly loaded the car. I had booked a place to stay just an hour ago, a small pub that had two rooms above it. I reasoned that booking a room above a public house ensured an easy walk back to my lodgings once I had enjoyed a few relaxing drinks at the end of a day. They served food, so it was a Bed and Breakfast where I would probably eat dinner most nights as well.

A week away to get my head straight. I would tell people tomorrow, once I was there. Was that cowardly? Probably, but it was a tactic that would prevent my parents or Big Ben or Amanda or anyone else from talking me out of it.

I closed the boot of my car, then closed the bonnet as well. The Porsche Boxster might look like it has no room for luggage, but the mid-engine design leaves a surprising amount of space both fore and aft. Enough for a suitcase, all the things the dogs might need, some sturdy walking boots and all the other paraphernalia I had packed just in case. I locked the car and went back to the house.

There were two small black and tan faces pressed up against the glass of the back door. The dogs had exhausted the list of tasks they had for the garden. I let them in, performed a final check around the house, making sure windows were shut, the fridge was empty, the bins were empty. I left the heating on as Jane would be using the house as an office while I was away. She was the only person I had told about my intention to abscond. I simply said I needed a break. If she had any concern about being left to run the firm, she chose not to show it.

I stood inside the front door, head cocked to one side wondering what I might have forgotten to do. I gave up after thirty seconds. If I had forgotten to pack something, I would have to manage without it. If I had forgotten to do something, it would have to be dealt with upon my return.

I whistled for the dogs, waited, then went to collect them from the sofa where they were pretending to be asleep.

They scurried to the car while I locked up the house, then the three of us set off for Cornwall on the other side of the Country.

We were going to Cawsand, a tiny fishing village on the Southwest coast that I visited and fell in love with as a child. I hadn't been back since but imagined I could already smell the sea and hear the waves breaking against the shore. As I pulled out of my road to point the car west, I could think of nothing but the peace and relaxation waiting for me at my journey's end.

Had I known the horror awaiting me there or the desperate situation I was leaving Amanda to tackle here, I would never have left the house.

Afterword

Hi there,

My inspiration for the plague of evil clowns came from a real event in the UK. It didn't get as bloody as I depict in this book and there were no murders that I recall, yet the story stuck with me, going around in what passes for a brain until I saw a way to use it myself.

My Blue Moon series riffs on traditional urban fantasy tales by taking the creatures and making none of them real. In many ways, it's a grown-up version of Scooby Doo and has been described as such by many readers. It's a comparison I enjoy hearing as that series was perhaps my favourite cartoon as a child.

At the time of writing this note, I have just completed my thirty-seventh novel and have been able to quit my dreaded day job to pursue a full-time career as a writer. Being able to do the one thing that I love to do, and make it pay the bills and beyond, is an immense privilege. I worked very hard to get to this point, but I recognise how blessed I'm, nevertheless.

The next book in this series, Dead Pirates of Cawsand, came about during a family holiday to Cornwall. For those who do not know where that is, Cornwall is the south-western tip of England, jutting into the Atlantic with miles of fantastic coastline. I was there, holding the hand of my toddler son and staring out to sea, when the idea of a skeletal pirate crew came to me. Cawsand, like so many Cornish villages, is separate from the other settlements around it. Cut off almost from the rest of civilisation, they must do things for themselves, and the police response time is slow. I believe I had more fun writing that book than any before or since.

I'll let you go now; I need to start writing book thirty-eight.

Take care

Steve Higgs

June 2020

vinci-books.com/deadpirates-cawsand

Tempest thought he deserved a holiday, instead he finds himself hip-deep in murderous ghosts before his second pint is finished.

Gold coins from a centuries-old sunken treasure ship have been found on the beach in Cawsand. This would be no cause for Tempest Michaels to take notice, but a man murdered by the ghost of a dead pirate come to claim back the gold? That ticks all his boxes.

Turn the page for a free preview…

Dead Pirates of Cawsand:
Chapter One

DEATH BY MISADVENTURE

Saturday, 29th October 2257hrs

As Philip stepped out of the pub, the cold air reminded him that it was late October, and he was on the seafront where there was nowhere to hide from it. It was a relatively still night but there was mist about already. He had expected it. Having lived by the sea his whole life, he took pride in knowing what the weather was going to do without the need to see a forecast. He pulled his coat tight about his body and zipped it all the way up to protect his neck.

'Don't let the pirates get you,' said a voice from behind him.

He turned to share the joke with the landlord who had come over to shut the door. It was closing time and Philip was the last one to leave. He usually was and prided himself on being a great customer.

'I think I'll be alright, Dave,' he replied with a laugh. 'It's a load of superstitious claptrap anyway.'

The landlord frowned as he replied. 'Try telling that to

those tourists last week. Or that nice Indian family that took over the old chip shop.'

'I hardly think they were set about by dead pirates, Dave.' He shuffled off in the direction of his house. 'See you tomorrow, Dave,' he called over his shoulder.

'See you tomorrow, Phil,' the answer drifted back through the mist.

Phil shuffled along the old, cobbled street back towards his house. He had lived in Cawsand all his life. He would die there too, he knew that and was happy about it. He had picked out his lot already, high up on the cemetery that overlooked the harbour.

The mist swirled around him as he turned away from the sea and headed inland. There were only two pubs in Cawsand, and he had to pass the other one both coming and going from his house to The Star. The other pub, the Sea Pilgrim, was owned and run by his sister-in-law which made it far harder for him to sneakily meet with Maggie Tanner. His wife knew he was having an affair, that he had always been having affairs. Clearly though, she was no longer bothered about it, probably even saw it as a relief that she was no longer expected to put in a performance herself. Her sex drive, what little there had ever been of it, had dwindled to nothing years ago. He was a stallion though. At almost seventy, he still wanted some action every night.

Not tonight though. Maggie had a headache she said, so their usual secret meeting had been cancelled. However, he had other things on his mind as he shuffled home: he was going to be rich. Maybe rich enough to leave his wife and move in with Maggie. A recent chance discovery had guaranteed his future, now he waited on a decision to be made. He would not wait much longer though. He had already issued his ultimatum, and they had no choice but to pay up.

A shadow moved ahead of him in the fog.

He stopped, peering into the murk. Had he seen something? The recent reports of ghostly pirates were making him nervous, that was all it was. Tourists and newcomers and superstitious rubbish.

He started moving again, then heard a noise behind him. He spun around or at least turned as fast as his decrepit, drunken body would turn. There was nothing there. At least, that was what he told himself, ignoring the fact that he could only see a few feet before the mist ate what little light there was.

He chuckled to himself for his foolishness. Shook his head and turned back to face the way home. Paying no attention to his feet he tripped over a cat as it came out of the alleyway next to him. It shrieked at him and shot across the street, the fright making his heart rate spike. He leaned against the wall of a house for support. His chest hurt suddenly, it felt tight, and he was struggling to breathe. Regret for a lifetime of drinking more than he knew he ought to dominated his thoughts. He sagged against the wall, thinking it was stupid place to die, then just as the pain in his chest was reaching an unbearable level, he let out a long, loud belch that seemed to start deep in his gut.

It went on for several seconds. When it finished, he wiped his mouth and stood up straight. Not a heart attack at all. His chest pain was gone all bar a lingering niggle. He chuckled to himself again, pushed off the wall and began tottering along the road once more. His house was just a few more yards away, just around the corner. Fishing in his pocket for keys, he saw another shadow in the mist ahead.

This time he ignored it entirely. Nothing but the moonlight playing tricks on his alcohol addled sight.

'Philip,' called out a voice in a creepy, singsong, off-key manner. It was behind him. He whipped around, but there was nothing to be seen in the impenetrable mist.

He looked about, worry gripping his pulse again and making it beat hard enough for him to hear it banging in his head.

'Philip,' the voice again. It called out from ahead of him this time. He spun around. Something moved in the mist and a figure emerged from the gloom, then another joined it. Both were dressed as pirates, complete with knee-high boots and hats. Each bore a cutlass in their right hand that looked wickedly sharp and eerily both were softly glowing as if lit from within. The scariest detail though was that they were both very definitely dead. They were virtually skeletal, their skin missing from their skulls and arms and wherever their ripped and rotten clothing had exposed what should have been flesh beneath.

Water was dripping from their clothing as if they had just emerged from the sea. 'Run,' the one on his left instructed. That the skeleton had no tongue and should not be able to make words didn't occur to Philip as he turned and fled.

With no idea where he was going, his only thought was to get away. Away from the horror in the mist.

The boat.

He remembered his boat. Ever reliable despite its age, Betsy would be his refuge. All he had to do was get there. Once he was cast off, they would not be able to get to him out at sea.

His pulse was hammering in his head from the effort of running, even though it was barely a stumbling jog. His chest ached from the exertion, but it was not far and all downhill. He checked behind when he reached the jetty, the pirates were still behind him, walking slowly, visible mostly due to the soft glow they were emanating.

Betsy was in sight though, right where he had left her earlier today. He tumbled onto the deck and scrambled to find a knife to cut the lines. There was one just inside the cabin, he kept it there for gutting fish when he caught them. So focused on reaching for it in the dark, he barely felt the cutlass cutting his throat. It was the warm liquid soaking his shirt that made him stop and look. Only when he looked at his hands to find them covered in dark sticky liquid did he question why his throat was stinging. He fell onto his back-side. A shadow came over him and he looked up. The night sky was obscured by two dark figures. His vision was blurring but they looked different from the two pirates that had been chasing him a moment ago. The pirates were the same size, these two were not. He wanted to say something, but his lungs were beginning to fill with his blood. Taking a breath was no longer an option.

As he sank to the floor, his pulse hammering in his ears, he wondered why they had singled him out. He tried to speak but a sudden blow to his chest silenced his question before it made it to his lips. He looked down at his body as an old, rusty-looking cutlass was pulled slowly back out of his ribcage. It made a comedic slurping noise as it came clear.

He wanted to chuckle, but a hand gripped his chin, forcing him to look up into the face above him. The face was mumbling something, whispering perhaps. He could barely hear it over the pounding in his ears. There was something about him having ignored a warning. Then his vision began to fade, and it no longer mattered.

Dead Pirates of Cawsand:
Chapter Two

RATTLER CIDER

Sunday, October 30th 1717hrs

The first swig of the pale liquid washed over my taste buds in a soothing kaleidoscope of flavour. At the bar, I had found myself presented with an array of options I was unfamiliar with. On a whim, I selected the Rattler pear cider, mostly because I liked the look of the pump with its snake motif. Plus, I was in the West Country and therefore drinking cider felt obligatory.

I downed half the glass in the first go while standing at the bar. I was thirsty from the journey, hungry and a little sore. The drive had taken longer than I had expected. It was only two hundred- and seventy-miles door to door, but the route took me down the A303, which even on a Sunday afternoon got snarled up as it went past Stonehenge and drivers gawked out of their windows at the odd collection of rocks. It was a single-track road for much of the journey after that, my speed dictated by tractors and farm vehicles and then, as I got deeper into Cornwall, by the narrow confines of the roads themselves, which were often too tight for two cars to pass.

The five hours I had planned for the journey quickly became six and although the dogs slept most of the way there, it was necessary to stop several times so that they might stretch their legs and exercise their bladders.

It was dark by the time I arrived. There was nowhere to park near to my lodgings, the tiny seaside village streets far too narrow for cars. There was a road that led through the village and in front the pub but a large sign on the way into the village made it very clear that visitors were to park in the car park and walk to their destination unless emergency or disability prevented them from doing so. Turning the engine off, my first imperative was to get both the dogs and myself out of the car. I was not certain where the pub was exactly, other than it was on the seafront, so I left my luggage behind and set off to find it.

Pulling at their leads, the two miniature black and tan dachshunds dragged me downhill towards the sea. The streets of Cawsand were lit by streetlamps as one might expect, but the narrow streets reduced the distance the light could penetrate, creating far more inky, dark shadows than one might expect. Even darker alleyways disappeared into an impenetrable gloom mere feet from their start point.

What I remembered of Cawsand was a picture-post-card-perfect little fishing village where rows of tiny, but brightly painted terraced houses wound around the steep cliff the village occupied. Undoubtedly evolving due to a natural harbour, the streets themselves were winding and unpredictable, side streets would suddenly appear to my left or right revealing yet more houses tucked away. I looked forward to exploring tomorrow during daylight.

I found the pub easily enough by the simple expedient

of heading downhill until I ran out of road and reached the water. Buzzing around my feet, the dogs were very happy to be somewhere new, the myriad unexplored smells causing them to dash here and there, constrained only by their leads. Where the road from the car park terminated at the seafront, there was a small pebble beach that could be accessed by stairs or by a ramp and the pub with its rooms was just to my left. It occupied an enviable position directly in front of the beach itself. I had probably sat outside it as a boy enjoying a bottle of cola with my twin sister though I had only a vague memory of doing so. There were no patrons of the pub sitting on benches outside it now though. It was a cool October evening so anyone visiting the pub would want to stay inside.

The dogs didn't resist as I pulled gently on their leads to steer them inside.

'Good evening,' I called out as I got to the bar. It was untended, even though there was a chap sitting at the far end of it, a half-empty pint glass in front of him and a paper in his hands. He looked up briefly, nodded in my direction but returned to reading his paper. He was the only person in sight. It was still early on a Sunday for the evening crowd, but the Dirty Habit back in Finchampstead would be full of customers at this time of day.

I heard footsteps approach from somewhere behind the bar. They were coming closer, clomping along wooden floorboards out of sight.

'Hello,' A lady said as she came through a gap in the wall behind the bar. She was close to sixty, or maybe slightly over, had a windswept face that spoke of living by the sea and she was quite short at what I estimated was a shade over five feet. Her hair was neatly styled in a shoulder-length bob and shot through with grey that she showed no interest in colouring.

'Hi,' I smiled at her. 'Tempest Michaels. I rather hope you have a room booked under my name.'

'Indeed, I do. I have been expecting you. I'm Gretchen, the landlady. I must say you were lucky to get a room. You called just moments after the last chap announced he was leaving earlier than planned. There has been quite a bit of interest recently with all that has been going on.' She didn't elaborate on what she was referring to. 'So, you are staying for five nights, leaving on Friday?'

'That is my plan,' I confirmed.

'And you booked the en-suite master bedroom bed and breakfast. You are going to enjoy the breakfast. My John makes it fresh to order every morning. He's such a talent,' she boasted. I assumed that John was her husband though she didn't say he was. The mention of breakfast made my stomach rumble lightly.

'How will you be paying, Tempest?' Gretchen asked.

'Credit card?' I replied, producing one from my wallet. 'Perhaps I can open a tab for drinks and food. Is the bar open?'

'Oh, yes. Would you like something now?'

'Indeed, I would,' I said, eyeing up the contents of the bar. 'I need to collect my luggage and the things for the dogs, but I would like a drink first I think.'

'Dogs?' Gretchen asked, her face a picture of confusion. She leaned forward and looked over the bar, whereupon she spied the two dachshunds sitting patiently by my feet. They saw her face appear and simultaneously started wagging their tails. 'Goodness, they are well behaved, aren't they?' she commented. 'I would never have known they were there.'

That exchange had led to Gretchen handing me a key to my room with instructions on how to find it, then showing me the range of drinks I could pick from. Ten minutes later I was placing the now empty glass of Rattler pear cider on the table in front of me and thinking that I should get my things from the car before I allowed myself the next one.

The room was easy to find and was a delightful space to spend a few days in. The bed itself was a giant four-poster constructed from solid oak. The uprights were beautifully turned in a spiral design and it had curtains hanging from each side so that the occupant could completely enclose oneself at night. In the days before central heating, I would imagine this feature was highly desirable. Less so now.

I left the dogs to sniff around the room and went to retrieve the luggage from the car. Finding my way to the car was easy enough, I just pointed myself back uphill, so despite the confusing, twisting streets and alleyways, I found the carpark again without becoming disorientated. Then, to avoid a second trip, I fiddled about until I could grab, hook or balance everything I had packed. Burdened by the weight of all the baggage, I struggled back downhill to the pub.

Looking about as I tottered along, I had to observe that it was jolly dark in the bits that the streetlights didn't penetrate. The moon was high in the sky though and quite close to full which created sufficient light to see by. I was curious to see how dark it would be on an overcast night and questioned whether the streetlights were on all night or perhaps went off at some point in the small hours. Did fisherman get up before dawn here? Centuries ago, they would have managed without streetlights, no doubt they could now as well.

There were lights on in most houses. In some, the curtains weren't drawn, so walking by the windows, I could see inside and had to make sure I didn't allow my eyes to linger too long on any particular dwelling lest I be spotted staring in. 'Would you like a hand?' asked a voice from nowhere which made me jump; I had not noticed anyone else about.

I turned slowly, a bit off balance by the weight of the items hanging from my arms to see an openly gay chap in his early twenties. He was wearing a full face of make-up, a pair of pink cowboy boots and ripped, bleached jeans that were so tight I wondered if he needed assistance just to get them on. He was just coming out of a house I had passed. 'Are you heading to the Sea Pilgrim?' he asked.

'I am actually. I'm staying there for a few days.' He was already walking towards me, raising his hands to relieve me of whichever items of luggage I could disentangle. I had received an injury to my ribs just over a week ago when I had a sort of job-related incident involving some men dressed as clowns. Several of my ribs had been broken beneath where my right arm naturally rests. They were healing but were still sore, so I was glad to reduce the load hanging from my right arm.

'Tempest,' I said, offering the man my hand as I put my suitcase down.

'John.' His handshake was rather weak – effeminate even, if I can use the term without being sexist.

'Were you on your way to the pub?' I was making conversation as silence would feel uncomfortable while the man was helping me.

'Yes. I'm the chef there. My mum runs it.' John was her son, not her husband.

'Oh. Well, I look forward to sampling your cuisine this

week. Can I expect a lot of fresh seafood dishes?' The thought of a freshly landed piece of plaice or a John Dory fillet made my mouth water. My stomach reminded me again that I had eaten all too little today.

'Oh, yes. My aunt provides me with a fresh catch every day. She's the parish councillor and supervises the fishing activities. In fact, she's responsible for all the boating activities out of the Cawsand harbour.'

'So, you have a quite a family legacy here,' I commented to make conversation.

He laughed. 'I guess we do. My sister Roberta is the local bobby, so we are all quite well known. Lived here all my life, apart from a brief, but wondrous career in the West End.'

'Acting?'

'No. I was a make-up artist. I thought I was going to be there forever, but my boyfriend cheated on me and he was the theatre producer, so I lost my job as well as my place to stay. I tried to make it on my own, but in the end, I just came home. It's lovely here though and my family are all local.'

At the door, I thanked him for his help, took back the bags he had carried and went inside. As I went up the stairs he was heading into the depths of the pub, probably to the kitchen.

I had to dump my bags to get the key from my back pocket. It was a chunky brass item that came attached to a square of metal that was almost the size of my wallet. I figured this made it harder to lose. I could hear the dogs snuffling at the gap under the door as I fiddled to open it and of course, they were climbing all over me as soon as I got it open.

Shuffling forward to prevent them from escaping

between my legs, I managed to get inside and close the door. I checked my watch: 1803hrs. I tussled briefly with leaving the luggage until the morning, but I was a stickler for routine and for being organised, so I picked the dogs up and placed them on the bed where I knew they would stay out of the way, then I tackled the task of unpacking.

Fifteen minutes later my clothes were hung up, toiletries were in the bathroom and the dogs' items were organised. It was finally pub o'clock.

Once we were back out in the corridor, the two dogs strained desperately against their leads. I could hear conversation coming from the bar downstairs. Lots of conversation. Now, it may be because my ears are attuned to hear such things now that I investigate the paranormal for a living but whatever the case, I heard the words, ghost, spectre, and pirate at least once while I stood at the edge of the room, looking around to work out where I was going to sit.

Dead Pirates of Cawsand: Chapter Three

A STRANGE TALE

Sunday, October 30th 1900hrs

The bar was packed. There had to be fifty people in it now, which meant that most of the seats were taken, and it was standing room only at the bar itself. Perhaps this was normal. As I made my way through the crowded room, watching to make sure the dogs didn't tangle anyone or get trodden on, I picked up snippets of the conversation. The chaps I was passing were all aged between late twenties and mid-forties with just one or two exceptions and there were only a couple of women present. Scanning their clothing and appearances I noted that those present were almost certainly not tourists as they weren't dressed to be out somewhere nice. They looked like they had been working. Their hair was windswept, their faces were red from the cold wind outside and they had on layered outdoor, rugged clothing.

I spotted an unoccupied table in the corner and made a beeline for it. It was a table for four, making me wonder if I might end up sharing, but to secure it, I hooked the dogs around a table leg, left my phone on the table and went to the bar to order food and a drink.

Waiting my turn, I heard the word *ghost* again and then someone said treasure. I stared at the line of spirits behind the bar and listened.

'... dived out past the headland today. I got a ping on the sonar, but it was just some old barrels that someone had dumped over the side at some point. I'm moving the grid inland tomorrow.' The speaker was to my right, but I couldn't see him, and I didn't want to turn and stare overtly at him.

Then another man spoke, 'I had no luck either. Did you hear that a ghost hunter has arrived in town?' My ears pricked up at that. I would hardly refer to myself as a ghost hunter but what was really startling was that anyone knew about me at all.

'Yeah, some multi-millionaire girl from up north,' replied the first. 'After the death on Saturday night, she packed her gear and came to Cornwall.'

'Never,' replied his friend. So, they weren't talking about me after all. However, there had been a murder, and someone thought there was a ghost involved. I had taken a break away from home to avoid all the ghostly daftness for a week. How had I managed to find it here already?

'Yeah, I hear she's quite the big shot. Brought a whole crew with her, flashy gear, expensive looking all-terrain vehicles. Jimmy saw them rolling onto the fields above the east headland by Kingsand earlier today. I reckon he must have meant old Graniff's land. He doesn't do anything with it anymore.'

'What did you hear about the murder then?' I was listening as acutely and as surreptitiously as I could manage without making my eavesdropping obvious. In so doing, I had failed to notice the landlady asking me what I wanted to drink until she asked again and touched my arm to get my attention.

Snapping back to reality, I said, 'Sorry, I was miles away. I'll take another Rattler cider please and the plaice for dinner.'

'Where are you sitting, love?' she asked.

'Just over in the corner.' I pointed. She placed the pint on the towel in front of me and disappeared into the gap behind the bar again. I sipped my drink but stayed where I was.

'...on his boat in the morning with his throat cut and stiff as a board.' I had missed a chunk of what they had been discussing.

'Who was he then?' one asked of the others.

'Well, I heard...'

The old chap I had seen sitting at the end of the bar when I first arrived interrupted. 'It was the landlady's brother-in-law, Philip Masonberg,' he said, having dropped his paper low enough to see over the top. 'The pirates got him. Don't go out there at night alone, chaps.' He met each of us with a meaningful gaze, looking at us over the top of his glasses. Then he flicked his newspaper once and hid his face behind it again.

A second of quiet passed, then the two chaps resumed their conversation.

'Have you seen anything? Of the ghosts, I mean,' one asked of the other. I turned a little now so that I could take a better look at the two men. They were young, or at least younger than me but probably still in their thirties. They were wearing the rugged outdoor gear that most others in the bar had on. Several of the other patrons had starting stripping layers off, I noted. It would be cool at sea if that was where they had all been, but in the confines of the bar, the number of people in here was raising the temperature. There were no distinguishing marks on the clothing of the two men to label them as working for a particular firm, nor was there anything remarkable about the features of either man. Both were of medium build and height with brown hair. They had most likely been out on the water for most of the day and were now enjoying a cold drink during their evening off.

Curiosity got the better of me. 'Excuse me, chaps. I could not help but overhear your discussion of ghosts. Can you tell me what it is that I have clearly missed?' I had moved away from the bar slightly so that I was in their field of vision when I started talking. I found it preferable to tapping one of them on the shoulder. They both stared at me, not in a threatening manner, but more with a look of surprise that I was so poorly informed. 'I arrived less than an hour ago,' I answered their unvoiced question.

It seemed to fill in a blank for them. The taller of the two, the one furthest away but facing directly towards me spoke first. 'You don't know about the pirates?'

'No. No, I don't,' I replied, hoping I would now get some answers.

'Well, don't go outside by yourself after dark, mate. Like the chap with the paper said.'

'Because of the pirates?' I confirmed.

'Because there are pirates out there and they are already dead and have come back to life to protect their treasure and they will probably kill you,' he said while flaring his eyes to show me how serious he was.

I took a sip of my drink, waiting to see if he had anything more to say on the subject. 'And you say that someone was killed by them recently?' I asked when he didn't speak.

'Old fella was found this morning. Run through with a sword,' he said while miming the sword action and pulling a face.

'A cutlass,' his friend cut in.

'Yeah, a cutlass,' he agreed. 'And there have been reports of ghostly dead pirates wandering the streets and scaring people for weeks now.'

'Ever since they found the gold,' his friend piped up again.

'Yeah, that's right.'

'What gold?' I asked.

'Crikey, mate. You don't know much, do you? It has been all over the news.' Now that he mentioned it, I did remember a short article on the national news a week or so ago about some gold being found. An old sunken treasure or something. I had probably been cooking dinner at the time and not really paying attention as I could not remember any more detail than that.

I pressed them for more information, which they willingly gave. A handful of gold coins had been found on Cawsand beach sixteen days ago by a chap out walking his dog. He was then spotted getting excited by the local copper who was out for a run at the time. Before anyone knew what was happening, the story was out and a fight over the ownership of the gold coins had begun.

A historian, probably with a dedicated career in marine tragedies was summoned from a nearby museum to examine the coins. It took him two days to confidently claim that they were lost when a ship called the Merchant Royal went down somewhere off the Cornish coast. The wreck had never been found, but now it looked like a storm, or something, had thrown the coins onto the shore and a gold rush of treasure hunters had beset the village hoping to make their fortunes.

The ghosts had appeared the next night – skeletal figures in pirate dress.

'They want their gold back. That's what I heard,' the man concluded in a hushed tone, leaning in to get closer to me like he was delivering a stark warning to stay away and be very afraid. I locked eyes with him for a moment. 'And they are going to hunt down anyone who goes after it,' he finished.

'But you are out trying to find more of it,' I pointed out.

He sniffed and straightened up. 'Yeah, well. Gold is gold.' He took a sip of his pint and checked his watch looking bored now.

It was all a bit odd. I thanked them both for their time and went back to my table to wait for my food. The dogs had gone to sleep on the old floorboards beneath the table. They looked up as I sat down but having seen that I was not carrying food to share, they saw no need to do more than that.

Dead pirates walking around the village looking for their gold, threatening people and stabbing one chap with a cutlass. That there had been a murder I believed. That it had been perpetrated by a centuries-dead pirate skeleton I could not accept. Sitting quietly and sipping my drink, I could already feel myself getting drawn into the mystery. With a sigh of resignation, I accepted that I was going to ask questions and investigate it for myself.

Fifteen minutes later, I was approached by a chap bearing my dinner on a plate. I had seen the same man working his way around the bar collecting empty glasses and serving dinner to other customers. The dominating feature was his muscular frame. He was a bodybuilder, if not professionally then he was most definitely dedicated to lifting some serious iron. His biceps bulged massively under his cheap, white shirt and his back formed a deep triangle that tapered into his lean waist.

'You waiting for fish?' he asked slowly.

'The plaice?' I attempted to confirm.

He stared down at the dish, the movement slow and deliberate, then looked back up at me, his expression unchanged. 'Fish,' he said again, placing the plate in front of me. It was indeed my plaice, a large piece, in fact, and exactly as I had expected the dish to look.

He seemed satisfied that the dish was delivered and wandered away feeling no need to furnish me with cutlery or condiments, or even a napkin for that matter. He seemed a little low on the ability scale, so I figured it might be simpler for me to sort such things out for myself. I got up and went back to the bar.

I waited to get the landlady's attention, glancing back at my fish hungrily and wishing I was already tucking into it. She spotted me, then tutted and rolled her eyes. She reached to a shelf behind her, producing the items I needed without me needing to ask for them. She indicated that she would bring them to me at my table.

'I see you met Thirty-three,' she said as she was laying out my knife and fork.

I raised my eyebrows in question.

'Our server,' she said as if that made anything clearer. 'The chap that speaks as if he's being played at the wrong speed. We call him thirty-three because when he speaks, he reminds you of a forty-five RPM record being played at thirty-three RPMs.' I was too young to have owned a record player, but I understood the reference. 'He's completely harmless and works for food and lodgings, but my lord he's as thick as they come.'

I shot my head around to stare at her, surprised she would be so negative about someone she employed.

'He's worked here for a few months. He just turned up one day. Walked in the bar looking for some work and has been here ever since, and it takes half the time to get the beer barrels in from the delivery van now because he carries them in three at a time.'

Thirty-three. It was a fitting name having listened to him speak, even if it was a little insulting and insensitive.

'What is his actual name? What do people call him to his face?'

'Oh. I don't know. He did tell me his name when he first arrived, but I forget what it is now. Everyone just calls him Thirty-Three.' She bustled off back to the bar, leaving me to enjoy my delicious fish, which was indeed delicious.

The dogs came out from under the table to stare intently at me. I was used to it, so I cooed at them between bites, assuring them I would find them a worthwhile treat later. As I scraped the plate to get the last few morsels, they began climbing my chair. I glanced across to the bar, checking that I was not being observed and put the plate down for them to lick clean. Then I finished my second pint and went to the bar for a third. The two chaps I had spoken with earlier were gone, replaced by two different men. These were much younger, perhaps twenty or twenty-one. They were talking about the ghosts and the spectral ship. Once again, I interrupted them to ask what they knew.

Grab your copy...
vinci-books.com/deadpirates-cawsand

About the Author

When Steve Higgs wrote his debut novel, *Paranormal Nonsense*, he was a captain in the British Army. He would like to pretend that he had one of those careers that must be blacked out and generally denied by the government, and that he has to change his name and move constantly because he is still on the watch list in several countries. In truth, though, he started out as a mechanic - not like Jason Statham in the film by that name, sneaking around as a hitman, but more like one of those sleazy guys who charges a fortune and keeps your car for a week even though the only thing you went in for was a squeaky door hinge.

At school, he was largely disinterested in all subjects except creative writing, for which he won his first prize at the age of ten. However, calling it the first prize he won suggests that there were other prizes, which is not the case. Awards may yet come, but in the meantime, he enjoys writing mystery and thriller novels and claims to have more than a hundred books forming a restless queue in his mind because they are desperate to be written.

Now retired from the military, he lives in southeast England with a duo of lazy sausage dogs. Surrounded by rolling hills, brooding castles, and vineyards, he doubts he'll ever leave, the beer is just too good.